SAVING SAMIEL

BINGO BRIDES
BOOK 1

JENIFER WOOD

A NOTE ABOUT CONTENT

I am a lazy reader and used to never read the content warnings. And then I realized I am also an *anxious* reader and would love a heads-up if things are about to get dark. This series is relatively light but I want to be sensitive to all readers. So, you can view this as a content warning, or you can view this as a menu.

Either way, *spoilers ahead.*

- Sexually explicit scenes
- Brides as prizes
- Demons
- Consensual non-consent
- Oral sex
- Marking
- Stuffing
- Knotting
- Impact play
- Anal play
- Chase/Primal play

- Tail play
- Scratching with non-human claws
- Choking (consensual)
- Bruising
- Violence (against a rival)
- Alcohol use
- Anxiety/panic attacks
- Occult
- Sacrilege
- Profanity
- Cigarette smoking
- Choking (against a rival)

If you have any specific content you are concerned about, you are welcome to reach out to me at authorjeniferwood@gmail.com.

To teenage Jen, you would be so proud.

CHAPTER
ONE

Annie

I'd never seen so many men with horns in one place, not even at the Devil's Ball in Tampa. That was the first thing I noticed: monstrous, cartoonish, jarringly archetypal. The second thing was the heat—pavement shimmering, a dry wind that felt like opening an oven not quite preheated. The bus rumbled away behind me with a fart of exhaust, and I was alone on the sidewalk, duffel at my feet, staring across the road at the fabled Devil's Throat strip.

Valley of the Damned didn't have a Welcome to Hell sign, but it had a thirty-foot billboard for Bingo Brides, with a demon in a white tux and a bouquet of pink roses. Kind of sweet, in a way. I wanted to laugh, but my throat felt too tight. Instead, I checked my phone for service (nope), then checked my reflection in the dark glass of the bus shelter. Two-tone bangs still sharp, lipstick immaculate, eyeliner winged and fierce. The Nevada sun lit my cheekbones the way I liked, but I regretted the glossy finish, already prickling sweat beads at my hairline. I shifted my bag to the other hand and stared at the courthouse clock across the street, which was stuck at 3:33, hands welded in a perpetual omen. I'm not superstitious, but that still got me.

I crossed Main, half expecting a demon to pop out of a manhole and photobomb my entrance, but the strip was deserted except for a couple of old ladies dragging folding chairs toward the Valley of the Damned Hall, their hair as blue as my favorite lipstick. Even the neon was off, giving the place a sun-bleached, post-apocalyptic charm. But after Tampa, I could handle weird.

Devil's Throat was a single block of false-front storefronts —saloon, pawnshop, diner, dollar store, jewelry spot, tattoo parlor. My destination was in the last building on the row: the bingo hall.

It sounded like such a joke, like the punchline to a meme. Except I'd bought a one-way ticket to Valley of the Damned because after two years as a nutritionist at a long-term care facility and a decade of dating men who described themselves as "intuitive" (eye roll), I had nothing to show for it except an Etsy collection of weird apology gifts. I needed something real. Or at least, real enough to scare me into wanting to wake up every day.

My last ex was a man named Seth—using the term *man* loosely. He was a barista with a demon tattoo and an anime-level fixation on being "bad." He'd moved into my place after a month, left beard trimmings in the sink, and used my expensive hair masks as lube. When I finally dumped him, he cried, and then asked if he could keep the air fryer. I only said yes because I wanted the last word in what was other-wise a two-year slog of petty, pathetic stalemates.

The morning after, he sat on the edge of my bed, red-eyed and puffy, wearing my old Misfits tee, and said, "You're the only person who's ever understood me." Then he moved out without so much as a backward glance, blocked me on Instagram, and replaced my number with a demon emoji in the group chat with friends.

I kept waiting for the regret to hit, but regret never showed. Instead, I'd cleaned under my couch for the first time in three years, watched horror movies alone with take-out, and realized I didn't miss Seth so much as the feeling of being needed, of mattering. He had always made me feel necessary, which I mistook for love. What I actually wanted was someone who made me feel alive.

Which is why I was here, melting in the Nevada sun, about to walk into a stranger's idea of Hell and win myself a demon husband. No more half measures. No more settling for "better than nothing." I wanted heat, not a slow simmer, and if that meant getting burned, so be it.

When I pushed through the glass doors, the AC blasted me in the face so hard I almost fell backwards. Not just cold —antiseptic and chemical, stinging the inside of my nose. The lobby was mostly linoleum, a vending machine grave-yard, and a mounted bull's head with glitter-glue tears running down its cheeks. A sign-in sheet and a stack of pens waited on the folding table. A doodle in the margin read, "DO NOT FEED THE DEMONS." I wrote "Annie H." and underlined it three times.

The hall itself was Vegas-big, with floor-to-ceiling windows and a dais at the far end. Rows and rows of Formica tables, each with a plastic bottle of ketchup-red bingo markers. I counted at least a dozen demon men in the back row, already in their assigned seats, horns in all shapes and sizes: goat, ram, antelope, devil-from-a-painting. Two had tails coiled like licorice ropes around their chair legs. Even sitting, they looked like a pack of linebackers at a tea party, hunched and tense. The rest of the room was empty, except for a woman in a mesh shirt and high-waisted jeans organizing bingo cards on a folding table.

She spotted me and waved. "Are you Annie?"

I nodded, too dry-mouthed to risk speaking, and drifted over. She was about my age, with dimple piercings and a magenta undercut, and there were black roses painted on her nails.

"I'm Mara, tonight's designated handler-slash-bouncer. Don't worry," she said, lowering her voice, "the demons are way more nervous than we are. They look scary, but they are all here for the same reason."

"Are you a bride?" I asked.

"Ha! Not unless brides have suddenly started wearing sweatpants and eating cereal at 2:00 p.m. I moved here with my wife five years ago. We just couldn't resist the irresistible charm of the local coffee shop's questionable Wi-Fi and the neighborhood raccoons' nightly garbage raids."

"Lucky them," I said. "The raccoons, I mean." If Mara noticed my hands shaking, she played it off with a wink and a shuffle of the sign-up sheets, like she was shuffling a tarot deck that could decide my fate. "How many of us tonight?" I asked, peering into the great linoleum tundra.

"Six, not counting you," she said. "Plus the usual lineup of demon bachelors, but we keep them separate until the program starts. Safety and suspense, you know? Over there" —she pointed at a round table in the corner, already half-full —"is the holding pen. Come on. I'll introduce you."

The other women looked up as we approached. They were nothing like the parade of would-be Stepford bachelorettes I'd expected. One wore a tie-dyed T-shirt that said "Eat the Rich, Marry a Demon," another had a spiked leather choker and a jacket patched with even more spikes, and another had a bandage on her arm and an expression that dared me to ask her how she'd gotten the injury. Quick glances and raised eyebrows, the instant calculus of potential allies, rivals, and drinking buddies. I was low on social battery, but the tide of nervous energy in the room made me want to match their wattage.

"Hey, you're new!" said the girl in the tie-dye. On second look, she was not, in fact, a girl at all but a woman with the sort of laugh lines that come from years of being the first to arrive and last to leave at every party.

I introduced myself and got a chorus of names in return: tie-dye was Jules, ex-bartender from Omaha; the choker-and-spikes-jacket was named Lark, and she worked in a tattoo shop in Portland (Maine, not Oregon, "the other one, the one with more ghosts"). The woman with the makeshift bandage called herself Erin and said she was "between gigs."

Mara snapped the worn clipboard against her palm like a judge's gavel. "Alright, mortals," she announced, eyebrows arched dramatically, "the fine print you should've read before showing up. Rule one: you've got a three-day trial period. You *must* consummate the marriage in those three days. If both parties agree to continue at the end—and I mean enthusiastic, notarized consent—you're magically bound to a ninety-day marriage contract. No takebacks, no refunds." She tapped her pen against the board. "Rule two: survive those ninety days still wanting each other, and congratulations! You're legally and supernaturally obligated to tie the eternal knot. We're talking forever-ever. Like, outlive-the-heat-death-of-the-universe forever." She grinned. "But hey, at least you get a toaster." No one laughed, not even Jules, who looked like the type to appreciate dark humor. The truth of it pressed down on us like the static before a thunderstorm. I gripped my own knees, and while I tried to project "unflappable party girl" at all times, my knuckles stood out white and obvious.

Mara handed out name tags—sticky rectangles with "HELLO, I'M A BINGO BRIDE" printed beneath a dizzy devil logo. As we affixed them, she hustled us through rules about safe words, emergency contacts, and the "conjugal cooldown closet," which was apparently stocked with Xanax, bath bombs, and emergency string cheese. She said it like running from a demon groom at midnight was something that happened a lot, and maybe it did.

Jules snorted. "What happens if we want to bail before ninety days?"

"If you break the marriage contract, there's paperwork, and an exit interview with the mayor, who is, unfortunately, also a demon. This may be a valley of demons, but it is also Nevada. They take contract law very seriously."

"Is he hot?" Lark asked, deadpan.

Mara shrugged. "I mean, if you're into politicians with obsidian skin and a tail like a hydraulic lift, then yeah, he's a total DILF. Personally, I think he cries himself to sleep at night, but who am I to judge?"

I watched Mara tick names off the clipboard, the little in-jokes and barbs ricocheting around.

"Next," Mara continued, "the bingo rounds are strictly supervised. If at any point you feel uncomfortable, raise the red paddle and I'll dismiss you from stage. Or at least cause a distraction so you can make a break for the parking lot."

Lark muttered, "And if it's the demon that's uncomfortable?"

Mara grinned. "Then he can raise a blue paddle, and we'll switch in some chamomile tea and a coloring book. Demons are not great with strong feelings, turns out." She shrugged like this was a universal disappointment.

"Third, and this is no joke—if you hit the jackpot at bingo, you're contractually bound to give the whole 'demon husband' thing a whirl for at least three days. Yep, that means either shacking up with your hellish hubby for a trio of days or at least showing up and pretending to like it. Think of it as a really weird college roommate situation, but with more brimstone and less ramen."

Erin raised her hand. "What if I win and then immediately get cold feet?"

Mara didn't even blink. "If you're worried about cold feet, don't set foot in the furnace. Seriously. Nobody's making you do this." She looked around the table, and I realized her eyes had gone hard at the edges, like she'd argued this before. "It's not like the trial is forever, and most of them can't cook for shit anyway, so you're more likely to die of food poisoning than blood loss."

Jules grinned, maybe remembering something, maybe just loving the drama. "I once made out with a demon at a KISS cover band show," she confessed. "Tongue was forked, he could tie a cherry stem like you wouldn't believe." She winked at me. "You'll be fine, rookie."

Mara handed out name stickers and markers, then led us to the dais. "Okay, let's get the introductions out of the way," she said, herding us onto a little stage with a frightful lack of ceremony.

On the other side of the aisle, the demon bachelors were neatly arranged at their own folding tables. If I'd been expecting horns and red skin as the main selling points, I was underprepared for the sheer spectrum of demon types. One had skin the color of a cigarette filter and eyes like slot machines. Another was so tall he had to slouch like a parent at a preschool recital, his horns only partly filed down. The rest were variations on a theme:

hands too big, expressions too naked, nerves as loud as ours.

"Ladies!" Mara called out. "Let's introduce ourselves, starting on my left!" Jules hoisted a paper cup as if it were a microphone, and took the plunge.

"I'm Jules, she/her, I make a mean Old Fashioned and I will absolutely talk your horns off about antique glassware. Signed up for this because I'm sick of dating apps and," she paused, "also maybe because I have a thing for guys with hooves. No shame." That got a ripple of laughter, even from the demons' side, one or two shifting in their chairs with what might have been a bashful flexing of their cloven feet.

Lark was up next, chin lifted. "Lark, also she/her, I'm an apprentice tattoo artist, and if you're gonna abduct me, at least be cool about it. I did not come all this way to get stuck with a basic demon." She glared down the line of bachelors and winked at the biggest one, who actually ducked his head and blushed—no mean feat for someone with a face like a weathered jack-o'-lantern and tusks.

Erin simply saluted the hall. "Erin. She/her. Not afraid of the dark, not afraid of commitment, allergic to kiwis. I like long walks on the beach and existential dread." Her smirk was a little crooked; I suspected she was the type who got funnier the more time you spent with her.

It went around the circle, quick and painless, and then Mara's hand landed on my shoulder, steering me gently to the front.

I felt my tongue stick to the roof of my mouth, a fine paste of nerves and Burt's Bees. The anticipation was almost enough to make me forget I had no issue with public speaking—I presented at health conferences all the time.

There it was—the whole room staring back, demons included, their eyes bright and expectant, their claws or clawlike appendages folded awkwardly in their laps. The whole setup was utterly absurd, and I couldn't help but laugh, which made my voice come out higher than usual.

"I'm Annie," I said, "she/her. I work as a nutritionist, but don't worry, I'm not one of the annoying ones. I promise never to say the word *cleanse* in your presence. I also like bingo, obviously, and... um... I can bench one-fifteen, which is pretty good for my size. So if you're looking for a bride who can open jars and also recommend the best snacks for a late-night crisis, I'm your girl."

Silence. Then one of the demons let out a low, throaty laugh that seemed to ripple down the line. I tried not to stare, but he caught my eye: red skin like a warning label, black veins like lightning beneath, and horns that looked less like Halloween and more like something you'd find on a Roman statue. He was built like a brick wall with a sense of humor, and when he noticed me noticing him, he grinned— not with his teeth but with the whole languid, deliberate set of his shoulders. His name tag, printed in block capitals, said SAMIEL. I wasn't sure how to pronounce it and was already mentally abbreviating to "Sam."

He caught me looking again, and this time, he stretched out his legs and propped them on the chair in front of him. I'd been trying not to gawk at the specifics, but the orientation packet did not prepare me for his feet. Not hooves, not quite, but massive, clawed, jointed in ways that made you want to Google "elk but make it demon." His ankles hinged in reverse, like a digitigrade predator, and the toes (three? four?) splayed out into four lacquer-black talons that looked sharp enough to dissect the metal folding chair. Then he shifted, and the enormous dark red wings unfurled slightly behind him. Dragon-like, leathery, with matching talons at each joint that glinted like garnets under the fluorescents.

My mouth went dry. Each movement had the casual, dangerous intent of an apex predator. I must have made a face—shock, fear, something else I didn't want to name—because his mouth twitched and he flexed both his claws and his wings simultaneously, like he was warming up for the world's most terrifying symphony.

Mara cleared her throat. "Well then! On to the main event. Let's get our bachelors up here and let the games begin." There was an awkward shuffle as the demons stood, which produced a symphony of tail-thwacks and the sound of dress shirts straining at the seams. They filed up to the dais, a living wall of color and muscle, and I tried to keep my eyes away from Samiel's feet, but the magnetism was relentless. He walked like he'd just been released from a maximum security gym, all shoulders and arrogance, but there was something else there—something almost shy about the way his eyes flicked from ceiling tile to exit sign to floor and only, very briefly, to me. The other girls took notice too, but if Sam felt the scrutiny, he hid it under a dangerous stillness.

The beauty of Bingo Brides was that it didn't pretend to be tasteful. We were all ushered up to the stage and seated on barstools that were lined up in a row. Jules got first pick at them, then Lark, then Erin, the rest of us filtered in behind. I sat where Mara told me, and letting my legs dangle because none of the chairs fit my height unless I wanted my skirt riding up to felony levels. I undid my duffel, fished out a notebook, and started a list in the margin. "1. Tall. 2. Red. 3. Looks like he could open a can of soup just by glaring at it." I didn't add "4. Would trample me barefoot and leave no evidence," but the thought lingered.

The rest of the introductions blurred, but I kept my eyes on Sam, trying to parse what he was thinking. I expected him to be staring back, maybe with a glazed-over "are you prey?" look or the slack-jawed hunger of every gym bro I'd met between Tampa and here. Instead, Sam looked faintly amused, like he'd seen this all before but was still enjoying the rerun, eyes crinkling at the corners. His horns weren't just ornamental, either—they looked thick enough to use as handles. For the first time since stepping off the bus, I felt the knot in my stomach loosen and spiral outward with every heartbeat.

Mara clapped her hands, startling the whole hall. "Alright, demons and dames, let's get to the main event. Demons, take your cards, we are ready to start the first round!"

A scuffle of chairs, the rustle of cheap polyester and heavy limbs. I found myself escorted up onto the stage as the demons took their seats. The other women murmured awkwardly, their confidence a little brittle now that the stakes were in play. I caught Sam's gaze. He was already looking at me, his thumbs circling slowly around the cap of his own bingo marker. If he'd ever played before, he was doing a good job hiding it.

A bell rang (actual brass, not digital), and the demons approached in formation, each one escorted by a VFW volunteer in a neon green OFFICIAL shirt. Samiel was in the first group, along with the slot-machine-eyed demon and a creature whose shirt stretched so tight across his chest it looked painted on.

Mara, now wearing a sparkly vest and the air of a seasoned cruise host, picked up the microphone and beamed. "Demons and dames, welcome to the hallowed tradition of the Hell's Valley Bingo Bride Mixer! You know the rules: if a demon gets bingo, he gets to claim first pick of the available brides. If no demon gets bingo"—she winked—

11

"we go to sudden death and draw names from the pit." The pit was a literal pit, a kiddie pool painted black, full of foam balls. Lark whispered, "I hope they clean that thing." Jules snorted.

Mara started the round. "B-12!" The room went silent as the demons peered intently at their cards, lips moving in silent prayer or calculation. There was something almost sweet about the way they hunched over, concentrating, like they'd spent the week rehearsing for this and didn't want to let down their friends back home in Hell.

Jules tapped her heel, humming under her breath. Lark cracked her knuckles, then her toes, which was more impressive. Erin rolled her eyes at each number, but she was the only one who looked genuinely at ease. Me? I watched Samiel. Every time Mara called a number, he'd mark it, then glance up at me, a slow, deliberate motion that made it feel like the two of us were the only ones in the room.

The tension ramped up with every B and G and O. Once or twice, I thought I heard the sound of someone's fangs grinding. A couple of the bachelors looked near bursting, their faces darkening from anticipation or blood pressure. I started counting how many numbers Samiel had left, as if I could will him to win by the force of my gaze alone.

It was the slot-machine-eyed demon who got there first. He pounded the table with such force the marker exploded in a red mist, then bellowed "BINGO!" in a voice that rattled the fluorescent tubes in the ceiling.

Mara, who clearly had nerves of titanium, only smiled wider. "That's our first winner!" she crowed, and the other demons clapped, some with claws, some with applause that sounded more like rocks tumbling downhill.

"Come on up, Gremory," Mara said, as if coaxing a kid to the front of the class for Show and Tell. Gremory rose, all eight feet of him, and approached the dais, looking both sheepish and victorious. He bowed to the audience, then fixed his gaze on the waiting line of brides.

He picked Jules. There was no hesitation: he extended a limb, palm up, and gestured with a kind of gallantry you wouldn't expect from a creature with a mouthful of fangs and a voice that could shatter glassware. Jules, to her credit, only blinked once before stepping off the stage, her heels clicking with the poise of a runway model who'd just been told the next person to cross the catwalk would be devoured.

They disappeared together through the side door, flanked by Mara. The rest of us—demons and brides alike—waited in a state of suspended animation. The air in the hall grew tight and electric, every shuffle of a card amplified in the silence.

Samiel scratched behind his horn and said, "That's a good match, actually."

I opened my mouth, ready to volley back something clever, but Mara was already launching into the next round. "I-21!" she called, the syllables ricocheting between the windows. Samiel's eyes locked on me, and for a second he looked like he might say something more, but then he dropped his gaze to his card and jabbed his marker so hard the table shook. I was about to make a little joke about competitive bingo, but then he did it again, and again, fast, like the numbers were falling exactly how he wanted—until, with a flourish, he slammed his palm down and yelled, "BINGO!"

CHAPTER
TWO

Samiel

The echo of my own voice sounded strange and exhilarating in the stale cold of the hall. I felt the eyes of every creature—human or otherwise—swing to me, calculating, appraising. My blood sang. I loved to win. I loved to take.

Mara beamed with the satisfaction of a game show host whose favorite contestant just hit the bonus round. "Samiel!" she said, stretching the syllables into something ceremonial. "Come on up and make your selection."

My seat groaned as I stood, wings flexing and then folding tight. I'd practiced this walk in the mirror, but the reality of it—the weight of expectation, the ache in the base of my horns, the low, heady pulse of the prize waiting—outstripped rehearsal. I took the stage.

I'd been waiting for this for forty years. Forty years, marked out in the slow drip of seasons, the endless shuffle of mortals through the Valley of the Damned, the bone-level chill in every room I ever entered alone. I remembered the day the mayor forbade me from participating in Bingo for my little goat prank. At the time it had seemed a tolerable stretch, a slap on the wrist for a demon used to eternity. But I'd been young, for a demon, and I didn't know how long forty years could really be. How much a body could crave even the smallest touch, even a brief glint of human attention. I watched the Bingo Bride events through the glass every year, the way a starving man might watch a banquet he could never taste.

I wanted a bride. I wanted to belong here, to have someone look at me and see more than the sum of my parts —horns, claws, wings, jokes that had outlived their punchline. I wanted to be necessary.

The remaining women all looked at me, but only Annie —Annie H., according to her sticker—held my gaze with any challenge in it. She was tiny, a slip of a thing, her body language a cocktail of nerves and challenge. Even standing straight, she didn't reach the bottom of my sternum.

Most of the other women had already calculated their odds and were looking past me. Annie, with her milkmaid skin and defiant maroon lipstick, regarded me like she was sizing up a used car with suspiciously low mileage. Something in the lift of her chin said, *You'd better not waste my time.*

It did something to me—something chemical—the way being near a live wire makes your bones thrum. My tongue split itself in anticipation, both ends writhing discreetly behind my teeth. My tail, which I normally had perfect control over, lashed once behind my knee and smacked a folding chair so loudly that even Mara startled. Embarrassing. I took a half step back, willed it to go limp, and tried not to think about what else was going stiff.

"Well, Sam, who'll it be?"

I made a show of looking over the bridal lineup—Lark,

whose spikes threatened to gouge my eyes; Erin, who was already doodling skulls on her name sticker; the other one, who looked at me like she was hoping I'd explode on the spot. But it was Annie I wanted. Her hair was a deliberate catastrophe, black ink on one side and platinum on the other, cut to frame a face so pale it verged on lunar. The eyes were startling: blue as chlorinated pools in July, outlined in sharp liner. The goth girl thing had never made sense to me before. She made it look like the only way to be, with a manicure that could slice a warranty sticker and an expression so controlled it vibrated a little at the edges.

I wanted her so badly it nearly doubled me over. But there'd be no violence here, not even the tender kind. Not yet.

I locked eyes with her and let myself smile. The trick was to keep my lips parted, just a little, so the canines glimmered but didn't threaten. I'd spent years watching humans, learning when to intimidate and when to court. She didn't flinch, not even when my forked tongue flicked out to drag a stripe of saliva, precise as a scalpel, along the edge of my fang. A dare, if she was looking for it.

"I'll take Annie," I said, voice even, hands loose at my sides. Behind me, the other bachelors watched like it was the finals of a brutal sport. Annie arched a brow, and for a moment I thought she'd refuse, right there in front of everyone.

Instead, she stepped forward, a deliberate, ice-cold glide, and offered her hand like I was supposed to kiss it or maybe try to eat it. I bent over, took her wrist in my palm—delicate, bones birdlike—and pressed my lips to the pulse point, letting the humidity of my breath linger longer than etiquette allowed. Her skin was feverish, a sharp contrast to the chill of the hall. I caught the scent beneath her perfume—

nervous sweat and some ghost of clove. It shot straight down my spine and pooled between my legs, an ache I had to lock down with everything I had.

"Charmed," she said, drawing the word out in a perfect, deadpan echo. She didn't pull away, not even when I held on for a beat too long. "So, are you kidnapping me for the three-day trial period right now, or is your zipper going to give out before we make it there?" She shot a laser-focused glance at the undeniable evidence of my enthusiasm.

I looked her up and down, slow enough to make it a point, then to the very obvious ridge pitching my pants. I could see the other women watching, peripheral vision a matrix of envy and amusement, but I didn't care. Annie had called my bluff in front of the whole damn hall. Beautiful.

"Zipper's industrial strength," I said. "But you're welcome to test it." The joke landed across her features like a shimmer of static. I knew what it meant to want to make an impression, to turn a room into your private theater. She was doing it now, and I respected the hell out of it.

Annie didn't look away. In fact, she let her gaze travel, slow and clinical, up the length of me before returning to my face. She arched a brow. "Not bad."

Mara cleared her throat. "Well then! If the couple would please proceed to the orientation suite—" She gestured to the far door with a flourish, then shot Annie a covert thumbs-up as we passed.

I offered her my arm; she didn't hesitate, looping hers through mine with a grip both polite and proprietary. Up close, the top of her head barely grazed my bicep. The irony of this was not lost on me: for a creature built to terrify, I was utterly undone by a woman half my size, who eyed me as if I were a haunted house—worth exploring, but not worth screaming over.

We strode down the side corridor, the carpet patterned in infernal paisley and sticky in the way of all casinos everywhere. I let my tail drift behind us, low and lazy. The tip brushed her calf and she didn't flinch, just shot me a side-eye that could have drawn blood.

"Nice tail," she said.

"Thanks," I said. "It has a mind of its own. You can punish it later if it acts up."

She snorted. "If you're looking for discipline kink, you're shopping in the wrong aisle."

"Noted." I let the word purr out, pleased to hear it catch on her. The door at the end of the hall was locked, but I only had to glare at it for a second before the ancient mag-stripe coughed and stuttered and gave up. I ushered Annie inside.

The parlor where we'd sign all our paperwork was a converted church basement, or so I guessed from the stained-glass windows depicting archangels brawling with monsters. The refreshments were mini cupcakes with purple frosting and cans of every off-brand soda in the Western states.

Annie grabbed a cupcake, peeled the wrapper off in a single spiral, and tossed it in her mouth in one bite. I had a soft spot for sugar, though I technically didn't need to eat as a demon. I ate the cupcake, wrapper and all.

Annie watched me chew the paper as if she'd just caught me eating glue in first grade. There was no judgment, though, just a flicker of curiosity. "They told us about demon food quirks in orientation, but I kind of assumed it was a sex thing."

I swallowed, grinned. "Everything can be a sex thing, if you want it badly enough." I leaned against the folding table, spreading my wings a little for drama, and let my gaze linger on the bruised line of her collarbone. Annie's eyes flicked to my wings, only for a moment. But I caught it. And I caught the shift in her scent. She was aroused by my wings —I'd have to keep that in mind. I opened my mouth to comment, but she cut me off.

"So," she said, "how's this supposed to work? Do we just shake hands and sign the prenup, or is there an obstacle course? A compatibility test?" She propped an elbow on the Formica, her chin in her palm, and gave a little smile that was all knives.

Well, if she wanted to ignore that moment where her facade dropped, I could save it for later. I pulled the packet of forms from the cinderblock bookshelf, each page pre-marked with color-coded stickies. "We're supposed to get to know each other. We have a whole set of questions." I word-lessly handed her the document and watched her eyes flick over it.

"Why did I come?" she read, more to herself, but then she looked up to answer me. "Because every guy in Tampa wanted to date his mother. Or his parole officer. Or both. Because I figured if demons were looking for brides, at least they'd be up front about it. I'm not scared of claws, or horns, or the fact you just inhaled that cupcake wrapper. I'm scared of boring. I'm scared of working the same job for thirty years and pretending to care about college football." She shrugged, feigning nonchalance, but her knuckles had gone white around the paper cup. "I want something real." She looked up at me, daring me to call her bluff.

The silence yawned open. I'd been told to keep things light, that mortals needed buffering from the full unfiltered demon experience in case they melted down or remembered, all at once, they were prey.

But Annie wasn't prey. Annie was a compact, spiked iron maiden wearing a smirk. I let the moment hang, studied her

—the way her jaw flexed when she thought I wasn't looking, the microtremble in her thigh as she braced against the folding chair, the way her eyes, even as they tried to glare holes through me, kept drifting down to my hands. Maybe she was imagining what I could do with them, or maybe she was imagining them around her throat. Either way, the thought made my mouth water.

"I want something real," she repeated, softer now, almost to herself. She didn't blink.

"Good," I said, "because I can't fake it. I've tried. It never ends well for anyone." There was a sick, bright pleasure in saying this aloud, in seeing her nod just once, as if that was the right answer and she'd have left if I'd said anything else. I leaned in, just enough to make her look up without having to move her whole head. "You're not what I was looking for," I told her, "but you're exactly what I want."

I saw the hesitation flicker in her and wondered if she'd ever been allowed out for air until now. Her mouth opened, then closed, the way a person about to step off a ledge sometimes inched forward and then remembered gravity. I could practically see the gears turning in her—how much to reveal, how soon, whether she'd regret it later. Maybe I should have felt superior, but instead I felt a rush of something almost like dread, because I knew exactly where she was coming from. It's a wide world of disappointment, and it takes a lot to put your chips down on hope.

We were both holding our breath through that moment of vulnerability. I opened my mouth, unsure of what was going to come out, when Mara walked in, more papers in hand.

She slapped the contract down with a flourish, startling us out of our staring contest.

"You two look like you're ready for the express lane," she

said. "Unless you want to try the compatibility questionnaire first. It's got questions about pets, politics, and eventual children. Not legally binding, but it's good for conversation."

Annie didn't even look at the glossy booklet. "Let's skip ahead," she said, like she was ordering at a drive-thru. "We can circle back to the deep stuff later." She grabbed a pen and flipped the marriage contract open to the flagged page. I watched her sign her name, the letters sharp and looping, no hesitation at the H, no flourish at the end. She passed the pen to me, and I took it, the plastic straining against my grip.

The pen left a divot in the line, a little meteor crater of plastic against the cheap government paper. I tried to sign delicately—I'd learned over time that mortals preferred the idea of restraint in their monsters—but the tip still punched through the first sheet and dented the second. Annie grinned, confirming that the performance wasn't lost on her.

Mara took the contract, flicked it once to flatten the signatures, and gave us the thumbs up. "Congrats, you two. You're officially three-day engaged. Have a cupcake to celebrate." She looked at her phone and stage-whispered, "Your chaperone will be along in about five minutes. I'd say use the time wisely, but I think you two are ahead of the curve."

"Chaperone?" Annie asked.

I plucked another cupcake, this one with black sprinkles, and watched her lick a smudge of frosting from her thumbnail. "The chaperone is mostly for show," I said. "Technically, he's supposed to keep us from murdering each other before night one, but mostly he just drives the shuttle and pretends not to notice." I smeared some frosting onto my tongue, leering just enough to get a reaction. Annie did not disappoint.

"Do the rules specify what happens during the shuttle ride?" she asked, eyes challenge-bright.

"The rules specify only that we arrive at the house conscious and in sufficiently intact condition to complete the orientation. Everything else is at our discretion." I let my tail curl around the leg of her chair, drawing her closer by increments.

She leaned in, conspiratorial. "So what's the house like? Spikes? Dungeon? Or is it one of those McMansion builds with bad insulation and ghosts in the crawlspace?"

I considered spinning her a line about oubliettes and howling basements. Instead, I told the truth just to see what she'd do with it.

"It's out by Lake Purgatory," I said. "They assign each couple a house for the three-day trial, but ours is… let's call it mid-century modern, with lake access." I let my tongue flick, quick as a match, just to see her eyes dart after it. "The mayor says it's haunted, but I think he's just trying to keep the brides from skinny-dipping. The water's cold, but the view is worth it."

She snorted. "Is that a threat or a promise?"

"Why not both?" I let my gaze rest on her, heavy as a hand.

"And what has to happen within those three days, Samiel?" she asked, and I knew the answer she was after.

I wanted to see if she'd flinch, so I didn't sugarcoat it. "We have to consummate. Within three days. It's the only part of the contract that isn't optional."

It was a litmus test, and I watched her for the tell: the blanch, the tick, the intake of breath that said the honeymoon was over before it started. Her eyes went wide for a quarter second—less shock than calculation. Then the corner of her mouth lifted, as if this confirmed a private suspicion.

"Is that a demon thing, or just a you thing?" she asked, voice low and sharp.

"Both, probably," I said. "But if you want, we can call it off now. No shame."

She pondered that, turning the thought in her mouth like a cherry pit. "I'm not a virgin sacrifice. I know what I'm doing."

CHAPTER
THREE

Annie

Mara left us with the cupcakes and a polite "good luck" in the same tone as "have fun storming the castle." Samiel didn't go back to the table; he just stood there, wings half-raised, as if he was ready to scoop me up and take off if the ceiling allowed it. I took a moment —finally, genuinely—to look at him.

He was beautiful, but not in the way that made you want to pose for a selfie. It was a more ancient, predatory type of beauty: posture like a centurion, skin the color of overripe cherries, the red so dark it was almost black along the veins at his temples and the crooks of his arms. His hair was long and glossy, the kind of black that reflected purple in cheap lighting, and did little to hide his ears—pointed like a wolf's, delicate and sharp even with the bulk of his body. The horns were even more intimidating up close, curving back and up from his forehead in a way that looked both ornamental and utilitarian. If you needed to impale a watermelon at thirty paces, Samiel could do it every time.

He caught me staring—like, really staring—and didn't look away. I'd grown used to men who performed "smoldering" as a kind of joke, a way to look hot while pretending not to care if you thought so. Samiel wasn't pretending. He studied me as openly as I studied him, and when I squared my chin in response, something in his eyes said, *Yes, good. Show me more.*

The silence didn't seem to bother him. He just stood there, wings shifting lazily, tail whipping the air in a slow S-curve behind his calves. The shirt he wore (black, of course, but with a pattern of tiny skulls embroidered like polka dots) was rolled at the sleeves, revealing forearms that would make most pro wrestlers weep with envy. His fingers, now idly shredding the paper of a cupcake, looked dexterous and unhurried, made for more than just brute force.

I wanted him. There was no intricate calculus, no six-point plan. I just wanted this demon to fuck me. Not metaphorically, not performatively, but in the precise, world-shaking sense. He'd looked at me like he could read the variations of my pulse from across a room, and now that I had a moment to catalog his physical presence—not just the flesh, but the gravity of him—I felt my own blood doing something new, something reckless. I let the thought hang, let it settle, and decided I would not wait for him to ask. I would ask first, just to see what he'd do.

But not yet. I wanted to draw it out, see if I could make him squirm.

The chaperone arrived exactly on cue: a demon with the shape and gravitas of a sentient filing cabinet, his badge reading "Clem" in listless handwriting. He escorted us to the parking lot, where a battered black shuttle bus idled in the sun. Samiel's hand found the small of my back, hot enough to burn through fabric even though I knew it was just skin. I didn't flinch. If anything, I pressed closer, the way you might lean into a thunderstorm just to see if you could out-stare the lightning.

Inside, the bus was empty except for the driver and the sticky ghosts of past passengers. I slid into a seat near the back and Samiel wedged himself in next to me, his body spanning the entire row and most of the aisle. The seat groaned in protest beneath him. His thigh, the width of a skateboard, pressed flush to mine, and his shoulder blotted out half my peripheral vision. The heat off his body was overwhelming—dry, elemental, like standing beside a kiln. I didn't hate it.

The chaperone made a show of pretending we didn't exist, picking at his phone and occasionally muttering into a walkie-talkie. Samiel draped his wing over the back of the seat, the membrane folding in on itself with the soft, leathery susurrus of a bellows. I could feel eyes on us from the parking lot, a few leftover bachelors and Mara, who leaned against the curb and watched with open curiosity.

The bus lurched onto the main drag, and we passed the bingo hall, the pawnshop, the little diner with blackout curtains and a hand-painted sign that said FRIED THINGS. There were no pedestrians, just heat mirages and bored-looking demons in lawn chairs, watching the day bleed out. It was the kind of place where you could disappear if you wanted.

Samiel's hand landed, casual as a cat, on my knee. He didn't squeeze or make a show of it—just left it there, a promise and a dare. I twisted my body to face him, my knee knocking against his. "So," I said, "are we supposed to make small talk? Or do we just sit here and wait for the urge to devour each other?"

He looked at me sideways, eyes brighter than polished

garnet. "I'm not good at small talk," he said. "But I'm told that's what humans prefer, so I can try if you want." His thumb drew a lazy circle on my kneecap, a microcosm of friction and heat.

"I'm thirty-two," I said, "so I'm at peace with awkward silence. But I do like to know what year my potential spouse was manufactured."

He blinked as if surprised by the question. "How old do I look?"

I studied him, the unlined red skin, the ink-black hair, the hands like sculpture. The only clues were in the eyes: some depth there, a sort of tiredness that felt older than language but not quite immortal. "You've got, like, two generations of damage. Forty, maybe? Fifty, if you moisturize?"

Samiel's smile went jagged, amused. "I arrived in 1985. They made us pick an age and stick to it for paperwork reasons. I was 'twenty-nine' for about thirty years. I guess that makes me, what, a vintage millennial?"

He winked, and it was somehow both self-aware and deeply, disturbingly sincere.

I tried to picture him in the 80s—shoulder pads, maybe a *Miami Vice* suit, the hair just as long but feathered, the horns a little more clandestine. "You don't look like you lost much sleep over Y2K," I said, and he snorted, a sound that vibrated straight through the vinyl upholstery.

"Technology's wasted on most demons," he said. "We only really care about three things: food, sex, and winning. Sometimes all at once." He gave me a look that was, somehow, both predatory and shy. It made my brain short-circuit for a second.

I waited for the punchline, but instead he sat back and let the silence breathe. I liked that about him. Most men, faced with my resume of failed relationships and barbed jokes, would fill the air with talk—about the weather or their jobs or the time they almost made it onto *American Ninja Warrior*. Samiel just sat with it. He flattened his hand on my knee and let his thumb travel up, slow and unhurried, to the place where my skirt bunched at the thigh. Not a grope—more like an invitation.

We left the "downtown" behind and headed up a gentle rise, the desert flattening out to saltbush and the distant shimmer of Lake Purgatory. The emptiness was vast, nuclear, the sky so blue it looked fake. I thought about how many generations of women before me had looked at a strange man and wondered if he would be the death of her. I wondered if any of them had done it on a courtesy shuttle with a demon whose tail appeared to have its own choreography.

"Tell me something," I said, pivoting in my seat to face him. "What happened the first time you came here? Did you, like, win the lottery and get a trophy wife, or did it all go up in flames?"

Samiel's grin took on a crooked edge. "You really want the story?"

"If it's embarrassing, absolutely."

He hesitated, then leaned in, dropping his voice to a hush. "First time around, I thought I'd hack the system. Everyone else was so desperate, so "—He gestured, as if to conjure the word out of the heat haze—" hungry in a way that doesn't impress anyone, especially humans. So I tried to cheat by using multiple cards. Didn't win, didn't even get Bingo. Bride went home with some other demon. I got stuck in town with nothing but regret and about twenty pounds of chicken wings to eat my feelings."

The story didn't line up. I narrowed my eyes.

"You're leaving something out, Sam." My voice came out colder than intended.

His expression thinned. "When the mayor realized I had tried to cheat, he was... reasonably upset."

The chaperone, Clem, snorted up front. "He turned Mayor Vepar's prize chickens into headless goats. Still hasn't lived it down."

"That was a misunderstanding," Samiel muttered. "And technically, the goats had heads. It was the souls that were missing."

Clem made a huffing sound halfway between a cough and a laugh. "Mayor doesn't care about the technicalities. He cares about goats with glowing eyes menacing the town council."

"You got banned from Bride Bingo," I said. "There's a term for that where I'm from. It's 'legend.'" The image stuck with me: a demon in time-out, inventing new ways to kill time and nurse a cosmic grudge. It softened him, just a little. Not that I'd tell him that to his face. I'd already learned he enjoyed the verbal sparring too much.

After a lull, something softer replaced the sarcasm in my voice. "You must have been really bored."

"Boredom is the natural state of a demon on Earth." The words came out wry, but there was pain under the lacquer. "That's why most of us either go native, or go feral."

I didn't let the silence close back down. "So what did you do for forty years? Eat wings, scare livestock, and brood?" I realized as I said it I was genuinely curious. Samiel was the first man I'd met in a decade who didn't seem to want to play a role, and it left me ferociously impatient to peel him down to the bone.

He flexed his claws, tracing a line along the faded upholstery between us. "I learned to cook," he said, almost sheepish. "Turns out, if you want to fit in, you need a hobby that doesn't involve fire or torment. Cooking was... achievable. I like the chemistry." He glanced sidelong at me, as if daring me to laugh at him, and when I didn't, he continued: "Took a job at the diner, too. Mostly on the grill, but sometimes I did front of house. Humans tip better when you smile, even if it scares them." The last bit sounded like an admission of guilt in a therapy circle, but I got the sense he was proud of it.

It was weirdly intimate, like a second date three hours into the first, fast-forwarding through years of bullshit. I wanted to ask what demons cooked for themselves, but I was busy imagining Samiel in a paper hat and apron, his claws wrapped delicately around a spatula, handing out pancakes to hungover casino tourists. It made me want to grin, so I did.

He must have caught the edge of it, because his tail twitched, and then he said, "What about you, Annie H? You never answered your own question up there. Why'd you come?"

"I figured demon marriage had to be less humiliating than regular dating," I said, "and I was running out of cities to start over in. You ever get that feeling? Like you've already lived through everyone in a hundred-mile radius?" I looked out the dirty window; the sky was so hard and blue, it looked brittle. "I want something that's not afraid to be ugly," I said, quieter this time. "I want someone who doesn't just pretend to get me but actually does."

It hung between us, the words heavier than the heat. Samiel's hand, already so much larger than mine, curled around my thigh with a gentleness that stung.

"I'm not afraid of ugly," he said.

Clem pulled the shuttle to a halt. Lake Purgatory was a mirage, milky blue and ringed with a sickly halo of white sand. The house sat on a rise above the lake, low and broad, a slab of poured concrete and glass that looked both ancient and freshly landed from the future. The walkway was a tongue of red flagstone, and the front door was flanked by two planters where the succulents were thriving. Samiel steered me toward the door like a gameshow host unveiling a prize package.

Inside, I had a split second of dissonance. I know he'd said mid-century, but part of me didn't believe him. I expected taxidermy, dungeon vibes, maybe a faint smell of brimstone. Instead, it was clean lines, orange shag rugs, a glass wall that led to a deck facing the water, and a floor-to-ceiling fireplace made of glittery volcanic rock. Eames chairs. A sunken living room. There was even a lava lamp, which Sam immediately flicked on for maximum ambiance.

I dropped my bag by the door and kicked off my boots, shaking the imaginary dust from my calves. "You were serious? I was expecting, like, pillories and iron maidens."

"Don't worry," Samiel said, trailing in after me. "The iron maiden's in the basement. I'll show you later." He said it like a joke, but I believed him just enough to make the hair on my arms stand up.

We explored in a loose orbit, the sound of Clem driving away fading. The kitchen was pristine, all steel and glass, with a double oven and a fridge big enough to hide several bodies. I opened it, half expecting nothing but Red Bull and raw meat, but instead it was full of actual groceries: berries, oat milk, charcuterie. Two kinds of hummus. I glanced at Sam and he shrugged.

"I did the shopping," he said, almost bashful. "Didn't know what you liked, so I got everything." He hovered in the entryway with the tension of someone who'd never hosted a guest before and wasn't sure when the party started. His wings tucked themselves in tight, as if he was still afraid to take up space. I wondered how long it took to unlearn that kind of caution.

I ran a finger along the countertop, then tossed the hummus onto the island. "So, Samiel," I said, biting into a carrot from the crisper. "What's the orientation protocol? Do we get the ten-cent tour? Or just skip straight to the trauma-tizing icebreakers?"

He ticked his eyes up to the ceiling, mock-consulting some invisible playbook. "Officially, we're supposed to review the terms of engagement, co-sign the safety agree-ment, and then attempt to create a shared meal as an exercise in "marital harmony." He made air quotes, and I tried not to snort carrot up my nose.

"And unofficially?"

His mouth curled, a slow tilt of mischief. "Unofficially, we can do whatever we want."

CHAPTER
FOUR

Samiel

I closed the fridge, bracing my palm on the door, and watched her devour the carrot. The way she chewed— quick, decisive, no hesitation—made me want to pin her against the stainless steel and see what else she'd bite. It had been literal decades since I'd wanted anything this much, and the feeling was both exhilarating and a little terrifying, like watching a storm charge up the valley toward your house and realizing it was never going to change course.

It was almost unfair how quickly she got under my skin. Her eyes held my gaze like the world had shrunk to a point between us, and when she bit into the carrot—deliberate, knowing—my body responded in ways I thought I'd trained out eons ago. Forty years of practice, and none of it prepared me for the taste of wanting. I wanted to chase her, to pin her, to see if her bravado would crack or just sharpen under pressure.

Instead, I followed her into the kitchen and feigned normalcy. She opened cupboards, found the espresso machine, and started the grind with the nonchalance of a woman who'd already decided she'd outlive her captor. Her skirt swished behind her knees, plaid and crisp, and her shirt was cropped just enough to bare a line of ivory skin when she reached overhead. I wanted to taste it, and the thought shocked me enough to make my tail twitch, knocking a spoon to the floor.

She watched it spiral, then bent—graceful, deliberate, like she knew I was watching. Her hand caught the spoon before it finished clattering, and she set it back in the ceramic caddy with a flourish.

"So, Samiel. What's on your bucket list for the three days? Besides the obvious."

She dropped it right there—no innuendo, just a fact. At some point she'd be naked and screaming in at least one room of this house, and the only question was which of us would be in more danger when it happened.

I let my tongue flick just a little, watching her eyes track the movement. "That depends," I said. "Do you want the real list, or the one I give the orientation committee?"

She set the portafilter back in the machine and leaned against the counter, arms crossed, the weight of her attention settling on my collarbones. "Show your work, demon. I'll spot the lies."

The honesty of her expectation was enough to make me nervous. I looked past her, out the window, at the blunt blue sky, then back down to the way her fingers drummed on her own forearm. "I want to see the lake," I said, surprised to find it true. "I want to cook for you. I want to play chess and let you win at least once, just to see if you're a good winner or a sore one." It all spilled out as if I'd been rehearsing, though I'd never dared to believe I'd get this far, never let myself hope I'd get to want anything beyond the basic, carnal minimum.

She stared at me like she was waiting for the punchline. "That's it? No bone-shattering, no world domination, no pranks on the mayor?"

I shrugged, feeling suddenly transparent. "I thought I'd have to work harder to seduce you," I admitted. "But you don't seem like the type who needs the hard sell."

She cocked her head, rolled her eyes skyward as if consulting a demon herself. "Samiel, I hate to break it to you, but you had me at 'industrial zipper.'" She took the mug, steam curling upward, and blew across the surface, treating it like the world's most dangerous potion. "Full disclosure, I'm not great at chess, but I promise to ruin your life in Scrabble." She held the mug between both hands, letting the heat scald her knuckles. Her gaze flicked to me again, unreadable.

Then, just as I opened my mouth to volley back, she cut in. "Sam, you want to fuck me, right?"

It was so blunt I almost dropped the cup I'd just pulled from the shelf. I'd spent forty years on Earth, witnessed human courtships conducted in coded language and cowardice, and here she was, stripping it to the bone and tossing it at my feet. Every layer of practiced charm dissolved under her stare. I opened my mouth and tasted the word before I said it.

"Yes."

"Then what are you waiting for?" She never raised her voice, but the words landed like a thrown gauntlet, soft and deadly.

I rounded the island in three long strides, and she didn't move, didn't flinch, just watched me with a half-smile that bared all her sharp little teeth. I touched her jaw with one hand, feather-light, testing; she tilted her head up, not yielding so much as inviting. Her pulse leapt under my fingers, wild as a trapped bird, and the hunger in me flared so bright I nearly lost my grip on the old self-control I'd been honing since Reagan was president.

Her mouth parted and I kissed her, slow at first—testing, then devouring. She tasted like burnt sugar and adrenaline and something sharp, like the white of a lemon rind. Her hands went straight for my shirt, curling in the collar and hauling me closer, a move so confident it made me want to laugh with delight. But I didn't, because already she was nipping at my lower lip, and all the air in my brain was being replaced by her.

She broke the kiss first, but only to breathe, and when she did, she grinned up at me with such outright challenge that it kindled something feral under my sternum. I curved my palm to the back of her neck, letting my claws just barely graze her skin.

"If you want me to stop," I said, "now's your last chance."

Annie's eyes narrowed, not in suspicion but in pleasure. "I'll let you know if you get close," she said, and then she was pulling my face down to hers again, greedy for more.

I caged her in against the counter, wings spreading for balance, tail flicking behind me like an exclamation point. She tasted me back, tongue darting quick and sure, and I let my own forked tongue slip out in return, a ticklish, forbidden thing I'd always been careful to hide. I could split it further up at will, or keep it just as a forked tip. I wondered how she'd prefer it. She startled at the touch—a tiny, involuntary sound in her throat, half-laugh, half-moan —and I nearly bit through my own lip. She pressed closer, her hands sliding up my chest, over the ridges of old scars and down along my ribs, winding under my shirt with no hesitation.

"Jesus," she said, when she finally surfaced, her breath gone ragged. "That thing you do with your tongue—"

I grinned, showing all my teeth this time. "Most mortals run from that," I said, and laid my forked tongue out for her, a slow, deliberate display. Both ends curled, tasting the air, then slid back in.

"Yeah, well," she said, eyes fixed on my mouth, "I'm not most mortals." She bit her own lip as if she wanted to prove it, then said, "Do it again."

I leaned in, tracing the border of her jaw with the two prongs, a line of sensation that made her eyelids flutter. I let the tips of my tongue tease her earlobe, then flick downward, tasting the line of her pulse. She moaned again, and the sound was so honest, so alive, that I had to brace both arms on the counter to keep from shaking. If there was a power dynamic here, it was torn to shreds and set on fire with every new touch.

I tasted Annie's last moan in my mouth, hot as a live coal. She pressed her hips into me, hard, like she wanted to grind bones as well as skin. I let her, every nerve in my body tuning to the way she fitted against me, the way she gripped my shirt as if she might tear me open and crawl inside. I held nothing back. My hands found her waist, then up, under the edge of her shirt, to the soft, exposed band of her body. My claws were blunt, careful, but they still left little red trails in their wake.

She arched like she wanted it rougher, and I gave her what she asked for: a full palm splayed across her ribs, then higher, cupping her breasts, the delicate weight of them making my whole body ring like a tuning fork. She gasped. I rolled her nipple between thumb and forefinger, not gentle, not cruel, but deliberate—an experiment and an announcement.

"Yeah?" I asked, voice gone ragged around the edges, face buried against her neck, hair spilling over her shoulder.

She bit my earlobe, hard enough to send a fresh spike of need through me. "Yeah. Do it again."

I did, and the shudder that ran through her nearly unmade me. I couldn't resist the urge to taste her, so I bent, nosed the collar of her shirt aside, and dragged my tongue (both tips, slow and forked) over the soft skin above her bra. The flavor was sweat and sunblock and a chemistry I'd never once encountered in Hell, and I wanted it on the roof of my mouth, in my blood.

"I want to suck you," I said, not bothering with euphemism, my voice a growl against her chest. "Taste all of you, every inch. Can I?"

She nodded, pupils blown wide, blue almost vanished. "You'd better."

Her shirt was gone before I knew what to do with the scraps of fabric. Her bra was black and lacy. I used my teeth, snapping the front clasp and letting the cups fall free. Her nipples were perfect, pink and already pulled tight. I caught one between my lips and licked, not rushing it, letting my tongue fork around it, tips circling in opposite directions, then sucked, slow and deep. Annie made a sound I'd never heard from a human before—part whimper, part satisfaction, as if she'd won a bet with the universe—and fisted both hands in my hair, yanking hard enough to make my eyes roll back.

"Fuck, Sam," she hissed, squirming against me, her thighs bracing around my hips. I could feel the heat of her, even through the layered fabric, and it drove me half-crazy. I didn't stop. I wanted her to know what she'd signed up for, wanted to leave her marked and shivering.

I moved to her other nipple, grazing it with my canine and then soothing it with a broad swipe of tongue.

She tilted her head back, exposing her throat, and her hands—small, precise—traced up my chest and past my shoulders, mapping me with the greedy, scientific curiosity of someone who'd been promised wonders and refused to be disappointed. I felt her palm on the base of my left horn, tentative at first, then a little firmer as she gauged my reaction.

It was the most intimate thing I'd ever felt—more than a kiss, more than sex. My horns were incredibly sensitive, and no one had ever bothered touching them. My knees actually buckled, a full system crash, the blood draining from my brain and slamming into a part of me that hadn't known touch in forty years. It was as though every nerve in my body was tuned to a single, shrieking violin string, and Annie's fingers—cool, clever—plucked it with the expertise of a concertmaster. My tail went rigid, my wings snapped open, and I made a sound in my chest that was closer to a growl than anything human.

Annie jerked her hand back, startled, but I caught her wrist before she could retreat. My pupils had gone full reptile; I could see it reflected in the steel of the espresso machine. I forced a breath, then another, but the craving flattened me. I buried my face in the curve of her neck, inhaling a hit of her scent, and said, "Careful. That's—" I choked on the word, tongue thick and useless. "Sensitive."

She was grinning; I could feel the upturn of her cheek against my brow. "Yeah, well, that's the idea." She reached for my horns again, and this time there was no hesitation—she cupped the base of the right one and dragged her nails up the ridged spiral, slow and devilish, and my vision went white around the edges. I groaned, a real, guttural thing, and gripped the counter to keep from collapsing around her.

Annie watched me, fascinated, as though she wanted to see how far it would go before something broke. She locked eyes with me, her tongue dragging slow across her own lip as she tested first one horn, then the other—twisting, kneading, squeezing with calculated cruelty. I shuddered, a full-body convulsion, and the ridge of my cock throbbed so hard it was almost painful. I'd had dreams like this, early in the exile, but never let myself imagine a human would actually touch me like she meant it. Never expected to feel the sweet, humiliating ache of being so—*needy*.

She leaned in, voice velvet over broken glass. "You like that?" Her fingers never let up, and if it was a game, she was already leagues ahead.

I gripped the counter until my claws scored white lines in the laminate, then hissed out, "If you keep that up, I am going to fuck you on this counter and apologize to the mayor later."

Her eyes glittered, undaunted. "Promise?"

She pressed against me, the press of her hips a direct, kinetic rebuke to the forty years of slow-play I'd been feeding myself. I wanted to savor it, but her hands on my horns made me reckless. I wanted all of it right now, wanted to rip through the pretense and get to the animal of it, the part that was just hunger and heat and the reality of someone else's skin. I picked her up with one hand—her legs looping my waist before I could even show off about it —and set her on the edge of the counter. She went for my belt, zero hesitation, nails black and perfect and clicking against the buckle.

I caught her wrists before she could undo it. "Annie—"

She looked up, eyes wide and unafraid. "What, you're going to try for a tender moment now?"

"I don't want to bruise you," I said, and I meant it. Her hands were small, her bones so breakable I could hear the delicate grind of tendon and cartilage under my grip. Human bodies were weak, and I had broken too many things to forget it.

She twisted her wrists in my hands, not to escape, but to tangle her fingers with mine. "I'm not made of glass, Sam," she said, breathless. "And if I was, I'd want you to break me anyway." She yanked my head down and kissed me hard enough that our teeth clacked. At that point, whatever shreds of restraint I'd been clinging to—habits, oaths, the memory of every HR orientation video I had ever been forced to watch—went up in flames.

Her thighs caged my hips, locking us together. She ground herself against me, skirt rucked up, black mesh underwear already damp and hot as a fever through the fabric. I wanted to rip them with my teeth, leave marks, but I forced myself to slow down, and let Annie keep control. She wrestled with my belt, tongue between her teeth in concentration, and for a dizzy moment I wondered if she'd just tear it off me with sheer force of will. Her nails scored the leather, then found the button beneath—and the look she gave me, up through her lashes, turned me inside out.

"Industrial zipper, huh?" she muttered, voice turned hoarse with want.

"Told you," I managed, though my lips were pressed against her neck, my hands braced around her hips, thumbs pressing into the tender line between thigh and ass. She popped the button, jerked the zipper down, and the sound—it was so loud in the kitchen, it was obscene. She dipped her hand inside my underwear and pulled my cock free.

She hooked her thumbs under the band of my briefs and yanked, determined, and I helped her—because if I didn't, I might explode through my own skin. She peeled them down, and I watched as her eyes widened at the sight of me: thick and veined black on red, with a knotted ridge at the base and the head shaped not quite like a human's, but certainly like nothing she'd ever seen before. There was a moment—an honest, gorgeous pause—where her whole brain clicked over, nowhere to file what she was looking at, and I almost laughed before her hand closed around me.

She stroked once, and it was bliss and agony, every nerve in me singing. The friction was electrifying, her palm hot and a little rough, and the way her fingers struggled to wrap around the full circumference made something animal in me roar for more. I leaned forward, one arm caging her against the cabinets and the other diving up under her skirt to palm the heat of her through the mesh. She gasped, not with fear but with delight, and her nails dug crescents into my bicep. I thought she might draw blood, and honestly, I would have let her. Annie's wrist moved with a confidence I recognized from my own kind—she pumped me slow, then fast, then slow again, studying the way my eyes shut and my breath snagged in my throat.

"You're so fucking wet," I said, and immediately realized I'd said it out loud. Not as a line, not even as dirty talk, just a pure, involuntary observation, and it made her laugh—a sharp, delighted sound that shot straight to my cock. She leaned in and bit my jaw, just hard enough to mark, and whispered, "You started it." Then she dragged my palm under her skirt, pressing my fingers to the soaked, sticky silk of her underwear.

I groaned at the feel of her, the way she was already pulsing and slick and so alive under me. I traced the seam of her underwear, then slid the fabric aside, not bothering with pretense, and pressed two fingers to her. She was hot—hotter than any mortal should be, and I felt something in me snarl with anticipation at the proof she wanted this as much as I did.

Her hand tightened on my cock, and she said, "Okay, I need a heads-up—no pun intended. Am I supposed to do something special with"—she pumped once, thumb tracing the knotted ridge at the base—"this part? Or is it like one of those gourmet hot dogs where you just admire the engineering and then bite down?"

It took me a second to realize what she was asking. I glanced down at myself, at the thick, marbled length of my cock, the head flared and almost spade-shaped, and the ridge at the base swollen and ridged like the handle of a battle-axe. The knot. I'd forgotten how the sight of it could stop a mortal cold. Annie's hand squeezed experimentally, then she surfed her thumb over the knot, curiosity and delight mixing in her face.

"That's an… upgrade," she said, voice uncertain for the first time, but only a little. "Is it, like, functional, or just for show?"

I almost wanted to say it was just for show, to make it easier, but I didn't want to lie to her. "It locks us together," I said, voice rough. "At the end. It's a breeding thing. Demon biology." The words came out hot, half-apologetic, but Annie's eyes only got brighter.

She ran her thumb over the knotted ridge again, as if she could memorize it with her touch. "How long does it last?" she said, and the way she said *how long* made me ache, the way she ground herself against the answer. "Full, or just tip?" She locked her eyes on mine, and I understood she wanted specifics, not metaphors.

"It's all or nothing," I said. There was a warning in my tone, and not a drop of apology. "You'll be stuck with me till it softens. Sometimes minutes, sometimes an hour if I'm—" I leaned in, tongue tracing her jaw. "Feeling possessive."

Her breath hitched, but she didn't pull away. Her entire body had gone pliant with anticipation, the animal part of her brain already signing the waiver before the rest of her caught up. She rolled the knob again in her palm, as if she wanted to test the friction.

"So it's really a breeding thing," she said, voice half-laughing, half-challenging. "Should I be scared?"

I curved my fingers inside her, feeling the way her body opened around me. "You should be prepped for it, at least," I said. "Once it starts, I can't stop." Decades of practice battling with the need to be honest, even if it made me look weak.

Annie's laugh was ragged, delighted. She fished my cock out again. "Copper IUD and the pill, Samiel. Double-barreled birth control. If you think demon sperm scares me more than the average man's, you don't know my exes."

The lust in my gut went white-hot. I lost the last of my restraint and hoisted her to the counter, letting her ankles hook my waist, her skirt hiking up to frame the soft skin of her thighs. She wasn't shy; she yanked her panties down to mid-thigh and grinned, mean and hungry, at the sight of me losing my composure.

I pressed the head of my cock to her, testing the wet heat with a slow, deliberate drag, letting the spade-shaped head spread her open. She bit her bottom lip hard enough for it to go white, but didn't break eye contact. I pushed in, slow, savoring every millimeter as her body shuddered around me. She was tight—so tight—and I had to grit my teeth to keep from slamming her straight through the backsplash.

The first inch was resistance, the next was pure give. She gasped, then let out a ragged, "Fuck, you're big," which made me want to ruin her with the rest of it, but I forced myself to go slow—let her adjust, let her own the moment.

"Want me to stop?" I asked, voice barely human.

She shook her head, wild and desperate. "No, no—just go, Sam, go—"

I pushed in farther, feeling her stretch, her breath hitch and then break into a whimper. Her hands clawed at my back, nails sharp, and I felt the sting like a benediction. I bottomed out slowly, the knot at my base straining against her entrance, not yet pressing in but promising. She arched her spine, face twisted up in agony and awe, and I let her acclimate, holding myself still inside her.

"Fuck, Sam," she said again, voice shredded. "You weren't kidding about the upgrade."

The words snapped something in me. I braced her hips in my hands and started to move, shallow thrusts at first, just the tip, letting her get greedy—letting her rock herself onto me harder with every motion. She was wetter than anything I'd ever felt, slick and hot and tight, and the sound of us echoed in the kitchen, obscene and gorgeous. Her breath came in gasps, then moans, and she never stopped watching my face.

I wanted to see how long she'd keep challenging me, but Annie answered that by pushing off the counter and dragging me—literally, hand fisted in my shirt—toward the living room. She didn't bother to fix her skirt, just hopped down, panties still looped at one ankle, and stalked ahead, not even checking if I'd follow.

I did. Of course I did. I would have followed her into a fire.

The sunken living room was golden in the low afternoon

light, thick carpet and all those glass walls. Annie turned and flopped onto the couch, legs spread, skirt bunched at her hips. She crooked a finger at me, a command, not a request.

"Come here."

I went, every muscle tight as wire. She lay back, propped on her elbows, and looked at me with a hunger that bordered on savage. I palmed her knee and spread her further, lining myself up again. She was so fucking wet, and so ready for me, and when I eased in the second time, she let out a sound so desperate I thought she might shatter from it. I bottomed out, my balls pressed to her, and the knot at the base of my cock throbbed against her entrance, not quite inside yet, just massaging a promise against the slick, swollen opening.

She arched her back, hair wild across the cushions, and said, "Don't you dare hold back." Her voice was ragged but clear, slicing clean through the haze of heat between us. "I want all of it, Samiel. Every fucking inch."

I did not need to be told twice. I set a rhythm—slow, heavy, grinding—letting my cock piston in and out, each thrust deeper, each retreat slower, letting her savor the obscene stretch. Her hands flew to my chest, nails raking down the skin, and her thighs shook around my waist, the beginnings of a spasm already rippling under the surface. She dragged me down for a kiss, her breath hot and sweet, biting my lower lip until I groaned into her mouth.

The knot of my cock swelled as I approached the edge, a slow, relentless pressure that built until it was almost unbearable. I could feel her clench around me, the muscles of her cunt fluttering in perfect time with the noises she made, like she was trying to milk every last drop out of me. Her hands found my horns again, this time holding tight as I pounded her harder, the sounds of skin and wetness and couch springs filling the whole goddamn house.

"Fuck—" she gasped. "—Sam—don't stop—"

I didn't. I couldn't. The last of my control snapped, and I drove in with everything I had, knot battering at her entrance until with a slick, obscene pop, it forced its way through. She screamed—no sound, just air and animal heat, her whole body going rigid as the knot tied us together, locking us in a pulsing, involuntary spasm. The velvet vise of her cunt clenched around me, milking out every ounce of sensation until the only thing left was white noise and the wild, shuddering aftershock of a climax that felt like it might kill me.

I held there, buried in her, my forehead pressed to the crook of her neck. Her breath was a staccato of little whimpers, body still trembling around the knot and the length of me inside her. I'd never felt anything like it, not once in four decades of pretending to be tame. My body wanted to rut, to claim, to stay inside her until the end of time. My mind just wanted to know if I'd broken her in the good way, or the bad.

She went limp, boneless and splayed on the couch, her chest heaving.

CHAPTER
FIVE

Annie

For a few minutes, all I could do was stare at the ceiling and count the sweat cooling on my skin. I'd had sex before—good sex, even—but this was something else, a whole-body reset button mashed so hard I felt my bones realign. My hips still tingled, oversensitive and deliciously bruised, and my heartbeat hadn't figured out how to slow down yet. I gazed down at Samiel beneath me, his eyes half-lidded and gleaming between triumph and awe. The corners of his mouth curled upward in a smile that was all teeth and satisfaction, like a predator who'd finally caught something worth the hunt.

He was still in me, and the knot was the most bizarre and intimate sensation I'd ever experienced. I tried to shift experimentally, and the movement wrung a sharp aftershock through my gut that made me giggle and gasp in the same breath. Samiel's brow furrowed.

"Are you okay?" he asked, voice pitched low, almost gentle. Maybe he was worried I'd break, or that he'd done something wrong, but the only thing wrong was how much I wanted to do that again. Like right now, if my legs would cooperate.

"Yeah," I managed, breathless. "I think you just rearranged my entire personality."

He blinked, uncertain, and then his mouth curved into a grin so disarmingly proud, I thought he might flex right through the couch. "I can fix it, if you want."

"No way," I said, finding his face with my hand. The skin was warm and just a little rough, like new suede. "I like it. I feel… optimized."

He exhaled slowly, and the tension in his body seemed to melt. I got the impression he'd been bracing for disaster and was only now letting himself believe he hadn't broken me. Not the way that mattered.

I wiggled again, experimentally, and the movement sent a shudder through both of us. The knot was still solid, keeping us joined, and the sensation was less possession now, more absurd intimacy—like a pinky swear made with every cell in our bodies. I couldn't help it; I started giggling harder.

He looked at me, puzzled. "Is it that weird?"

"Oh, it's weird," I said, struggling to breathe, "but so am I. I think I'm into it." I flexed around him, just to see what would happen, and Samiel's eyes rolled back in his head for a split second before he managed to pull it together.

"Careful," he said, voice rough. "If you do that, we'll be here all night."

"Is that a promise or a threat?" I ran my hand up the side of his face—I couldn't get over how hot he ran. I wondered if having a higher body temperature was a demon thing or a Samiel thing. "Or is this just standard for demon marriages, the whole *knot and lock* thing?"

He leaned in, nuzzling just under my jaw, all careful teeth and steady breath. "It will soften eventually. I just... didn't want to let go." The admission was so naked, it made me dizzy.

I snorted, which wasn't the sexiest response, but he didn't seem to mind. "I mean, if you're going to keep me here, you could at least let me see the lake. You promised a view."

He huffed a low sound, somewhere between a purr and a laugh. "That I can do. There's a hot tub on the back deck. Clothes optional."

I tried to wriggle in excitement and nearly saw stars. "You're going to have to carry me. My legs don't work anymore."

He carried me—knot still firmly lodged, my ankles locked around his waist—to the patio door. The glass was warm against my bare back. Outside, the raw sky had softened from brutal blue to the bruised lavender of early evening, and the lake below shimmered in a way that looked inviting—but Samiel had warned me it was brutally cold.

The outdoor air was still desert-hot, but the wind licked goosebumps across my skin where the sweat had dried. There was a hot tub in one corner, half recessed into the concrete. The water steamed, a blue and white cauldron with a sign on the side: PLEASE SHOWER BEFORE USE.

Samiel maneuvered the few steps up, before lowering us both in, me still wrapped around him. I hissed as the hot water hit my skin, feeling the delicious sting. Samiel groaned as the heat hit him. "God yes," he said, voice raw and unguarded. "This is almost as good as—" He stopped, then smirked. "Well. Almost."

I laid my head on his chest, his heartbeat a drum beneath my ear. The water lapped between us, washing away the sweat and ache, but nothing could rinse away the feeling of belonging that had settled in my bones. My body still pulsed where he remained inside me. I pressed closer, chest to chest, my arms finding their way around his neck like they belonged there.

The silence between us was the good kind, just the hush of two people recalibrating.

For a while, we let the surface tension and the hiss of the jets do the talking. Somewhere in the valley, someone had started a bonfire, the woodsmoke drifting in a lazy spiral over the water. Bats looped through the air, chasing dusk-crazed bugs. It was perfect, almost aggressively so, and I felt myself relax into it—not just the bath, but the whole idea of being here, of letting myself want something without the constant snarl of skepticism gnawing at the corners.

Samiel's hand found the nape of my neck, rubbing circles. Not possessive, just… gentle. I'd been bracing for claws and fangs, for some kind of cartoon villainy, but all I got was a thumb kneading where the tension pooled behind my skull.

"Should I be worried this is the happiest I've ever been on a first date?" I mumbled, barely loud enough for the bats to overhear.

He chuckled and the vibration of it, deep in his chest, hummed through my cheek. "Humans always worry when they're happy," he said. "It's one of your top three hobbies. Right after self-sabotage and inventing new flavors of potato chip."

He rolled us a little so I was half-floating, my head on his arm, and used his free hand to fish a leaf out of the water. He examined it like a jeweler, then flicked it over his shoulder.

"Okay, so what are demons' top hobbies?" I asked,

letting my fingers trace the waterline along his ribs. "Besides, you know. This."

He made a thoughtful noise, like he was reading the question off a card. "Number one is cheating at board games. Number two is making up new rules to board games so you can't technically call it cheating. Number three is pretending we're not vulnerable, even when we are."

"Sounds a lot like humans," I said, and dipped my pinky in the swirl between our bodies, marveling at the way our skin looked together—his, unearthly and dark, mine pale as a peeled grape in the haze of the evening. Even the water felt different on us. He steamed; I pruned.

"Maybe that's why they keep trying," Samiel said. "Matching monsters to mortals. See who can outlast the experiment." His voice was so soft I almost missed the edge of longing in it.

I wanted to say something grand, something to shatter the moment open, but this didn't need a speech. I just pressed my forehead to his, the horns cool and smooth against my hairline, and let the hush do the rest.

A minute passed, maybe more. My body felt right for the first time in years, perfectly weighted and perfectly suspended. Eventually, I felt Sam's knot soften and his cock slip out of me, leaving me feeling hollowed out.

I felt suddenly loose and floaty, limbs light, like I could just drift in the tub forever. I stretched out my legs and watched the foam swirl around us, pink from the sky above and tinged blue from the LED at the bottom of the tub. Samiel tucked me under his arm, easing my body to rest against the line of his, which was oddly comforting, like we'd done this a hundred times before. He stared out over the deck rail and the sand and the distant glassy lake. I followed his gaze, and for the first time in maybe a decade, I allowed myself to just sit in the moment.

The sunset was ridiculous. The sky laid itself open in layers—coral, then orange, then a seam of purple so dramatic it looked like a digital filter. The clouds above the lake glowed from underneath, and the water reflected a smear of molten gold that rippled and broke against the shore.

It was so beautiful I had to look away, because it made my heart clench in a way that was embarrassing. I distracted myself by letting my hand wander along Samiel's ribcage, mapping out the grooves under his skin. He shivered a little, and I felt a spike of satisfaction—maybe I wasn't the only one knocked off-balance.

"So," I said, making my voice as casual as possible, "what's the protocol after this? Do we light a ceremonial candle? Sacrifice a neighbor? Announce our engagement to the HOA?"

Samiel's hand tightened a fraction on my shoulder. "Now, we survive our chaperone check-in at noon tomorrow, and otherwise..." He gestured at the world, at the lake, at my still-wet thighs and the way I blinked up at him. "We do whatever the hell we want. Three days, no interruptions. They're strict about it—the town is off-limits, phones don't work very well this close to the portal, and nobody's allowed to interfere unless we're dying or on fire. I asked. They said dying was preferable."

I grinned, picturing the mayor with a clipboard and a fire extinguisher, ticking off *asphyxiation by demon dick* on his incident report. "So we're marooned together, is what you're saying."

He shrugged, a ripple of muscle and nonchalance. "Marooned implies you want to leave."

I snorted but didn't argue. The idea of being stuck here for three days with nothing but a demon, a haunted lake, and a fridge full of snacks felt less like a punishment and more like a gift.

"I think I can handle it," I said, and nudged my head under his chin. "You're a pretty decent island to be marooned on."

He made a sound in his throat, almost a purr. "I can do better than decent. Just..." He hesitated, and his hand came up to cup the back of my skull, careful as if I were truly breakable. "There are some things I'm supposed to do. Some... tests. But I want to wait. Surprise you. If that's okay."

I tilted up, squinting at him through the steam. "Tests? Like compatibility challenges, or are you going to try to drown me and see if I float?"

It was a joke, but Samiel's hesitation was real. "A little bit of both, maybe." He ran his thumb along the edge of my ear, a rhythm meant to soothe, but his eyes stayed locked on the horizon.

I wasn't sure why, but I liked that he didn't want to give it all away at once. There was something weirdly respectful about it. He didn't want to scare me off, or maybe he didn't want to scare himself, but either way, he wanted to do it right. It made my insides do that little flip they only ever did after the credits rolled on a good horror movie, the kind where you got exactly what you came for but still weren't sure if you'd sleep tonight.

"Okay," I said, after a while. "Surprise me, then. But if it's a trust fall over the lake, I'm pushing you in first."

He chuckled, and the sound was so human, it almost startled me. "Deal. But you should know, I can't drown. Not even if you held my head under."

I snorted. "Now I have to try, just to see the science."

The temperature fell off a cliff after sunset, desert warmth bleeding into a blue-black cold that sank through the deck and bit every patch of exposed skin. I shivered, and Samiel, without a word, shifted his wings to create a windbreak, then pulled me almost all the way onto his lap. The way his body radiated heat made it feel like he'd absorbed the sun and was now parceling it out, molecule by molecule, for my benefit alone. There was a weird comfort in the way he held me, not possessive but present, like I was an answer to a question he'd spent years trying not to ask.

We stayed like that until the jets cycled off and the hush of the valley swept back in. Eventually, the chill crept back into my bones, the desert night reasserting itself. I shivered, and Samiel immediately lifted me out of the tub, wrapping me in a towel so oversized, it may have doubled as a tent. He carried me back inside without a word. The glass doors whooshed shut behind us and for a second, I thought I heard the echo of my own scream ricochet off the lake. There was a moment of vertigo as Samiel held me suspended above the carpet, wings braced for balance, his eyes black with want— and then the towel slipped, baring me again, and he tucked it around me like a secret.

My stomach, always the loyal saboteur, seized the moment to make its needs violently known. It let out a noise so outrageous and prolonged it sounded like into a new species of lesser demon. The sound vibrated between us, echoing off the glass and the concrete, and I felt my cheeks heat up in the way only hunger and the total dissolution of dignity could produce.

Samiel arched a brow, the corner of his mouth twitching. "That," he said, "sounds like a threat."

I peeled the towel up higher on my chest, pretending it

was armor. "You'd better feed me before I eat you. And not in the fun way."

He set me down gently, feet barely touching the shag rug, and then let his hands linger at my waist for a beat too long. "What do you want? I stocked for every contingency."

I considered. "Surprise me. But nothing processed. I want real food. I want, like, dinner." The admission sounded juvenile, but Samiel's face broke into a lopsided grin like I'd just passed a test he wasn't sure I'd studied for.

He stalked into the kitchen, flicking on the lights with his tail. He rummaged in the fridge, and I watched the play of muscle at his back, the way his wings tucked in but quivered at the tips every time I shifted the towel and exposed a patch of thigh. Maybe he noticed; maybe he just liked the idea of me watching. Either way, he moved like a man who wanted to be caught.

He lined up ingredients on the butcher block: eggs, a block of cheese, a small pile of green onions, a suspiciously perfect tomato, sourdough bread. He looked at me over his shoulder and said, "Do you like breakfast for dinner, or is that too on the nose?"

"Breakfast is my favorite dinner," I said, still swaddled in towel, perched on the nearest barstool. "If you can make a decent omelet, you can have my soul. For three days, anyway."

He cracked eggs with a single-handed flourish, no shell shards anywhere, and started whisking them with a ferocity that nearly matched the way he'd fucked me. The skillet heated, the cheese grated itself beneath his claws, and in less than five minutes he had a perfect, golden curd folding over itself on the plate. He layered in tomato and chive, then slid the whole thing to me with a proud, almost bashful smile.

I took a bite. It was flawless, creamy, the cheese barely

melted inside so it oozed with every forkful. "Oh my god," I moaned, louder than necessary. "You're wasted on the bachelor circuit. You could run a restaurant with food like this. Five stars, would bang again."

Samiel grinned, a slow, prideful curl of his mouth. "Give me another night. I'll show you what I can really do." The words came out dark and deliberate, like a promise—though I couldn't be sure if he meant the food, the fucking, or both.

I dared him with a look, then devoured the rest of the omelet in greedy, undignified bites. By the time I finished, the towel was slipping dangerously low, and my skin had developed that prickly, post-hot-tub hypersensitivity that made everything feel faintly electric. I shimmied off the stool and let the towel drop to the floor, just to see if Samiel would react.

He did. His eyes flickered over my body in a way that was both clinical and avaricious, as if he wanted to log every contour for a report later. He wiped his hands on a towel, then stalked toward me with a predatory patience I was already learning to recognize as his baseline.

"You waited too long to eat," he said, voice low but edged with something like scold. "You always do that?"

I rolled my eyes but couldn't hide the flush. "I forget sometimes. Deadlines, distractions, existential dread. I'll eat when I'm hungry, or when it's in front of me." I shrugged like it was nothing, but he didn't let it slide.

He caught my chin between his thumb and forefinger, not hard, just commanding. "Don't do that again," he said, and the heat in his words made my knees want to buckle. "You're not allowed to starve yourself around me. If you go more than six hours, I'll hunt you down and make you eat whether you want to or not." The promise was dark and unyielding, and for a second I wondered if this was what it felt like to be cared for, or possessed, or both. The scary part was—I didn't hate it.

He watched my face for signs of resistance, and when he saw none, he released my chin and bent to pick up the towel. He draped it over my shoulders, infuriatingly gentle after all the predatory heat of his stare. "You're going to need your strength for tomorrow, Annie. I have plans."

I snorted, trying to play it off. "You're giving me the full demon experience, aren't you? Next you'll be planning out my macros and hiding protein powder in my drinks."

He flicked an eyebrow. "I could. Do you want a smoothie?" He said it with such serious intent that I laughed, a real, honest sound that bounced off the concrete and glass of the kitchen.

"I'm a nutritionist," I reminded him, "and the only time I ever eat like a nutritionist is when I'm too tired to make food, or too stubborn to admit I need it. So yeah, breakfast for dinner is basically my superfood."

Samiel's brow creased, then smoothed. "You are a nutritionist," he said, my statement jogging his memory.

I nodded, licking the last bit of cheese from my fingers. "I do remote consults for a lot of tech people—paranoid types, mostly, who want cheat codes for not dying young. Half my job is explaining to grown adults that coffee doesn't count as breakfast, and the other half is convincing them that the human body is not a blender you can run on Red Bull and existential dread alone."

He watched me push the empty plate away, his eyes tracking the movement. "So your whole job is telling people how not to kill themselves with their own appetites?" His claws tapped the counter, a touch so careful it made my heart spasm.

"That, and making them feel okay about having one in

the first place." I dabbed at the corner of my mouth with my finger, catching the last bit of egg. "I mostly see clients by Zoom. It's all spreadsheets and shame spirals." I paused, realizing I'd just demolished his perfect omelet without coming up for air. "It's weirdly intimate, telling people how to eat. You get to see all their secrets, you know? I watch them hoard their granola bars and guilt like it's currency. That's the fun of it—getting to see how people really live, not how they want you to think they do." I ran my finger along the empty plate, collecting the last traces of melted cheese, and considered the demon in front of me, who was already eyeing the fridge like he was planning his next culinary seduction. "Honestly, you're the first person who's ever made me eat after sex. Usually it's the reverse."

After a while, the edge came off. I slumped over the counter, resting my forehead on the cold marble. "I'll have to get my license transferred if this thing sticks," I said, a lazy mumble.

The words were half-joking, but Samiel's gaze sharpened. "You'd move here? Permanently?"

He waited, not breathing, not even shifting his weight, as if a single wrong move would scatter the hope so palpable between us.

I didn't mean to say it yet, but it was out in the open now and there was no taking it back. Hell, it had been the point all along, hadn't it? I'd applied for the nutritionist job at the stupid Lake Purgatory wellness center before I even bought my bus ticket. I'd researched the licensing board and filled out the paperwork. I'd stalked the town's sad excuse for a social media presence just to see if the grocery store carried oat milk or if I'd have to settle for the shelf-stable kind. All these little acts of hope, stashed away as insurance in case I met someone who wasn't a disappointment. And now, with

Samiel's eyes locked on me, I realized I'd been pulling for this outcome the whole time, even when I was pretending to be too cool to care. If I was honest, I'd been more afraid of not finding something worth staying for than of the valley itself. The rest was just inertia and self-defense.

"Hey." His voice was softer than I expected. Samiel reached across the counter, gathered my fingers into his hand, and just held them—thumb stroking the backs, claws kept carefully away from skin. "You don't have to decide." He said it like he meant it, but there was a tremor there, a hunger to believe maybe he wasn't just a one-night monster after all.

"You'd like it here," he said, voice soft as the dusk outside, but then, catching himself, straightened his back and went for casual. "The town's small but weird. Nobody cares what you wear or who you fuck."

I looked up at him, at the face that should have scared the shit out of me but instead made my teeth ache to bite. His eyes—open, raw, almost pleading—held mine like he was afraid I'd vanish if he blinked. My heart hammered against my ribs.

"Is it always like that for you?" I asked, voice barely above a whisper. "When you're with someone, I mean. Or was that..." I trailed off, letting the question hang between us, not sure if I was ready for the answer, but needing to hear it, anyway.

For a second, Samiel looked at me like I was the last train out of the city, and he was the only idiot left on the platform. His mouth curled, uncertain. "That was my first time," he said, which was almost laughable, except the words hit with the force of truth.

I tried not to choke. "You mean, first time with a human?"

He shrugged, a self-conscious roll of muscle under skin.

"First time with a bride. First time it felt like it mattered." He looked away, his gaze catching on the dark window as if he expected to see his own reflection and didn't want to. "Most demons don't get picked. Or they get picked by someone who wants the tourist version—a weekend of stories, a novelty. They don't...want us for us. It's easier to stay on the bench."

I didn't know what to say to that. I'd always thought of myself as the benchwarmer, the second-string girlfriend or the rebound or the good story, if you wanted to look edgy without actually committing to the lifestyle. The idea that Samiel—seven feet of muscle and menace, with wings that could block out the sun and claws that could rip through steel—could feel unwanted almost made me want to laugh. Except he said it with his eyes cast down at his own massive hands, voice dropping to a rasp that cracked at the edges, and the crimson flush that spread across his cheekbones said he'd never meant to let that vulnerability slip.

I watched him, really watched, as he busied himself clearing the counter and wiping down the glassy surface with a bar towel. His movements were careful, deliberate, the way a man might shift his weight in a room full of glassware he'd already been accused of breaking. Even in this house, even alone with me, Samiel was tethered—pulling in his wings, using the slow rhythm of busywork to keep his claws off my skin. Maybe some part of him still believed he was a walking hazard, an accident waiting to happen. I recognized the feeling. I'd spent most of my life trying not to be too much, only to wonder if I'd accidentally made myself into nothing at all.

It hit me then what I wanted out of this—what I needed, beyond the sex and the dare. I didn't say any of this—didn't want to spook him, or worse, make him think I was after some kind of project or redemption arc. Instead, I kicked off the barstool, licked the brine from my lips, and closed the distance between us. His back was still turned, wings tucked so tightly that the edges trembled, and I reached out—careful, this time—and ran my hand along the velvet membrane where it joined his shoulder blade. He shivered, startled, but didn't pull away.

CHAPTER
SIX

Samiel

Her hand, cool from the marble, traced along the join of sinew and skin at the top of my wing. No one had ever touched me there—at least, not without intention to wound; not without gloves, or the insulation of intimidation, or the clinical curiosity of the town's infernal physician. Annie's touch was exploratory, as if she'd found the seam of a new world and wanted to pry it open with her fingers. The shock of it almost buckled my knees.

My first thought was: *don't flinch*. The second was: *what if I do?*

She didn't rush. Her nails grazed the leading edge, right where the flesh thinned and you could see the black thread of veins spidering beneath the surface. No one, not even another demon, had ever lingered there. It was where our armor ended and our risk began. The spot was so sensitive that the entire wing trembled under her touch, shivering in a way that was almost embarrassing. I tried to hold as still as possible.

The sensation was so acute, I almost missed what she said next, the sound of her voice muffled by my own pulse.

"Do you let anyone else touch you like this?" Her tone was playful but edged, a knife wrapped in velvet. "Because I'm not in the market to be another notch on some industrial-strength zipper, Samiel."

I blinked, struggling to parse the words through the static in my skull. The question didn't offend; it cut. She was watching me in the glass, eyes locked on the shudder of my wings, daring me to lie. I didn't.

"No," I said. "No one." I let the word vibrate in the open air, let it shiver out of my chest and into her hand. "No one ever." I meant for it to sound like a boast, but it came out hushed and small.

She held my gaze in the glass, searching for cracks. "Good," she said. "Because I don't want to be the training wheels for your next bride. Or your rebound from existential exile."

There was an edge of something unfamiliar in her voice —not jealousy, but a kind of stubborn pride, the territory of a woman determined not to be just another experiment for a creature built to survive centuries of them. She kept her hand on my back, but her spine stiffened, and in the glass I saw her chin lift just a hair.

I rolled the words in my mouth, tasting their weight. "I've never had a bride. And there won't be a next," I said. "You're it, Annie."

She gave a noise halfway between a laugh and a scoff, but it came out bright, like the sour snap of a green grape. "You say that like it means something. Like there aren't a thousand other girls with bad dye jobs and irreparable emotional damage queued up just waiting for their demon experience."

A flush crept across my face, hot enough to burn. "Maybe, but they're not you." I said it with finality.

She stared, her eyes full of disbelief and something else—fury, maybe, or the kind of hope that erodes itself before it ever gets a foothold. The touch on my wing stilled, but didn't leave. In the glass, her pale arms looked almost spectral against the red-black lattice of muscle and membrane, and I wondered if she saw what I did—a creature so vulnerable in its want that it could only be a kind of suicide to admit it.

"Prove it, then. Don't just fuck me like I'm the first. Make me feel like I'm the only." Her fingers closed tight at the base of my wing, nails biting in, and the simultaneous spike of arousal and panic made me want to howl.

She tugged me to face her, a brisk, efficient motion that belied her size. Even after what we'd just done, even with my pulse still rabbiting in my throat, I went like a lamb. A horn caught in her hair; she untangled it with a practiced snap, then wrapped both arms around my neck, her wrists crossed and locked behind me. She pressed her mouth to mine, patient and merciless, the taste of her still bright on my tongue, and when I kissed back, I tried to flood her with every lonely year, every ounce of longing I'd ever learned to hide. She seemed to sense it. She broke for air, all fierce little gulps, and looked me dead in the eye.

"Sam," she said, "can we do it in a bed this time?" Her voice was light, bordering on a tease, but I caught the flicker underneath. *Let's make it count, let's do this right.*

I wanted to say something cool, a line she'd remember, but all that came out was, "Yeah. Yes. Of course."

My hands, which could have ripped the counter in two, cupped her face with a care that bordered on reverence. I gathered her up, wings arching for balance, and carried her through the house. She weighed nothing. No—she weighed exactly what she ought to, a perfect counterbalance to the heaviness I'd carried inside me for decades.

The bedroom was at the far end of the hall, and I was unprepared for how much it looked like a magazine ad from the 1950s—tasteful, not tacky, a king-sized bed with a button-tufted headboard, walnut dressers, and a pair of globe lamps that cast honey-colored halos onto the walls. The comforter was a watermelon-pink paisley, faded from a thousand washes, and the carpet—yes, real, actual carpet—was so plush that Annie's toes disappeared in it as soon as I set her down. On the far side of the room, a sliding glass door opened onto a balcony, the lake glimmering in the darkness beyond.

For a moment, neither of us spoke. Annie wandered to the bed, trailing her fingers along the coverlet, her eyes wide and a little dazzled. She looked so small next to the enormous bed. I hovered on the threshold, taking in the sight of her, still in a towel, in the room we would be sharing for the next three days—that is if it all worked out. I was hungry for her, but wanted to let her lead. I'd spent the last forty years smothering my want.

She perched at the edge of the bed, towel crimped tight around her, and gave me a look that was equal parts challenge and invitation. I couldn't tell if she wanted me to pounce or keep my distance, but the uncertainty only added to the tension, stretching it taut as a guitar string.

"You know," she said, tilting her chin and feigning a casualness I recognized as armor, "I always do things in reverse order. Sex first, then intimacy. I like to know what I'm getting into before I get to the part where we talk about our parents and our favorite childhood pets." She let the towel slip a little at her collarbone, as if to make her point. "Keeps the expectations low, and the surprises good."

I laughed. Her logic was flawless. "So what comes after sex and intimacy?" I asked, following her in, looming deliberately just inside the doorway. The honey glow caught every line of her, the war paint on her eyelids almost shimmering. She looked at me not like prey, not like a test, but with a hunger that mirrored my own.

She grinned, a flash of teeth and cosmic ulterior motives. "Usually? Snacks. Then overthinking. But I think we already covered both of those, so..." She stretched out, arms above her head, the towel giving up its last pretense at modesty and falling away from her body. The motion was so deliberate, so unhurried, that it made me want to worship her every inch. Even demons had their gods. Mine was suddenly laid out on a melting paisley comforter, staring the devil in the face and daring him to do his worst.

"Come here, Samiel," she said, her voice dropping to a register that made the rest of the world go mute. "You're thinking too much."

She was right, but the words still landed like a talon on my chest. I crossed the carpet, slow but inexorable, and let the bulk of my presence fill the room. She watched me, eyes drinking in every motion—my hair loose down my back, my skin dark and humming, the way I hesitated at the foot of the bed like I was waiting for an invitation.

Her fingers curled into the edge of the mattress, knuckles whitening, and I realized with a jolt that she was just as flayed open as I was.

I didn't try to be smooth. I just bent and laid my hands on her knees, skin to skin. Her legs parted, a reflex or an invitation—maybe both.

"Are you cold?" I asked, because the goose bumps on her legs looked more like a topographical map than human skin.

"No." Her voice didn't waver. "Just waiting for you to decide if you're going to kiss me or eat me."

"So what if I can't choose?" I said, and I swept her up.

I pressed her knees wide, then slid my hands, palms open and reverent, up the warm planes of her thighs. Annie's skin was so delicate next to mine, tender parchment packed tight with nerves. I let my thumbs trace the trembling muscles above her knees; she shivered under my touch, her eyes huge, pulse a little drumbeat at her throat. I didn't rush. I wanted every inch.

Annie let her head tip back, hair fanned out across the pillow, and her eyes slid shut as I traced featherlight lines up to her hips. She smelled faintly of sweat and ozone and the clover-wet slick of lake air off the deck. I inhaled her, let the want fill all the empty places.

I lowered myself, careful as a cat, and laid my mouth just below her navel, tasting the fine spray of heat that radiated there. I kissed a line down, barely grazing the skin, not stopping until my mouth hovered over the pale thatch of hair above her cunt. Even now, I could sense the tension in her, the way she was bracing in case I'd turn cruel or careless. I forced my own body to breathe, to slow down, to get this right. I let my forked tongue taste her, one tip tracing the seam, the other circling, and Annie gasped—a sound so sudden and involuntary it cracked open something in me.

I took my time. I let her feel every split second, every scrape of my tongue, every measured exhalation. I lapped at her, slow at first, a ticklish feather of sensation, then deeper, pressing one end of the tongue inside while the other flicked upward to catch her clit. The possibilities were endless with a tongue that split on command. She grabbed the sheets, fists twisted tight as tourniquets, her voice punching out of her in these little staccato bursts, not even words at first—just gasps, then my name, then "fuck, Sam, don't stop." I didn't. I could have done this for hours. I *wanted* to do this for hours. I wanted to know the precise ratio of pressure-to-pleasure that would break her mind, make her forget the long line of mortals and monsters and disappointments before me.

She arched, hips rolling hard, and her hands shot out, one tangling in my hair and the other gripping my horn like she was white-knuckling a roller coaster. The pain was exquisite—it tipped me into a fever that made my whole body buzz. I let her use me for leverage, let her ride my face, let her show me exactly how she wanted it. The air was thick with her heat.

Her thighs clamped around my head, a vise of muscle and need, and Annie's voice lost its sarcasm, lost its edge—it was just pure, keening want.

"Fuck, Samiel, you're going to kill me," she gasped, her hand scrabbling at my scalp, nails finding new purchase as she tried to outpace the pleasure. "Holy fuck, what—what even is that—oh my god—" The words tumbled out, raw and unguarded, and I realized with a pulse of pride that I was the first to make her sound like this.

I doubled down, letting the split ends of my tongue work in tandem—one tip swirling her clit, the other plunging into the sweet, clenching heat of her pussy. She bucked hard, and her whole body seized, a coiled spring releasing, and she came with a violence that would have embarrassed her if she'd had enough brain left to process it. She clamped my face tight to her, hips rutting up, a ragged scream scraping out of her throat. I felt her pulse on my tongue, a slick, shuddering flood, and I drank it in, greedy for every drop.

She tried to pull away, even as her legs locked around my

neck like a python, but I wouldn't let her go. I pressed her down, hands braced on her hips, and lapped at her through the aftershocks, tongue working as her body shivered and spasmed, her nails raking bloody crescents into my forearms. "Fuck—Sam—god, stop, it's—" she pleaded, but her cunt fluttered on my tongue, desperate for more even as her brain begged for mercy.

I drew back just enough to breathe and she tried to clamp her thighs shut, but I gripped them, hard enough to leave finger marks.

"Not done." I growled, and went right back in.

She yelped, a high, shattered sound, and twisted so hard she nearly bucked me off. But I was stronger, and she knew it, and the shock of my tongue—slick, relentless, unmerciful—sent her into a second wave that crashed over the first, her body convulsing in a way I could only describe as seismic. This time, the orgasm ripped through her so hard she forgot how to breathe. I felt her fingers lock on my horn, squeezing until my vision went white at the edges, and I moaned into her, letting the vibration shudder up her spine.

Annie tried to say my name, maybe to beg off, maybe to spur me on, but it was just a strangled vowel, a prayer in a language that only made sense in the dark. She lay on the bed, legs splayed, arms thrown wide above her head, sweat streaking the hollows of her belly and neck, as I traced my tongue up through the last aftershocks, licking her clean.

And when it was done, when she was wrung out and gasping with her cheek pressed to the pillow, I rose over her, bracing my knees on either side of her hips. She opened her eyes, dazed and ocean-blue, and reached for me without words. I let her drag herself up my body, let her catch her breath against my chest, let her kiss me with the wild, spent mouth of a woman who'd been cracked open and found the world on the other side.

I kissed her back, slow and soft. After all that animal want, the simplicity of a kiss—just lips and tongues, just the slow melt of bodies finding their way toward each other—stopped me dead.

"You taste better than anything I've had in forty years," I said.

Her eyes glittered, sharp and delighted. "You're about to get so sick of hearing me scream your name."

I grinned and started to answer, but she pressed a finger to my lips, then ducked under my arm and slithered off the bed. She landed in a controlled fall, knees thudding softly into the carpet, and before I could ask what she was doing, she'd already wrapped both hands around the base of my cock.

She looked up at me, eyes bright with reverence and mischief. "My turn," she said. "Relax or I'll bite."

I'd been inside a thousand fantasies, lived out every permutation of pleasure, but nothing came close to the sight of Annie kneeling, hair a mess, gaze daring me to break. She stroked my cock, one hand working the shaft, the other cupping my balls with a gentle, decisive grip. She bent her head and licked, slow and deliberate, lapping a line from root to the spade-shaped head, then swirling her tongue around it like she was taste-testing gelato. She didn't hesitate —not even as her lips parted to take the head, the flare of it stretching her jaw wide enough that her eyes watered on contact. She pulled back, breathless, and squinted up at me with a look of mock accusation.

"You're fucking huge," she said, voice half-muffled by the still-wet shine on her lips. "I mean, I saw it, but I didn't think..." She wrapped her hand tighter around the base, then squeezed up to the knot, as if confirming its existence with a scientific grip. "Jesus, Sam, how did you even fit this in me?"

I laughed, helpless against the pride and the hunger in her face. "You're the one who said not to hold back."

She bit her lower lip, eyes fixed on the cock in her fist. "I did. And I meant it." Then she tipped her head, lined up the head of my cock with her mouth, and took me in one slow, steady swallow, her tongue curled around the ridge, savoring the stretch. She bobbed once—twice—then pulled off with a gasp, eyes wide and wild.

"Holy shit, Samiel," she said, dazed, "this is going to ruin me for everyone."

She dove back in, lips sealing around the head, hand working the shaft in perfect counterpoint. Each time she took me deeper, the muscle in her throat flexed and her eyes fluttered, as if she couldn't decide between oxygen and the need to be full of me. Her other hand cupped my ass, nails digging in just enough to make me snarl, and the shock of sensation threatened to send me over the edge before I was ready.

I braced my hand at the back of her head, not guiding, just anchoring her there, and she worked me, hand and mouth, with a patience that was both worship and threat. I could feel the pleasure coiling up, dangerous and tight, and when I reached the brink, I didn't want to drown her in it— not yet. I wrapped my fist in her hair and, without thinking, tugged her off with a snap.

"Stop," I barked, voice guttural. "Annie—look at me."

She blinked up, eyes wide, lips glossy and open. "Did I do it wrong?" she asked, the tease in her voice undercut by the need painted across her face.

I shook my head, breath coming ragged. "You did it too well. I want to be inside you, not on your tongue." I hauled her up, both hands locked around her waist, and tumbled her backward onto the bed, pinning her wrists above her head. She squirmed, delighted, and spread her legs without hesitation, the invitation so clear it would shame the devil.

I lined myself up, dragging the slick head of my cock through her folds, circling her clit with slow, deliberate passes. The heat of her was unreal—hotter than the Nevada night, hotter than the core of a star. I watched her face, watched the way her eyes pinched shut and her jaw went slack when I teased her, the way she arched her back, hips canting toward me, greedy for friction.

"Ready for round two?" I asked, voice thick.

She didn't even open her eyes, just reached down and grabbed my ass, nails digging in. "If you don't fuck me right now, I will start screaming until the mayor comes to evict us."

I laughed, but she was dead serious. I pressed the head against her, not entering, just holding there until the anticipation made her whole body tremble.

"Please, Sam," she said, voice gone hoarse and hungry. "Please."

That did it. I pushed inside, slow at first, then with a steady, brutal pressure that made her gasp and claw at my arms. She was so slick and tight, my cock fit like it was made for her, every inch a victory over the emptiness I'd carried for centuries. I let her feel every pulse, every twitch, every stretch. Her legs locked around my waist, urging me deeper, her heels digging into my back; the pain was lightning, pure and sweet, and I fed on it.

I set a rhythm, hips pistoning so hard the bed frame slammed against the wall. Each thrust drove a grunt from my chest, a moan from hers, the sound of us rising like a tide and drowning out everything else. She met every drive, every withdrawal, her body greedy for the collision, arms wound around my neck like she was never going to let go.

Her hands found my horns, and when she gripped there, using them for leverage, something snapped inside me. I buried myself to the knot, pinning her to the bed by the weight of my hips, and watched her scream my name into the crook of her arm. I rode her, relentless, one hand braced on her throat—not squeezing, just holding the flutter of her pulse under my palm, a tactile reminder that she was real and alive and mine for the taking. The other hand clamped her hip hard enough to leave a print. Her whole body bowed up to meet me, a perfect tension, and when I rammed in again, the knot forced its way inside with a wet, obscene pop.

She convulsed around me, legs trembling, mouth open in a silent howl. I felt her come, the pulsing rhythm of her cunt milking my cock, desperate to wring out every drop. It knocked the breath from my lungs; I broke, slammed once, twice, and then exploded inside her, wave after wave until my vision starbursted and my whole body locked up. I pressed her to the bed, both of us shaking, and held there, unwilling to move, unwilling to let go even as the knot swelled and locked us together again.

She clawed at my shoulder, nails biting deep, and when I finally looked down, eyes focusing past the blur, she was watching me with a kind of triumph I'd never seen before. Her cheeks flushed, lips bruised, hair wild and tangled around my handprint on her throat. She looked ruined in the best possible way—like a temple after the right god had come through, all the walls knocked down and the air full of lightning.

"That," she managed, after forever. "That was worth it."

I tried to laugh, but all that came out was a ragged pant. I thought about every moment of loneliness I'd ever hoarded, and every empty comfort I'd ever settled for, and felt them all burn away in the heat of her body. If I could have poured myself into her, bones and memory and all, I would have.

We lay there for a long time, fused at the hips, skin creating new constellations of sweat. I rolled to one side, careful not to wrench the knot that tied us together, and Annie went with me, still breathing hard, her heartbeat pounding an insistent counterpoint against my chest.

She pressed her face to my throat, her breath feathering the skin, then licked a sweat-salty stripe up my jaw. "I think you broke the bed," she observed, voice gummy with endorphins. "I definitely heard something snap."

I couldn't help but laugh, and the movement low in my diaphragm made the knot twitch inside her, drawing a whimper and a giggle up her spine. "Sorry," I said, though I wasn't, really. "I can fix it in the morning."

"I'll hold you to that," she said, curling tighter into my side. There was nothing defensive or self-protective in the way she tucked beneath my wing, nothing held back. We lay like that, the lake splayed out in starlight just past the balcony glass, her breaths feathering soft and slow against my skin.

Her hand found mine, fingers weaving through like she was braiding string. I closed my eyes and let myself memorize the smallness of her grip, the way her thumb circled my knuckle, over and over, as if trying to polish it smooth. What a gift, I thought, to simply be held, to have someone anchor me to the world.

For a long time, we didn't speak. Annie's pulse slowed and her breaths evened, but I could feel the ache in her hips where the muscles still fluttered in aftershocks. I watched the moon roll across the lake, listened to the scratch of her breathing as it tangled with my own, and let the world outside shrink to the radius of her embrace.

Somewhere in that hush, her hand fell slack. Her breaths evened out and turned weightless, an animal surrender, and I realized with a strange pride that she trusted me to hold her as she faded. I tucked her closer, one wing draped fully over both of us now, making a tent of velvet and shadow. It was the safest I'd ever felt. I wondered if Annie would say the same, or if she'd wake in the morning and realize it had all been a game.

I didn't want to sleep. I wanted to watch her through the night, guard the perimeter of this fragile new world we'd built.

Instead, I reached for my phone on the nightstand, careful not to disturb her, and texted Mara. "She's staying if I have any say in it. Prepare my house. Office space for her work. Women's pajamas. Whatever humans need." I caught the last of Annie's breath in my lungs and let go, finally, of the last discipline and vigilance that had kept me upright for four decades, my phone still warm in my palm.

CHAPTER
SEVEN

Annie

The next morning, the sky was still half-dark when I surfaced from sleep. The lake was a sheet of mercury, the house silent except for Samiel's slow, seismic breathing. His arm was a dead weight across my waist, the wing folded over our bodies like a very expensive, slightly leathery comforter. The air was cool, and my skin was clammy in the way that meant I'd sweated through the sheets at some point. The clock on the dresser glowed 5:44 a.m.—which, for my poor Florida-ruined circadian rhythm, might as well have been noon.

I tried to extract myself without waking him, a doomed effort. His grip tightened, claws prickling lightly against my hip, and he made a noise in his chest—a rumble that sounded more like a cat than a hellbeast. I stilled, heart hammering, and waited to see if he'd open his eyes. He didn't. Instead, he nuzzled deeper into the crook of my neck, tail snaking up the length of my thigh and looping possessively around my knee. The forked tip twitched against the back of my leg, a lazy, reflexive motion that made me shiver despite the sheets. For a second, I let him hold me, let myself enjoy the safety of being wanted this much, the gravity of another body keeping me affixed to the planet. But eventually the reality of a full bladder and muscles sore from use—deliciously, profoundly sore—made it impossible to stay pinned.

"Sam," I whispered, trying to pry the tail loose.

He muttered something unintelligible, the vibrations traveling through his chest into mine. The tail only tightened.

I tried again, this time with a gentle twist, and he made a grumpy, guttural noise—a sound that might have been "no" or "mine" or just a growl at the interruption. I snorted, then wiggled harder, finally dislodging myself from the demon octopus. The tail unwrapped with a reluctant spiral, and Samiel's claws retracted, but his face contorted into a scowl of pure, petulant loss. I braced for him to wake, but all he did was burrow into the tangle of sheets and let out a monumental sigh, like it was the last breath he'd ever take until I returned.

I padded to the bathroom, bare feet sinking into the plush pink carpet. The master bath was the size of my last apartment, with a soaking tub in one corner and a shower big enough for a five-person bachelorette party. Everything was tile and glass and chrome, but instead of feeling like a hotel, it had a weird warmth to it—a tray of little succulents by the window, stacks of mismatched bath towels rolled into a pyramid, a basket of sample-size bath bombs next to the tub. I wondered if this was Sam's doing, or if it had been staged by the town's infernal hospitality committee. Part of me hoped this was what Sam liked—soft things, good light, small comforts in a world that was otherwise engineered for disappointment. I wondered what his actual house was like.

I stepped into the shower and cranked the handle, expecting standard-issue lukewarm, maybe with a sulfur edge. Instead, the spray was perfect. Tropical hot, thunder-storm pressure. The kind of water you'd want to live in. I let it hammer my skin, watching the bruises and bite marks bloom purple and rise across my chest and hips. I touched the one on my neck, traced the line of teeth with my finger. It wasn't an accident. He'd marked me, and I'd let him.

I pressed my forehead to the tile and let the steam erase the last traces of doubt. I wanted this—wanted him, wanted the town, wanted the possibility of waking up every day to the kind of hunger that made you feel alive in the marrow.

The water scalded in all the right ways, waking up muscles that had gone soft and lazy overnight. I let the needles of heat work the ache from my thighs, the ghost of Samiel's hands lingering at every seam and hollow. My hair was a disaster; I lathered it twice with the house-brand shampoo, which smelled faintly like cinnamon and some-thing more feral, maybe clove or patchouli. I wondered if Samiel had picked it out himself.

When I finally shut off the water, my skin was flushed and alive, my brain clearer than it'd been in months. I toweled off, wrapped my hair up in a twist, and padded back into the bedroom.

Samiel was exactly where I'd left him, except the scowl had resolved into a look of half-conscious satisfaction, his face mashed into the pillow like he was dreaming of some-thing that agreed with him. One wing hung off the side of the bed, the other arched protectively over the spot where my body had been. The sight of him—sprawled, enormous, totally vulnerable—squeezed something unfamiliar in my chest.

I realized abruptly that I had nothing to wear. My skirt and shirt from yesterday were in a heap by the kitchen, and my duffel—if it had even made it off the bus—was a total mystery. I wrapped the giant towel more tightly around me and tiptoed out to the living room.

My duffel was waiting just inside the front door, upright and prim like it had been delivered by a very considerate poltergeist. The sight made me weirdly happy; it meant the town's infernal hospitality program was at least as efficient as Amazon Prime, and possibly more so. I dragged it to the sunken living room and unzipped it, taking inventory. All the clothes I'd packed for three days in Hell: black mesh tanks, a denim vest with "Feral but Friendly" embroidered on the back, ripped shorts, five pairs of fishnets, a black bikini, a bottle of sunscreen, and—because I never learned— a spare umbrella. There was also my makeup bag, a folding travel mirror, and two hardcover books I'd already read.

I dressed without ceremony, picking out the threadbare shorts and a mesh top, then layering on the vest for good measure. My hair, still wet, hung in two-tone strings along my face; I pulled out my blow-dryer and makeup bag, deciding to finish getting ready in the guest bathroom. I didn't know how much longer Sam would sleep, it was still early. I opted for minimal makeup, not feeling like I needed my full armor of face makeup, and then headed to the kitchen to find breakfast, and, more importantly, coffee.

The fridge yielded oat milk and a suspiciously artisanal espresso blend. I hunted through the drawers for a tamper, found one shaped like a demon's fist (which I appreciated), and set to work. The hiss and spit of the machine, the clatter of mugs, the comfortingly human monotony of making coffee—these were the rhythms I understood. I could almost pretend I wasn't in an architectural fever dream on the edge of a haunted lake, waiting for a demon to wake up and decide whether to eat me or just make me pancakes.

I heard the creak of the hallway floorboards before I saw him. Samiel appeared in the kitchen, utterly naked, sleep still dragging at his features. His hair was tangled and wild, and there were pillow lines pressed into his cheek. He looked softer than last night—less like a demon and more like a giant, confused postgrad who'd woken up in the wrong dorm.

He blinked twice, registering the daylight and the smell of coffee. "You left," he said, voice hoarse.

"I had to pee," I said, filling the mugs. "And then I had to shower, because I had sex with a biohazard and wasn't sure if I was going to turn red in the wash."

He padded over, picked up the mug I'd already poured for him, and took a careful sip. His eyes rolled back in pleasure, the veins at his temples glowing momentarily. "You make coffee like a god," he said, "which is ironic."

He set the mug down and looked at me, really looked, and for a second, I saw the demon stripped away, just a man left holding the memory of something he thought he'd lost. "Thank you," he said, and I could tell he meant more than the coffee. "I... didn't like waking up alone. I thought maybe —" He paused, mouth twisting, uncertain how to finish. "Never mind."

I let the silence ride for a beat, then filled it. "You thought I'd bail after two rounds? Please. You think I'd pass up another shot at that knot?" I grinned, but his face didn't smooth. The uncertainty in his eyes felt older than the desert.

I closed the space between us and pressed my lips to his

bicep, just above the angry blue print my nails had left the night before. "I'm not going anywhere. Not for three days, at least. You're stuck with me." I looked up at him, found the right words. "Promise."

His eyes flickered, and the tension in his shoulders melted—not all the way, but enough that I could see the relief under it.

"Good," he said, his voice soft but anchored with a ridiculous seriousness. "Because if you left, I'd be forced to hunt you down. It's against protocol, but I'd do it anyway." His tail curled around my ankle, a little shackle of warmth.

"Is that a threat, Samiel?" I raised both brows, letting a playful chill creep into my voice.

"No," he said, entirely grave. "It's a plea bargain." He stepped closer and anchored his arms around me, careful with the claws, careful with everything.

I let him hold me for a long minute, coffee warming our hands, steam pooling around our faces. The silence had weight, but it wasn't uncomfortable; it was the shared hush of two people who'd survived something and were waiting to see what came next. His chin rested on the top of my head, the horns framing me in a weird, cathedral-like way that I found more comforting than I'd ever admit. When I finally pulled back, I kept my hands pressed to his ribs, felt the heat and the steady drum of his pulse.

"You need a shower," I said, tilting up to look at him. "You're still covered in—" I gestured, then let my hand drop. "Well. Me."

He grinned, but there was a hint of shyness, like he'd only just realized he was naked. He didn't cover himself, though. Just straightened his spine and stepped back, arms loose at his sides, utterly unselfconscious. "You're not going to run?" he asked, tilting his head. "You'll wait?"

I pretended to consider it, sipping my coffee with the slow deliberation of a contract negotiator. "If you're gone more than ten minutes, I get to eat all the pastries in the fridge and pick the music for the rest of the day."

He grinned, showing the crooked canine. "Deal." Then—because some instincts died hard—he hesitated in the doorway, eyes locked on me. "Promise?" The word was so naked, it almost hurt.

"I promise," I said, matching his seriousness. "I'll be here when you get out."

He vanished down the hall, wings sweeping a low arc in the morning sun.

Alone, I took inventory of the kitchen's offerings. There was a tray of pastries, all suspiciously intact—someone, maybe Samiel, had gone to the trouble of slicing and fanning them, like they were expecting a panel of judges for the *Nevada State Bake-Off*. There were croissants in both sweet and savory, scones, strudel, something that looked like a poppyseed cake, and a pile of cheese Danishes so plump, they glistened like they'd been shellacked for a food commercial. It was far better than any hotel breakfast I'd ever scavenged at a conference.

But pastries didn't count as breakfast. Not for me. I needed protein, or I'd get shaky and irritable by noon, and no amount of sugar or caffeine could fix it. I went back to the fridge, scrounged eggs, spinach, a log of goat cheese, and something labeled "bacon" in three languages, one of which was, I suspected, not spoken on this plane of existence.

I set to work, rolling up my sleeves and gathering pans, bowls, and a cutting board. Cooking for myself had always been an act of survival, but cooking for someone else felt almost ceremonial. I chopped the spinach (fine, so it didn't go limp and slimy in the eggs), whisked the eggs until they glistened, and crumbled in a ridiculous amount of goat cheese. If there was one thing I knew about men—even demon men—they'd eat anything as long as you drowned it in cheese and salt. I opted to skip the haunted bacon, but maybe I'd work up to it by Day Three.

It was strangely peaceful, moving around the kitchen, the brightening lake catching more sun by the minute and the air still holding a nighttime hush. I lined up the plates, brewed a second round of espresso, and had just slid the omelet into the pan when I heard him return.

Samiel's hair was wet and slicked behind his horns, and he wore a pair of black sweatpants that looked like they could split at the thigh seam if he even considered lunging.

I plated the food and slid it across the island to him without comment, then watched as he stared at the eggs like he was trying to solve them.

"What is it?" I said, genuinely curious. "Are these... like, off-limits for demons? Is there a secret mortal taboo about goat cheese I should know about?"

He blinked, then shook his head, incredulous. "No. No taboo. Just—nobody's ever made breakfast for me." He picked up his fork with the exaggerated caution of a man handling an heirloom or a live grenade, then cut into the omelet, unleashing a molten ribbon of cheese and spinach. He chewed, swallowed, and then closed his eyes in something like reverence.

"Jesus," he said, "you could overthrow governments with this."

I laughed and dove into my own plate. We ate in silence for a couple of minutes, forkfuls and sips of coffee filling the space. At some point, as the food did its work, I felt something in me click into place—like I could finally imagine the morning after being a real thing.

Samiel polished off his food and then, without warning, he dropped the fork and closed the distance between us in a heartbeat, his hands settling on either side of my face. He bent and kissed me, and this time it was neither sex nor ritual. It was a thank you. He lingered, lips soft and unhurried, and when he drew back I saw—just for a second—the debris of a century's worth of longing, swept clean and replaced by something as simple as breakfast.

We leaned against the kitchen island together, staring out at the lake, both of us a little embarrassed by the sudden intimacy or perhaps just unsure how to fill it. I fiddled with my coffee, felt the heat in my cheeks, and realized I was blushing for the first time in years.

"So," I said, tracing a finger around the rim of my mug, "do we just wait for the chaperone to show up and grade our relationship? Or do we get to do something fun before the mandatory check-in?" I tried for casual, but the thought of being "graded" made my shoulders tense up in a way that was only partly a joke. I'd spent my whole life on the edge of some evaluation—school, work, relationships, therapy intake forms—but this was the first time the stakes felt so high.

Samiel considered, then grinned. "The mayor's due at noon for the check-in. Until then, we're supposed to 'bond in a naturalistic setting,' which mainly means not traumatizing the gardeners or causing property damage." He eyed the patio door, then me. "If you want to see the lake, now's the time."

I was already moving. There were cravings that didn't make sense until you were in the presence of certain landscapes—salt water, sand, the shimmer of heat over flat land —and Lake Purgatory, for all its devil-branding, called to me like an old, bad habit. I wriggled into my sneakers, palmed two more pastries from the kitchen, and watched Samiel roll his shoulders, wings stretching and flexing. He let them fan out, the span catching the slanted sun and turning the kitchen into a cathedral of red and shadow. He looked like something built for flight, some prehistoric beast that had been tricked into domesticity but never fully tamed.

We stepped outside. The morning was already heating up, the sky an impossible, chemical blue, the air carrying the faint, metallic tang of the lake. Our little house perched on a bluff, the concrete patio giving way to a switchback trail that snaked down to the shore. At the bottom, the sand was fine and bone-pale, almost white against the water. The lake itself was a color you only saw in dreams or in the aftermath of a chemical spill—cobalt near the bank, then shading to an oil-slick black at the center. The surface was dead calm, not even a shimmer from the wind.

Samiel stalked ahead, barefoot, his tail carving a lazy S behind him. He turned once to see if I was keeping up, then waited, hands shoved in his pockets, looking uncharacteristically shy.

The shoreline was studded with black rocks, a few drift-wood benches, and a rickety public dock that looked like it had been built as a Boy Scout project and then abandoned to the elements. But further down, maybe a hundred yards from the house, was a second dock—private, slick with dew. Tied to it was an actual rowboat, the kind you saw in stock photos, all white with a rim of faded blue, two oars resting inside and a picnic basket wedged under the center bench. I blinked, not sure if it was a mirage, but Samiel saw my stare and grinned like a man holding a royal flush.

"I said I wanted to show you the lake," he said, voice pitched low. "I asked Mara to set up a lunch for us, knowing

—or hoping—we might sleep late." He rubbed the back of his neck with his clawed hand.

I let out a laugh, sharp and delighted. "Should I be worried about a boat ride with a demon? Is this how the next ninety-day bride goes missing?"

He slipped a hand around my waist, guiding me with the same casual authority he used to manhandle a skillet. "If I was going to drown you, I'd at least wait until after dessert," he said, and the way he said it made me want to bite his shoulder for the hell of it.

We picked our way down the trail, the air getting heavier with the funk of lake minerals and some odd, floral under-note that might have been from the patch of wild sage clinging to the slope. The dock groaned when we stepped on it, but Samiel didn't even blink. He braced the rowboat with one clawed hand, offering me the other to step in. I pretended not to notice the way he tested the boards, just in case they tried to give out under my weight.

He helped me in, steady as a rock, then pushed off with a single, shockingly graceful move. The boat glided free of the dock, and for a second, I let myself pretend I was in a different kind of story—a summer camp romance, maybe, or the opening to a horror movie. All I knew was that I felt seen, and not just in the predatory, hungry way. More like Samiel had been paying such close attention that he knew what kind of morning would make me want to stay here forever.

He rowed with slow, powerful strokes, the muscles in his forearms flexing under the thin membrane of his skin. The oars dipped in and out of the water so smoothly that there was barely a ripple. I sat on the prow, knees tucked up, the air cool on my face but already promising to burn off by noon.

After a few silent minutes, he paused, let the boat drift, and reached under the middle seat. He emerged not with a knife or a bottle of demon whiskey, but with a can of SPF 100 and a folded black-and-white umbrella, the kind tourists used on the Vegas Strip when their skin couldn't take the sun.

He nudged the umbrella open, set it in a clamp to shield my shoulders, and handed me the sunscreen. "I read the orientation packet," he said. "I know humans… fry."

I took the bottle, warmth blooming in my chest. "You're not worried about your own skin?"

He grinned, showing one fang. "I could bake at four hundred for six hours and only get hungrier." He squinted into the sun, eyes gone almost gold around the edges. "But I didn't want you to burn. Or to be uncomfortable." He said it so simply, so unadorned, that I wanted to cry a little and also tear his sweatpants off and ride him into the bright, indifferent eye of the day. I settled for smearing sunscreen down my arms, then my legs, watching the way Samiel's eyes flicked to my hands, tracking every movement.

"You did this for me?" I said, not just the umbrella, but the whole thing—the basket, the rowboat, the gentle sacrifice of his own dignity to make a mortal woman's morning perfect.

He shrugged, like it was obvious. "You said you liked breakfast. And lakes. And not being turned into a cautionary tale about melanoma."

I set the bottle aside, then edged forward, feet braced on the hull, and kissed him square on the mouth. It was clumsy, off-balance, and made him nearly drop the oar, but he steadied the boat with one hand and kissed me back, soft mouth ridiculous on that face. When I drew away, the lake was spinning, and not just from the change in weight balance.

"You're pretty thoughtful for a demon," I said, voice low.

Samiel's face went oddly serious. "The least I can do," he said, "is keep you safe." There was a weight to the way he said it, like he was making a vow. I wondered if he knew how good he was at it—how completely the sense of danger that had always stalked me had been reclassified, redirected, until it no longer seemed like something outside myself but something I could manage, or even want.

I sat back, watching the water. The lake was still empty, the mirror-surface unbroken except for the wake of our little boat. Far up on the bluff, the house looked tiny. I tried to project myself a decade into the future—see if I could imagine myself still here, still on this dry, haunted shore, eating goat cheese omelets and rowing out onto the water with a demon who made sure I never wanted to leave.

Samiel rowed us across the cove, his face set in an easy half smile. When we reached the far side of the lake, the water changed. It darkened, ribbons of black and indigo twisting beneath the boat, as if something ancient and patient waited at the bottom. The air chilled, or maybe it was the way the shadow of the cliffs leached the warmth from the sun. A finger of dread prickled along my spine—not fear, exactly, but the flutter of nerves that comes just before impact.

He beached the rowboat on a crescent of dark sand, hopped out with a demon's casual disregard for sharp rocks, and anchored the boat with a twist of rope around a boulder. He turned, offered me a hand, and I took it—half expecting him to haul me into the freezing water for a joke, but he only steadied me.

The cold was real, but the sun on my back kept it bearable. A breeze picked up as we walked, the sky overhead bright and the cave mouth ahead a slit of pure black in the soft sandstone. I could smell the minerals, the live edge of the water, and underneath that, something like ozone or the promise of fireworks.

Samiel grabbed the basket, leading the way. His hand, rough and warm, never let go of mine. We scrambled up a short, steep slope where the sand gave way to stone. At the top, the world fell away beneath us—just a dizzy drop to the water, the town a toy set across the shimmering expanse.

"Watch your step," Samiel said, navigating the ledge with a confidence that was both reassuring and a little show-offy. He led me to the mouth of the cave—a slit of black so deep the sun couldn't touch it—and ducked inside, dragging me with him.

The temperature dropped by ten degrees as soon as we entered. I blinked, letting my eyes adjust, and found that the pitch darkness wasn't so much empty as densely packed, full of the blue-black shimmer of minerals and water seeping from the rock.

Beneath our feet, the cave floor sloped gently down, then opened up into a chamber that glowed with an impossible, underwater light. I braced for the usual damp rot of lake caves, but the air was clean, almost cold enough to taste. Samiel knelt, scraping his claw along the wall. It sent up a flare of phosphorescence that painted the stone in lines of neon blue.

"Sulfur mostly," he said. "Magnesium, arsenic, bits of cosmic history. It's why the water doesn't ever get warm, even in August. It pulls heat straight out of the air." The words sounded rehearsed, but I could tell that being here meant something to him. The way he crouched, shoulders hunched to duck the roof, was almost reverent.

I stepped closer, toes curling against the sudden chill. The light from the cave mouth faded behind us, replaced by waves of ghostly blue radiating off the walls. I reached a hand toward the mineral graffiti, letting my palm hover a bare centimeter from the surface. It thrummed, a vibration that ran up my bones. "It's beautiful," I said, not quite whispering.

He looked up at me, something tentative in his face. "Most mortals just see a hole in a rock. They don't notice the way it glows." He reached out, not quite touching my wrist, just lingering nearby.

I edged deeper into the cave and nearly lost my balance; the floor dropped away in a shallow bowl, rimmed with pale sand that looked imported from another world. In the hollow, maybe a dozen feet across, a pool of liquid shimmered so blue that it seemed lit from below. The air over it was colder, and every ripple threw turquoise shadows onto the ceiling. I squatted at the edge, toeing the sand. It was shockingly soft—like powdered sugar, or the dust from a well-loved plush toy.

Before I could ask him if it was safe, Samiel had set down the basket, stripped off his shoes, and rolled up his pant legs to the knee. He stepped right into the water, bracing for the cold and grinning at me through the shiver.

"You have to try it," he called. "It's like swimming inside a gemstone."

I hesitated, then followed, wading in up to the ankle. The shock nearly took me out at the knees.

"Holy shit," I gasped, "it's freezing. Are you trying to kill me?"

Samiel just laughed, full-voiced and echoing off the cave walls. "If I was, I'd have better methods." He splashed a little, then beckoned me deeper. "I'll keep you warm," he promised, and the way he said it made the cold not just tolerable, but exciting—a dare, a shared secret in the dark. I kicked ahead, splashing him, and he caught me around the waist, pulling me so my back pressed his chest. The temperature difference—the chill of the water, the infernal heat in his hands—made me shudder, but I didn't want to wriggle away. I wanted to see how good it could get.

He tucked his chin over my shoulder and whispered, "See that ledge?" I followed his gaze up to a shelf in the rock wall, maybe ten feet above the water, jagged but perfectly flat on top. "That's where we'll eat."

And with no further warning, he hoisted me out of the pool and set me on the sand, as if I were a pool toy and not a whole person. He scrambled up the wall, claws anchoring in the rock, and came back with the basket. Without breaking a sweat, he one-armed me up to the ledge and then joined me, grinning, as if this was as natural as breathing.

The ledge, despite its height, was wide and slightly concave, with a perfect view back down into the shimmering cave pool below. The surface was gritty with pale dust, but the basket came equipped with a thin, checkered blanket—classic red and white, which made me laugh out loud. Samiel laid it out with excessive care, anchoring the corners with river rocks, then opened the basket with a flourish that would have shamed a Vegas magician.

Inside, there was a spread: little jars of pickled things, a loaf of honest-to-god bakery bread, cheese and charcuterie, paper-thin slices of something that looked like prosciutto but glistened purple-black around the edges. There were strawberries, bigger and redder than any I'd seen outside of a Photoshop ad, and two glass bottles of something clear and bubbly. Samiel fished out two cups—actual glass, not plastic

—and popped the tops with a flick of his thumb, pouring them without a drop spilled.

I sipped, expecting wine, or at worst, some horror of spiked mineral water, but it was sweet and subtle, more like an iced cider than anything else. I breathed in the cold, the faint salt of his skin close beside me, and felt the last of my nerves dissolve.

We ate in near silence at first. Samiel offered up everything, breaking the bread and slathering it with cheese, handing me the first strawberry, then the next, never taking for himself until he'd watched me taste and approve. It wasn't like being courted, exactly, more like the world's most overqualified bodyguard had decided to feed me until I surrendered.

At last, when the edge was off my hunger and I'd shifted to lying back on the ledge, staring up at the mineral-lit roof of the cave, I let myself ask the question that had been floating beneath the surface. "Why me, Sam?"

He wiped a trace of cheese from his thumb, then flicked a glance at me that was as raw as sunlight. "Because you never blinked," he said. "Not even at the start. Most people, when they see a demon, they look for an out, or an angle. They imagine how they'll use it, or how they'll survive it. You just... looked. And then you laughed."

He shook his head, the movement almost shy. "I've never known anyone who didn't need to be convinced. You made it easy to want you."

CHAPTER
EIGHT

Samiel

I used to think I was cursed with want. That I would always be hungry—hungry for touch, for novelty, for a taste of chaos in a world so stiflingly governed by order. Even after forty years in exile, I'd never found anything that could quiet the gnaw in my chest. Not until Annie. Not until the act of providing became, for the first time, not a bribe or a con or a means of getting what I wanted, but the actual endgame—the reward in itself.

Watching her pluck the berries from the basket one at a time, her lips stained with juice, I felt a satisfaction so complete, it was almost religious. She took the bread I offered, tore off a piece, and handed back the larger half, like she didn't notice or didn't care about making things even. She chewed quietly, eyes lit from below by the cave's neon glow, utterly unselfconscious.

I was waiting for the anxiety to spool up, for the ancient alarms to start blaring that it could never last, that if I let myself taste this—it would rot in my mouth. Instead, I felt a violence of protectiveness so hot and sudden, I nearly snapped the glass in my fist. The compulsion to keep her safe, keep her here, keep her fed and watered and wanted, was so unfamiliar that for a second, I mistook it for rage. But there was no fear in it. Only a kind of nuclear certainty: if any force in this valley, or this world, tried to touch her without her permission, I would tear the bone from its body and salt the wound.

It wasn't just physical. It was everything. I wanted Annie safe from the hunger that had gnawed at her all her life—the men who'd left her cold, the loneliness she wore like mail, the expectation that nothing good would stick around. I wanted to be the answer, not another disappointment. I wanted to be the one who kept every promise, who made her laugh every morning and let her fall asleep knowing she was cherished. It was primal, and it was permanent. I didn't care if it sounded pathetic. I sat with the truth and let it fossilize in me.

She wiped her sticky fingers on the blanket, then glanced up at the cave mouth, thoughtful. "Are you always like this?" she asked, as if reading my mind. "So full throttle?"

I considered. "No," I said, voice low. "But I am with you." It wasn't a line. It wasn't even what I thought I was going to say, but it was right. Annie squinted at me like she was looking for a punchline. Finding none, she just shook her head and smiled.

We lingered on the ledge until the cavern's blue glow started to dim, replaced by the diffuse gold of the real sun slanting in from above. Every new sound—a distant hum of a motorboat, the shifting of pebbles on the ledge—felt like a timer winding down on our little pocket of suspended time. Eventually, Annie sat up. She stretched her arms overhead, spine arching like a cat's, and looked over at me with a glint of mischief.

"Do we just stay here forever?" she asked. "Because if you have a plan for how to get me back up that wall, I'd love to hear it."

"I'll carry you," I said, not bothering to make it a joke.

She snorted. "You just want to show off." But she came to me easy, letting me bear her weight as we descended the ledge—my arms a cradle, her head tucked into the crook of my neck. I thought I'd get used to holding her, but every time felt like a first—no diminishing returns, only the novelty of finding her in my arms again and knowing she was still real.

When we reached the sand, Annie squirmed loose and did a little shake, knocking the powdered dust from her calves. "Okay, what's next?" she asked. "I'm assuming the mandatory bonding itinerary is more than just carbs and spelunking."

I set the basket down, wiped my hands on my thighs, and hesitated. I'd read the welcome packet—memorized it, actually, starved for any sliver of structure. The next phase was called "the Chase." It was both a test and a joke, a rite that dated back to the earliest days of The Valley of the Damned and the original demon-human pairings, when everything was still uncertain and both parties needed a quick, nonlethal way to establish boundaries. The rules were simple: she ran, I chased. If I caught her, I got to do whatever I wanted.

If she made it back to the house, she got to write the rules for the next day. The packet said it was supposed to promote "healthy conflict resolution and mutual trust." It had not, however, explained how to tell your new maybe-wife that you were about to hunt her through the desert at sundown and, if you caught her, pin her to the sand until she begged.

I eyed Annie, gauging whether she'd think it was fun or just feral. She was wiping berry juice from her chin with the back of her hand, expression pure curiosity.

I wet my lips. "Have you heard of the Chase?" I asked, careful with the words.

She rolled her eyes. "Not unless you mean the credit card company. Or… wait—" She sat up straighter, the glint in her eye sharpening. "Is this a demon thing? Like, a literal chase?"

I nodded, slow. "It's tradition," I said. "The rules are, you get a head start. The runner can hide, double back, whatever. If you make it to the designated safe zone—which is usually the front porch or a marked rock or something—you win. If I catch you, I win." I tried to keep the heat out of my voice, though the thought of chasing Annie through the dusk made my blood burn. "If there are limits, you say them now. Otherwise, it's fair game."

She considered this, eyes narrowed, gnawing a thumb-nail like she was weighing the merits of a challenge. "What exactly do you get if you win?"

My face went a little deadpan, because the real answer was, *You. Every way I want, until you can't walk.* But I also didn't want to scare her off. I kept my voice light, let the threat of it linger just behind the soft sell. "If I win, I claim you for the rest of the night. No take-backs, no mercy." I let my gaze flick down her body, then back up, as if I was measuring exactly what she'd be giving up if she lost the bet.

Her breath hitched, a little, and she grinned. "Claim me how?"

I shrugged, as if it were nothing. "Any way I like."

She snorted, but the sound was edged with anticipation. "You're really going for it. Full monster."

I shrugged, as if it were nothing, but the silence after hung sharp as a razor. Annie kept her eyes on me, and I let her watch, let her see the want without a mask for once. I could have filled the cave with promises and reassurances, could have defaulted to some canned line about boundaries and safety words, but instead I just watched her think. Her eyes ticked back and forth, reading me like a page, and in that breathless quiet I realized she didn't want to be talked into it. She wanted to decide for herself.

The standoff lasted a half-minute, maybe less. Then she grinned, fast and feral. "Deal. But if I win, you have to answer three Truth or Dare questions, no loopholes, no demon logic."

I nodded, letting the teeth of her challenge sink in. "Agreed."

She stood, dusted off her hands, and looked down at the cave pool, the shock of cold already forgotten. "So what's the safe zone?"

I didn't have to think. "The door of the house. If you touch it, you win. If I catch you first…" I shrugged, but the thrill in my chest was a wildfire. "You know how it ends."

She laughed—a sudden, delighted bark that bounced off the cave ceiling and sent a little shiver through the water. "Okay, but I want it to be fair. I get a full minute head start. And you can't use magic, or fly, or whatever weird demon tricks you're hiding."

I held up my hands, palms open. "No tricks. Just me, and whatever I can do on foot." The hunger was plain in my voice, and I didn't bother hiding it.

She considered, then said, "At sundown?" Her eyes never left mine.

I let the smile break across my face, slow and irrevocable. "At sundown."

We climbed the bluff together, pacing the last incline at a half-jog and trading the basket back and forth when the grade got steep. We could have gone slow, and maybe I should have, but I was wired with the thrill of the idea—and Annie, despite her smaller stride, matched me step for step, grinning with the wildness of someone who refused to be outpaced. By the time we reached the patio, sweat slicked our skin and the adrenaline was enough to make my claws itch for her again. But the clock on the kitchen oven blinked 11:32.

She dropped the basket inside the front door, then pivoted with a finger raised. "I need, like, eight minutes to shower and not look like I got sandblasted by a horny demon before the mayor shows up."

I caught her around the waist, pressed my mouth to her ear, and murmured, "Six minutes. Or I'm coming in after you."

She snorted, "Then you'll have to explain to the town's number one bureaucrat why there's a naked demon in the master bath."

Six minutes later exactly, she emerged in a fresh black slip dress, hair damp and finger-combed, eyes outlined with a defiant swipe of kohl. I heard the click-click of her boots on tile and felt my pulse pick up, stupid as it was. The way she stalked into the kitchen, chin up, face scrubbed and open to the day, made me want to pin her to the nearest surface and tell the mayor to come back in ten. Instead, I busied myself loading the dishwasher, resisting the urge to fix my hair, put on a clean shirt, anything to look more presentable. The last thing I wanted was to look like I was trying too hard for a goat-faced pencil-pusher and his clipboard.

I wiped my hands on my sweatpants—no time to change, so I was still in the sweatpants, still shirtless—and tried to look unruffled as the doorbell sang out its three-note jingle.

Annie shot me a look that was half warning, half mischief. "You look like a college athlete who just got up for his first ethics seminar."

I grinned, baring teeth. "Let's hope the mayor grades on a curve."

She rolled her eyes and went to the door, swinging it open with a flourish.

Mayor Vepar was even smaller than I remembered, which was saying something. He stood barely five foot three, with a build like a keg of beer in a three-piece suit. His head was mostly horn and beard, the eyes beady and gold set deep behind steel-rimmed glasses. The goatee, once black, had gone to salt and pepper, but the effect was more "Satanic distinguished professor" than "mall Santa." His hooves clicked sharply on the tile as he entered, not bothering to wait for an invitation.

He gave Annie the up-and-down, a long, unnerving look that started at her boots and cataloged every inch up to the tip of her liner-flicked lashes. Annie didn't flinch, just arched an eyebrow and held the look, like she'd been stared down by bureaucrats before and wasn't impressed by the horns or the tiny, cashmere vest.

"Ms. Harris," he said, voice nasal and precise, "you seem well-rested for a woman who barely survived her intake interview."

She grinned, baring her teeth, and I nearly flinched at how much she looked like she was ready to bite him. "Your staff made it clear I'd need my energy for the next round."

The mayor didn't smile. "That's the spirit." He produced a clipboard from the folds of his suit, along with a ballpoint pen so glossy and black, it looked as if it had been dipped in oil. He flicked his gaze to me.

He squinted at me for a long, uncomfortable moment, clicked the pen, and said, "Mr. Samiel. Everything in order?"

I braced for reprimand—maybe a comment about my attire, or the visible scratch marks on my chest, or the fact that we'd left a carnage of cheese rinds and berry stains across the picnic blanket in the entrance hall—but the mayor's gaze slid past me, focusing entirely on Annie.

"Ms. Harris," he said, pen poised over the form, "you are aware you may end this arrangement at any point in the next seventy-two hours? Without consequence or retaliation?"

She nodded, unflinching. "I read the fine print," she said. "I'm not here under duress." Her voice was dry as a Nevada summer, but the mayor wanted more.

"Can you confirm for the record that Mr. Samiel has not coerced, manipulated, or compelled you through infernal means—explicit or implied?" The question was so formal, I could smell the legalese simmering off it.

Annie blinked, then tilted her chin up so her gaze met the mayor's dead-on. "No, sir. I let him do everything to me of my own free will. Twice." She paused, then added, "Three times, if you count the kitchen."

The mayor's mouth opened, then snapped shut. For a moment, the only sound was the gentle hiss of the espresso machine.

"Duly noted," the mayor said, and I watched the tip of his pen tremble just a fraction as he recorded Annie's answer. "And I assume, Mr. Samiel, for the record, you are satisfied with the progress of the arrangement thus far?"

I tried to play it cool, but Annie's words had kicked my nervous system into overdrive. I could feel the tips of my ears go hot. "Completely," I said, voice low and uncooperative. "There have been no—incidents." I could hear the mayor's pen click in approval, but he kept his eyes on Annie.

She didn't flinch, just squared her shoulders and said, "He's been a perfect gentleman." Then, with a sidelong look at me: "Mostly."

The mayor pursed his lips, considering. I felt a familiar dread needle up my spine—forty years of mandatory check-ins, of always being the one under review. I'd expected it to be different with Annie here, with an actual chance at a match, but the old panic had been hibernating just beneath the surface, waiting for the moment when everything could still be taken away.

The mayor shuffled his pages, eyes never leaving Annie. "You will, of course, participate in the Chase this evening?" He said it like a threat, but the question was directed at her.

Annie grinned like she'd been waiting for the prompt. "Oh, absolutely. It sounds like a blast. But what I want to know is—is it just a Samiel thing, or do all the demons here do it?"

Mayor Vepar's lips twitched, barely suppressing a smirk. "It's policy. The tradition is older than the town itself. If you read the orientation materials, you'll find it was originally designed to give both parties a measure of recourse." He paused, shifted the clipboard to his other hand, and fixed his gaze on Samiel. "Some of the more... aggressive types found the Chase cathartic. For the less physically inclined, it's symbolic. Either way, the end is the same: negotiation, followed by reconciliation." He said the last with a sardonic twist, like he doubted any negotiation would last more than a minute against a demon built like a linebacker.

Annie turned to me, eyes sparkling, and asked, "So what

are the odds you'll actually catch me?" She made it sound like a joke, but I could see the question behind her eyes: *what will you* do *to me if you win?*

I smiled, but it felt like borrowed confidence. "You look like you do cardio," I said, eyes flicking down her frame before I could stop myself. "I'm guessing you don't just run from commitment."

She arched a brow, unconvinced. "But?"

I hesitated, and in that half-second of pause, I realized what was really eating at me. The Chase was tradition, yes, but it was also risk. It was the last test, the real one—the kind that couldn't be rehearsed or papered over with jokes. It was the hinge point where Annie would either decide she liked the monster in me, or she'd see it for what it was and run until she hit the state line.

I wanted her, needed her, with a ferocity that was starting to scare me. I worried that if I let her see it, she'd flinch. Or worse, she'd pity me.

I shrugged, making it an afterthought. "I'll chase you," I said, voice low. "I'll run you to ground. But I won't touch you unless you let me." The line was a bluff, a dare, and I watched her eyes go sharp with want.

The mayor's gaze flicked back and forth between us, reading the room with predatory precision. "Excellent. If there's nothing further, I'll check back at dawn." He tucked the clipboard under his arm and left, hooves ticking on the tile, the door snicking shut with finality.

We stood in the silence, the shadow of the mayor's visit lingering. Annie broke first, crossing the kitchen and opening the fridge, as if the world could only be reset by the ritual of snacks. She rooted out a bottle of mineral water, cracked it, and regarded me over the rim of the bottle.

"You're going to win, aren't you?" she said. "You've already decided."

I watched the motion of her throat as she swallowed, the way her jaw flexed with calculation. The answer was so obvious it almost felt stupid to say it out loud. I could pick her up and pin her to the fridge in less time than it would take her to scream. The only suspense was in how she'd make me work for it.

"Yeah," I said, honest. "I'm going to win."

She grinned, but it was all teeth. "Then you'd better make it worth the chase."

CHAPTER
NINE

Annie

Samiel let out a slow exhale, as if he'd been waiting for a sniper on the roof to take the shot and, having survived, now had to remember how to breathe again. He reached for my hand but stopped halfway, as if uncertain whether I'd bite. I took the lead, threading my fingers through his, the tips of his claws cool and peculiarly gentle against my palm.

"We've got hours until sunset," I said, tilting my head just enough to catch the doubt in his eyes before he could stuff it down again. "And you planned the lake, the picnic, the cave. Which means the afternoon is mine." I yanked him toward the living room by the hand, ignoring the way he balked in the threshold, as if the idea of being surprised was more dangerous than anything the town's demon mayor could come up with.

He tried, once, to protest. "You don't have to—"

I cut him off with a look. "You cooked, you carried, you

rowed me across a possibly haunted body of water. Let me pay you back."

The house was cool and a little dim, all the shades drawn against the furnace-bright Nevada sun. I let go of Samiel's hand at the foot of the couch, then pointed at the TV remote.

"Sit," I ordered. "Watch."

If he was surprised, he covered it well. He folded himself onto the couch, wings tucked, and waited as I rummaged the shelves beneath the TV for the stack of DVDs I'd noticed last night. It was all classics: horror, romance, cult comedies. I flipped through the spines, then held up two—*When Harry Met Sally* and *Evil Dead 2*.

Samiel blinked, then pointed at the latter, a hesitant smile breaking over his face.

"Excellent choice." I popped it in, then flopped onto the opposite end of the couch, keeping a safe three feet of distance, which for him was basically the range of a handshake.

The opening credits rolled, chainsaws and screaming, and I watched his face as the movie got going. At first, he was rigid, arms crossed over his chest, as if he expected the TV to be a booby trap. But about ten minutes in, as Bruce Campbell's hand started to attack him, Samiel's mouth opened in wonder. The laughter that followed was a full-bodied, stunned bark, as if he'd never been permitted the luxury of a joke at a monster's expense. He tried to contain it, but by the time the disembodied hand was jabbering through the walls, he was doubled over, tail whapping the far armrest, tears gathering in the corners of his eyes.

I pretended not to notice, but the sight of a six-foot some-thing demon rendered helpless by slapstick horror was its own kind of phenomenal. I paused at one point, for snacks, and he asked as I headed to the kitchen, "I don't get it. Why would you make a horror film... funny? Isn't the point to scare?"

I grinned, returning with popcorn. "That's the trick. Fear is a joke, half the time. Laugh at it, and it can't eat you." I drew my knees up, hugging them as the next scene shrieked across the screen. "Besides, if you're going to survive Hell, you might as well enjoy the ride."

He nodded, trying on the idea. "So, it's like... a challenge to the darkness?"

"A dare," I said, "with popcorn and bad effects. It's tradition."

The movie escalated. So did we. The first time our knees touched was an accident, a consequence of the couch being too short and Samiel needing to sprawl his legs out to avoid cutting off circulation to his demon-sized calves. The second time was on purpose, and I felt a spark when he didn't flinch or apologize, just nudged back with a small, deliberate pressure. Our hands found each other again, and this time fingers laced, my thumb worrying the callused ridges on his. Every time something in the movie made me jump or cackle, the grip got tighter, like we were both waiting for a cue neither of us wanted to miss.

The movie wore on, my head full of buzz and static, eyes starting to water from both the relentless gore and the weird, low-key sweetness of sharing a couch with someone who didn't judge me for reciting every single line ahead of the actors. Around the midpoint, I felt the gravity between us shift. Samiel was inching closer, slow and careful. His thigh pressed against mine, a solid, unmoving heat. I pretended not to notice, but my whole body was on high alert, every patch of skin waiting for the next contact.

At the climax, when Bruce Campbell finally chainsawed the monster and screamed in victory, Samiel whistled—a sharp, delighted sound that made me jump. I laughed, and he turned, eyes wide with joy. He looked at me like he couldn't believe he was allowed to be here, watching movies and eating snacks with a woman who wasn't afraid of him—or wasn't yet. The next second, he caught himself, and looked away, as if he'd remembered he was supposed to be scary.

I broke the tension by heaving a throw pillow at his chest. "You ever see a movie before? Or is this a first-timer thing?"

He caught the pillow, squished it between his elbows, then shook his head. "Only old sitcoms and cooking shows. They said it was safer, less likely to make us... nostalgic." As soon as he said the word, he grimaced, like he'd stepped on a truth he hadn't intended to spill.

"God, you poor disaster," I said, flopping back so my head landed in his lap. "You've been missing out. You haven't lived until you've seen a man chainsaw his own hand off for the greater good." I twisted to look up at him, my head pillowed on his thigh. "What else have they been keeping from you, Samiel? Do you even know about the cultural magic of Shark Week?"

He blinked. "I thought that was a military program?"

I howled and slapped his leg, the shock of muscle and heat making me linger a second. "You sweet, sweet idiot. We have so much to cover." I grinned, feeling weirdly triumphant that I could actually teach a demon something. "Next up, reality TV. After that, memes."

He looked down at me, a half-smile curling at his mouth. "I want to know it all. If you're the teacher."

I swallowed. "You're really not going to get tired of me?"

He shook his head, all gravity. "Never."

I wasn't ready for the weight of that word, the way it fell

into my chest like buckshot and scattered there. So I reached for the remote, changed the channel, and queued up a YouTube playlist called "Internet's Dumbest Home Experiments." I didn't think about it—I just wanted him to see what happened when regular humans dared the laws of nature with nothing but a jug of Diet Coke and a dream.

Samiel's eyes went comically wide as the first video started—a pair of sunburned idiots pouring Mentos into a two-liter, the resulting geyser arching into the neighbor's lawn. He howled, a delighted sound that startled even me. The next clip—microwaving a can of soup until it detonated —had him doubled over. He watched in slack-jawed awe as the homepage cycled through every permutation of destruction: watermelons in blenders, slingshot-thrown bowling balls, the slow necrosis of an off-brand marshmallow left in a trunk through July.

For a moment, I forgot to overthink. Just watched the light hit him, the way his face animated with every new disaster. I wondered if all the demons in Hell's Valley watched the world like this, hungry to understand the rules of a game they hadn't been allowed to play in years.

After the fifth or sixth clip, Samiel just blurted it out. "Are humans always this... reckless?"

"Absolutely," I said. "We have a genetic compulsion to see how close we can get to death without making it official." I shot him a sideways look. "You're not going to tell me demons don't have their own version of this, right? The 'hold my beer' impulse?"

He shook his head in awe. "But you tape it. And post it for others to... learn from?"

"Or just to laugh at. Cultural immortality. You either get famous or die trying." I leaned into him, propping myself up on one elbow, unable to stop the smile that kept sneaking around the corners of my mouth. "What, is this not how you pictured your first forty-eight hours with a bride? Watching rednecks explode watermelons for science?"

Samiel's hand came up, cupping the side of my face. "I never even dared to picture it," he said, voice thick. "This is better."

Before I could find a quip, he dipped his head and kissed me. Not the feral, devouring thing from last night, but a slow, hungry melt, lips parted just enough to trap the sound of my own gasp in the space between us. His hand slid into my hair, thumb tracing my cheek as if to memorize the shape of me. I let myself fall into it.

I'd been kissed in plenty of ways—sloppy, efficient, bored, even sometimes desperate—but never with the kind of focus Samiel brought to the table. He kissed like he'd been dreaming of this specific moment for so long that he didn't trust the world not to snatch it away. Like he was trying to remember every detail: the taste, the heat, the way my teeth scraped his lip when I bit at him just hard enough to make him hiss.

He angled his body, shifting under the weight of my head, then with a single motion he dragged me up and onto his lap, the movement so fluid that I barely registered the transition until I was straddling him, knees pressed to either side of his hips. The mesh of my shorts prickled against his thighs, and his hands bracketed my waist, not possessive but supportive, like he was holding something that might jump or shatter if he wasn't careful.

We made out, open-mouthed and ferocious, his tongue hot and forked. My hands climbed to his hair and horns, loving the way he shivered when I gripped them. I wrapped my legs tighter around his hips, grinding down so the throb inside me matched the one I felt, heavy and thick, under his sweatpants.

Samiel wasn't gentle, but he was careful, as if he'd studied the geometry of my body and calculated the exact amount of pressure it could take before bruising. He pulled me closer, one hand gripping the small of my back, the other snaking up my side to cup my breast through the mesh. His palm was rough, callused, but he moved slow, thumb tracing tight circles around my nipple until it peaked hard against the thin fabric. I moaned into his mouth, shameless, and felt his cock harden to full size beneath me—so solid I wondered if it might just tear clean through the seams of the pants if I moved too fast. I rocked forward, grinding along the length of him, and the pressure of it made me gasp, made him bite down on the curve of my shoulder with a low groan.

With an effort, I pulled back, hands braced on his shoulders, my breath coming shallow and hard. "Sam," I managed. "Fuck, I want you, but—" I shot a look at the clock on the far wall, numbers burning orange: 3:49 p.m. "If we don't eat something now, you're gonna have to carry me back after the Chase. I'll pass out the minute you win."

It was not a lie. I was already lightheaded, my muscles gone strange and floaty from too many hours of adrenaline and popcorn and him. But also, I didn't want to lose the momentum. I leaned in, bridging the distance between our mouths, and nipped at his lower lip before whispering, "If you let me die of low blood sugar, I'm haunting you for the next four decades."

Instead of laughing, Samiel went oddly serious. "You won't," he said, voice low. He adjusted me in his lap, as if the weight of me was nothing, then reached for his phone—

which, I now noticed, was vintage enough to have actual buttons and a matte-black case battered by years of use.

"You want pizza?" he asked, thumbing the speed dial with a rapid, almost anxious dexterity. "Or is that too... basic for the last meal of the unclaimed?"

I gawked. "You're kidding. There's a pizza place here?"

He shrugged, but I caught the sly flicker of pride in his eyes. "Hell is full of surprises." He hit the final button, and the phone chirped as it connected. The voice on the other end was so loud and surly that I could hear it from where I sat, still perched on Samiel's lap.

"Devil's Throat Pizza, what the fuck do you want?"

Samiel's face lit up with malevolent glee. "Two larges. One with meat, all of it. One plain cheese, extra garlic, extra sauce. And mozzarella sticks. And—" He glanced at me, question in his eyes.

"Peppers. Hot ones," I said, channeling every yearning from every sad Florida pizza delivery. "And ranch. Like, a tub."

He repeated my order verbatim, pausing only to add, "If you mess up the mozzarella, Clem, I'm coming down there." He hung up with a sharp click, then set the phone aside now that it had performed its duty.

"You heard the demon," I said, giggling. "We're getting mozzarella or there will be blood."

Samiel's eyes—still black-limned from the last round of hunger—softened. "You have to have carbs and cheese for the Chase. The whole point is to run, isn't it?"

"*The whole point* is to get caught," I said, and the words came out so quickly, I almost clapped a hand over my mouth. His mouth curved like the line of a wolf's yawn.

"If you want to lose on purpose, I'll make it worth your while," he said. The suggestion in his voice made my thighs

112

tense up, my mind blanking out anything but the thought of being pinned under him, back in that bed or maybe against the cool of the kitchen counter.

"I didn't say I wanted to lose," I said, "but if I do, it'll be because I underestimated you. Or, I don't know, because I tripped on a fucking tumbleweed." I grinned, tempting him to call my bluff. "But if you win, I expect you to make good on every threat."

Samiel's eyes lit with a fever I'd never seen in a man, mortal or otherwise. "I'll make sure you remember it. Every second." The promise was so blunt, it left my stomach flipping, but not in the bad way. I wanted it; I wanted him to win. I wanted to see what he'd do with me once he had permission to stop being careful. I wanted to know what it would feel like to be claimed—not as a bride, but as a prize. Even the idea of losing felt like a victory, if it meant more of this: more of him, more of the buzz, more of the way he looked at me like I was the only person on the planet who mattered.

The doorbell rang and I jumped up to answer it, finding a familiar face on the other side. Clem—the same demon who'd driven us to the house—stood there with pizza boxes balanced on one palm. His eyes lit up when he saw me alone, his eyes lingering on my braless chest.

"Well hello again, unclaimed," he purred, leaning against the doorframe. "Thought I'd deliver personally." He stepped closer, voice dropping. "You know, if tall-dark-and-horny isn't working out—"

I gave him my coldest, most withering look, the one I reserved for men who still called women "chicks" in emails.

"You're cute, Clem, but if I wanted a pizza guy with boundary issues, I'd go back to dating humans." I took the boxes from his outstretched hand, but he didn't move, just leaned in closer.

I thought he'd let it drop. Instead, he reached out and, with a single claw, traced a slow line down my cheek. His claw was shockingly cold, precise as a scalpel, and I jerked back, pizza boxes tilting dangerously. He caught my eye, a mocking, yellow glimmer in the center of the slit pupil. "That's a shame," he drawled. "I always liked a girl with a taste for danger."

I opened my mouth to shut him down for good, but something flickered in the periphery—heat, pressure, a weather change in the house's atmosphere. Before I could finish my next breath, Samiel was in the foyer, moving so fast the air actually whooshed.

His hand closed around Clem's throat, claws dimpling skin but not breaking it, and pinned the other demon neatly against the wall. The pizza boxes teetered in my arms. Clem didn't struggle; he just grinned sideways at me, as if we were in on some private joke.

"Hey, boss man," he wheezed, voice gone thin. "I was just—"

Samiel didn't growl. He didn't need to. He bent in, his lips brushing Clem's ear, and said, "Deliveries are curbside only at the house, remember?" His voice was a razor blade wrapped in velvet.

Clem's feet dangled a good two inches off the ground, but he didn't drop the smirk. "She invited me to the porch. You got a problem with your bride greeting the help?"

Samiel squeezed, just enough to make the cartilage crackle. "I have a problem with my property being touched by anyone who isn't me." The words, so cold and simple, sent a flash of heat through my chest that was part terror, part joy. There was no pretense in it. No pretending they weren't monsters.

Clem's eyes rolled, making a show of it. "It's just a little fun, Sam. Don't get your horns in a twist."

Samiel let go, the sudden absence of pressure making Clem sag like a wet towel. "If you touch her again," Samiel said, voice flat as the surface of the lake, "I'm sending you back to Hell. In pieces. Understood?"

Clem rubbed his throat, gave a wheezing cough, then fixed his smirk on me. "Worth it," he mouthed, then turned and slunk off the porch, shoes scraping the tile. The door clicked shut behind him.

For a second, Samiel watched the empty hallway, fists flexing and unflexing at his sides. I set the pizza on the kitchen counter and just looked at him.

"Jesus, Sam," I said. "He was being a creep, but you didn't have to go full Liam Neeson on his ass."

He didn't look at me, just stared at the door like it might open again if he blinked. His shoulders were bunched up around his ears, and his hands shook a little.

"He touched you," he said, voice low and thick.

"And?" I said, a little sharper than intended. "I can handle it. I've been in HR meetings scarier than that demon." I wanted to laugh it off, to drag the mood back to lightness, but it didn't work. Samiel's jaw clenched, and when he finally looked at me, his eyes were black all the way through, like someone had poured ink into them.

"You aren't supposed to have to handle anything," he said. "Not with me here." He tried to soften it, but the words just hung there.

I blinked, not sure whether to be flattered, annoyed, or both. "I'm not glass, Samiel." I crossed my arms, trying to keep my voice steady. "I know you want to protect me or whatever, but I don't need a bodyguard. I need a..." I trailed off, the word *partner* burning behind my teeth, too much and too soon.

He looked stricken, like I'd slapped him. "I'm sorry," he said, but it fell flat. "I just—forty years, Annie. I've had to watch every inch of this town, every day, knowing if I so much as looked at a woman wrong, I'd be straight back to Hell. I guess I forgot how to do just enough." He scrubbed a hand over his face, the claws almost grazing his eyelid. "I can dial it back. I will."

I stared at him. All that want, all that hunger, and he was still terrified to fuck it up. I made a decision then. I needed to be honest about who I was, too.

"Look," I said, moving closer. "If you're really going to be my demon, then you have to trust me to take care of myself sometimes. Not every touch needs to be a duel to the death, okay?" I reached out, lacing my fingers through his, the veins on the back of his hand still pulsing with leftover adrenaline.

He squeezed back, hard. "Okay," he said, "but you're still mine. I'm not letting go."

I rolled my eyes, but not unkindly. "Fine. But if you ever try to alpha-male another pizza guy, I'm switching to vegan." The threat was empty, but he flinched anyway, and I laughed, the tension finally breaking.

We ate our pizza on the kitchen floor, backs against the fridge, the smell of garlic and tomato and scorched dough so crisp, it shredded the roof of my mouth.

After a while, I noticed the silence had changed. Not bad, just... heavier. I finished my third slice and wiped my fingers on the crust, then glanced at the clock, the window, the weirdly empty blue outside.

"You ever think about what happens after this?" I asked.

"Like, after the Chase. After today, after the matching." It came out quick, and I hated how small my voice sounded in my own ears.

Samiel looked at me, the stillness in his face suddenly alive with panic. "You mean, if you... stayed?" He said it so tentatively that I felt the bones of my chest cave in a little.

I nodded, forcing myself to go on. "I mean, what does 'mine' even look like out here? Am I supposed to just let you break every pizza guy who looks at me funny? Or are we going to have to, like, set ground rules?" I tried to joke, but it didn't sound like one.

He was quiet for a long time. "I want to hurt them," he said, his voice dropping to a register that vibrated through the floorboards. "Anyone who touches you, looks at you wrong—I want to tear them apart." His jaw clenched, tendons standing out along his neck. "But I won't. For you." He hunched his shoulders, massive wings folding in tight against his back like a shield. "I'll try to do better. I don't want you afraid of me."

I reached out, my hand covering his where it tensed against the floor. "I'm not. I just... I want to be more than a thing to be protected. I want to be your equal, not your precious." I said it before I could lose my nerve. "I want to know if you'd still want me if I could fight my own battles, if I didn't need you at all."

He stared at our hands, then up at me, and for the first time the black in his eyes was all soft, no sharp edges left behind. "I want that," he said. "If you could tear the world in half, I'd just want to watch." He squeezed my hand, claws retracted, all careful control. "But I need to know you'll let me fight for you sometimes. Not because you need it— because I need it."

I breathed out. "Deal," I said. "But you have to promise

not to kill any more delivery guys. Or at least wait until after they bring the food inside." He laughed—a real one—and for a second I saw how it could work, this thing between us. Not a standoff, but a partnership made of challenges, of who could love harder or be braver without giving up any ground.

We finished the pizza, leaving a mess of napkins and crusts on the kitchen floor. The sun dipped behind the valley's edge, stretching shadows across the living room. Samiel gathered everything with demonic efficiency, then turned to me, eyes gleaming in the darkening light.

"Should I get changed?" I asked, half-joking. "Or is this one of those things where you want to see if I can outrun you in mesh shorts and free tits?"

He paused, gave me a once-over—the kind that should have felt objectifying, but on Samiel was more like a tailor's appraisal than a pickup artist's leer.

"You should wear something you can run in," he said, voice careful. "And shoes. There are goatheads in the sand— seed pods, not actual goats," he clarified. "But you can wear whatever you like. I'll find you no matter what."

The way he said it—matter-of-fact but edged with pride —made me want to test him. I pictured myself in those fishnets, bare legs flashing white against the dusk, and wondered if he'd hunt me harder for the spectacle. Or if he'd tear them off just to prove the point. I decided to split the difference and pulled on my shortest running shorts and an old, baggy band shirt and bra, then laced up my sneakers. I left the makeup as it was—the ghost of black eyeliner, the sweat-glow on my cheekbones, a mess of two-tone hair frizzing from the earlier shower. I didn't want to look perfect for the game; I wanted to look like myself. My heart hammered against my ribs as I caught my reflection in the hallway mirror—cheeks flushed, pupils wide, hair wild. I thought of the way his eyes had burned with his fingers wrapped around Clem's neck, how the veins in his forearms had stood out like ropes. My mouth went dry. Would he look at me that way as he hunted me through the desert? Would I feel those hands closing around my wrists, my throat? The thought made my skin prickle with goose bumps despite the heat, fear and something darker twisting together in my stomach.

CHAPTER
TEN

Samiel

At 6:59 p.m., the air outside was still radiating heat from the day, but under it there was a tremor—a fine sizzle like electricity just before the power hum went dead. I stood on the porch with Annie, waiting for the second hand to click over, feeling the hair at the nape of my neck bristle with anticipation. The sun, half-submerged behind the mountains, poured molten gold over the sand, turning every rock and weed into a silhouette.

I glanced at Annie, taking in the sharp line of her jaw, the way her hands flexed open and closed at her sides. "You sure about this?" I asked, voice pitched low.

She grinned, all teeth and nerves. "You're the one who said no takebacks."

"Fair enough." My wings flexed, a slow unfurl that stretched the membrane almost edge-to-edge with the patio. I caught the movement in the glass of the sliding door behind us, a blur of red and black that made me look less like a man and more like a warning.

Without warning, I scooped Annie up and launched skyward, the sound of my beating wings drowning out her yelp.

"I'll fly you to the start point and then give you a minute head start," I whispered into her ear as I flew. She clung to me as the desert stretched out below us. "If you make it to the deck before I catch you—you win." Knowing there was no way she would. Sure, we had agreed on rules and parameters, but what were rules to a demon?

We reached the outcropping of rocks where I would deposit her. I was to let her have a sixty-second head start, no more, no less. The wind off the valley hit us, hot and grainy, as I set her down on the bald cap of a boulder and let my hands linger long enough to leave fingerprints.

She pulled free, steadying herself on a ledge, and looked over her shoulder at me—eyes huge, mouth a dark slash in the late sun. "You going to tell me the rules again?" she asked, half-joking.

I just smiled, teeth bright, and shrugged. "You know them. You run. I hunt. If you make it to the deck before I catch you, you win. If I catch you…" I let the silence hang, let her imagine it.

Her nostrils flared, and I could smell the spike of her adrenaline, bitter and electric. She wiped a sweaty palm on her shorts, then squared her shoulders toward the house far below—tiny as a Monopoly piece at the edge of the first switchback.

"And you really won't use tricks? No demon magic, no—"

"I told you. No tricks. Just legs and willpower." I locked my gaze on her. "But do you trust a demon to keep up his end of the bargain?"

She didn't wait for a second warning. She spun on her

heel and dove off the boulder, sprinting down the scree with a reckless speed that made my own heart hammer. I watched, letting the clock tick, counting each second like a drumbeat against my ribs.

I wanted her to run. I wanted to see how far she'd go before she realized I was already at her heels. And in that minute, all I could think about was the flash in her eyes when Clem laid hands on her, the way my own hands had closed around his neck without a thought. I could have snapped Clem like a chicken bone, shredded him to pulp in front of her, and the only reason I didn't was because I didn't want to see that flicker of fear in Annie's face. Not even for a second. But the urge was there—instant, pure, and so right it felt like a law of physics.

Maybe I was more monster than man after all. Maybe the mayor had good reason to keep us on leashes. Maybe I'd never learn how to turn that part of me off.

Or maybe Annie already knew. Maybe she wanted it, the same way I wanted her: total, animal, unyielding. The thought made a bright hunger explode in the back of my throat, not for food or air but for the chase itself, the knowing that I could have her, that I was allowed.

At forty-two seconds, I caught a flash of her hair in the sagebrush, just before she vanished behind a thicket of mesquite. At forty-three, the breeze shifted, and I could smell her sweat and the raw, salt-sweet tang of her skin, a trail that read like a love letter written directly to my cells.

Sixty seconds. I launched off the rock, wings snapping full, and the updraft nearly wrenched me backwards—I caught myself, caught the wind, and rode it, using every muscle in my back to push forward, toward the blur of motion that was Annie hurtling through the desert.

She'd chosen the narrowest path, all scree and switchbacks, a descent that would have shattered a human ankle if taken at this speed. She was clever, using the landscape to her advantage, knowing I couldn't use my wings to just drop straight down without risking a crash. But she'd underestimated the way my body remembered this valley—the curve of the ravines, the crumbling seams of old ore paths, the scabbed-over wounds of a hundred abandoned mining trails. I mapped her route in my head as I dove, using the air to slingshot from ledge to ledge, always keeping her in my peripheral vision.

She crossed the first flat with a burst of speed that made me grin—a straight shot of pure animal will, legs pumping, arms driving her forward like she was running for her life. I let myself savor the spectacle—the wildness, the refusal to play prey—and followed, every nerve ending tuned to the frequency of her.

Halfway down the switchback, I caught the blur of her hair again, a ragged comet of color against the silver scrub. She'd cut off the trail and was booking it across a shale field, loose stones skittering underfoot. I landed on a ledge above, crouched low, and waited to see if she'd look back. She didn't. She just kept moving, head down, lungs heaving. The sight stoked something in me that was more than hunger—it was awe. I could have glided in, closed my claws around her and pinned her to the sand, but the way she ran—every stride a fuck-you to the idea of being claimed—made the old, cinder-black part of me want to let her run, let her believe she might win, just for the taste of her hope when I finally took her down. I circled overhead, wings stretched to catch the dying thermals, my shadow rippling over the ridges in long, slow sweeps. She was fast. Not trained, not graceful—but fast. I waited, crouched on the rock, every nerve screaming, every inch of me tuned to the flick and beat of her pulse.

Then I dropped.

Wind hammered my face, the taste of her in it—sweat, the ghost of her perfume from the night before. Every sense sharpened. I banked hard, using my wings to ride the wind shear above the ravine, then folded them and dove straight down the shale, clawed feet skidding, hands digging for hold. I ate up the distance between us in seconds. She must've heard me—a human would've, anyone would've—but she didn't break stride.

I was on her before she hit the creekbed, a full-body collision that snatched the breath from both of us. She spun to the side, off-balance, but I caught her mid-scramble, palms bracketing her ribs as I pinned her to the packed dust. The scree bit into my knees, Annie cursing and panting. I hoisted her off her feet and spun her, slamming her chest-down into the scrubby dust.

The pebbles bit into her knees, and her palms splayed for balance, but Annie never begged—I loved her for that. She bucked to throw me, but I pinned her flat, one hand splayed between her shoulder blades, the other raking down her spine. Her shirt tore with the barest effort, my claws slicing it open from neck to hem. The fabric fluttered away; her back arched, pale and ridged with muscle, and every inch of her screamed to be marked.

I braced her hips in my hands and yanked her shorts and underwear down in one motion. The sound—cotton surrendering to force—was obscene, and I knew she heard it, knew she felt the air against her skin, the threat of exposure. I could smell her: sweat and the spike of terror and the thick, sweet undercurrent of arousal. She was even before I'd touched her.

She tried to twist around, to snarl something back at me, but I pressed her head gently into the crook of her elbow, careful not to slice her with the claws. I let my weight rest against her, pinning her, and ran my tongue up the length of her spine, slow and deliberate, tasting the grit and salt. She shuddered—whether from fear or anticipation, it made no difference.

"Sam—" she gasped, voice muffled by the crook of her arm, but there was anger beneath the desire. "You used your wings." Her elbow jabbed backward, catching my ribs. "That wasn't the deal."

I let her have a single breath of warning before I spread her thighs. Burying my face between her legs, my forked tongue forced her folds apart, lapping at her clit and then slipping lower. I savored the taste of her—raw and alive—as she bucked and sobbed into the dirt. Her scent, rich with arousal, filled my nostrils, spurring me on.

She writhed beneath me, hips jerking between fight and surrender as I licked her cunt, relentlessly teasing her swollen bud. Annie's nails raked the ground in a primal rhythm that matched her erratic breathing. She bucked her hips against my face, a wordless plea for more.

My tongue skillfully split and coaxed her open, thrusting in and out of her slick heat until she shuddered under the weight of impending orgasm. I sensed the moment before it hit, feeling the pulse in her thighs and the tension in her abdomen. Her orgasm ripped through her, unguarded and beautifully messy as she cried out, trying to muffle the sound with her fist.

I didn't wait for the last tremors to subside before lining up my hard cock with her entrance. She spasmed around me as I entered her, tight heat gripping me like a vise. I slammed her back down onto the dirt-packed ground, pinning her pelvis down with my own. Burying myself to the hilt, I felt every ripple of her contractions around my shaft.

"Say it," I growled in her ear, voice rough with lust. "Say who owns you."

She twisted her head to look at me, hair plastered to her sweat-soaked face. A defiant smile played on her lips as she hissed, "Fuck you."

I grinned wolfishly and surged my cock all the way inside her wet cunt. I wasn't gentle; I could feel the stretch, the way her cunt resisted and then yielded, the friction a perfect, desperate ache. She screamed, but didn't tell me to stop. I set a rhythm, fucking her so hard that the slap of skin of my balls against her echoed off the rocks, every thrust a statement, a claim, a signature in the wet heat of her. I gripped her ass with both hands, claws dimpling the skin, and pulled her onto me, forcing her to take every inch.

"Mine," I growled, and the word rattled out of me with a hunger I'd never felt before. "All of you, Annie. Mine."

She sobbed, "Yes, yours," and arched her back, offering herself up like a prize to a conqueror.

I leaned over her, spine bowing to bring my mouth to her ear. "I'm going to knot you here, in the dirt, where anyone can see. I'm going to fuck you until you can't walk, and then carry you home." The words came out as a snarl. I bit her shoulder, careful not to break the skin, and the taste of her salt sent me reeling.

She bucked back to meet me, hips slamming into my groin on every stroke. Her hands clawed at the dirt, scrabbling for any purchase, but I left her no room—just the friction, the stretch, the relentless pulse of my cock as it hammered her open. She was drenched, her body milking me, and I felt her tighten again, the start of a second orgasm building from the ruins of the orgasm that had just ripped through her. I wanted to make her sob, to wring out every last drop of defiance until she was nothing but want. But she'd earned a little mercy, too.

I hooked my arms under her, hauled her up so her back arched and her ass pressed flush against my hips. I flipped her with a single heave, pinning her on her back so she could see the sky, could see me. Her legs fell open, revealing her swollen, glistening sex, pink folds slick with need. I hooked my hands under her knees, spreading her wider until she whimpered, then drove into her with agonizing slowness, savoring each inch as her tight heat enveloped me. Her eyes locked with mine, pupils blown wide with desire, her wild hair framing her flushed face as her lips parted in a breathless moan that sent fire racing down my spine.

I leaned in, mouth by her ear, and whispered, "Tell me if you need me to slow down." My thumb brushed a strand of hair from her sweat-slicked temple, even as my hips remained mercilessly still. Her breath hitched, fingers digging into my shoulders.

"I will," she gasped, eyes half-lidded and glazed, "but if you stop, I swear I'll kill you."

I licked the shell of her ear, tasting sweat, and started to fuck her again—hard, then harder, letting the smack of our bodies echo off the stone, receiving all the confirmation I needed that she was still with me. I braced my palms on either side of her shins and bent low, letting my weight press the backs of her thighs tight to the ground. Her chest heaved, nipples peaked and flushed from the chill and from being fucked open so shamelessly. I dipped my head and caught one in my mouth, drawing it deep with such force she jolted and cursed my name. I suckled hard, pulling blood to the surface in dark blooms beneath her skin. Her areola disappeared between my lips as I worked, leaving the flesh angry and purple when I finally released it.

Her other breast received the same treatment—my mouth creating a violent constellation of bruises that would mark her as mine for days. She screamed as I sealed my claim with a final, possessive pull, but her cunt spasmed around me and I felt her gush, the wet heat flooding out over my balls and down the crack of her ass.

Her eyes fluttered shut as I dragged my tongue across her collarbone. "Are you going to mark me up everywhere?" she gasped, her voice breaking on the last word.

"Every. Single. Inch," I growled against her feverish skin, moving to her neglected nipple. I drew it between my lips and sucked until she arched off the ground, the suction leaving a perfect crimson ring. "By the time I'm done, your body will remember only me."

She writhed beneath me, fingers finding my horns, using them to drag my mouth harder against her breast. "Fuck, Sam, I—" Her words dissolved into a broken moan as my teeth grazed her sensitive flesh, the sound vibrating through both our bodies like a shared current.

I dragged my tongue over her nipple, feeling it harden against my teeth. "Tell me who owns this body," I growled, my voice vibrating against her flesh. "Tell me who's ruined you for anyone else."

She writhed beneath me, her back arching off the ground as her hips rolled against mine, taking me deeper. Her eyes locked with mine, pupils blown wide with surrender.

"You," she gasped, her nails digging crescents into my shoulders. "Only you. God—I'm yours." Her confession broke on a moan as I thrust harder, claiming her with my body as she claimed me with her words.

I moved my hand between us and found her clit with my

128

thumb, pressing hard enough to make her mine. Her body convulsed beneath me as she shrieked, her inner walls gripping me like a vise. I owned every inch of her now.

"This is mine," I growled, working her clit in relentless circles while driving my cock deeper with each thrust. Her body slid against the dirt with each powerful stroke, her resistance futile. "You'll come when I command it, as many times as I want." I caught her nipple between my teeth, tugging in rhythm with my thrusts. "And I want more." She raked desperate fingers across my skin.

"I can't," she sobbed, even as her body betrayed her, trembling on the edge of surrender.

"You can," I said, and pinched her clit hard between my thumb and finger. She howled, eyes rolling back, and her cunt went molten around me, squeezing and milking my cock with every pulse of her orgasm. I fucked her through it, relentless, letting her sob and gasp and beg until she went boneless underneath me.

When she finally stilled, I pulled out, flipped her onto her stomach again, and shoved her hips up so her ass was high and her face pressed into the dirt. I lined up and thrust back into her with a single savage stroke that sent my heavy sac slapping against her swollen clit. She screamed—wordless, pure—as I felt my knot begin to swell, stretching her entrance with each brutal thrust. I grabbed a fistful of her hair, yanked her back until her spine bowed like a drawn bow, and buried myself to the root. My balls smacked rhythmically against her, each impact drawing a desperate whimper from her throat as the knot locked us together, sealing my claim.

Annie's hands clawed at the ground, nails carving desperate furrows in the dust as she arched back to meet each thrust. Her face gleamed with sweat, tears catching the moonlight on her flushed cheeks, but her moans were pure surrender. With every stroke, I claimed another piece of her —her gasps, her trembling thighs, the way her body yielded and tightened around me in perfect rhythm. My knot swelled, stretching her, owning her from the inside out, and when I growled "Come for me," her release shattered through her like a command fulfilled, her pleasure mine to take and give as I chose.

I gripped her hair, yanking her head back until her throat arched taut beneath the moonlight. "Look at you," I growled against her skin, rough with hunger. "Your body knows who you belong to." I dragged my tongue along the pulse hammering in her neck, before grazing my fangs over the tender spot where her shoulder met her throat. "The way you tremble when I'm inside you—" My words dissolved into a feral sound as she clenched around me. "You're mine to hunt, mine to claim, mine to ruin. And you're fucking perfect."

My hands braced her, one on her shoulder, one on her hip, and I rocked into her, knot swelling impossibly larger as her cunt fluttered around me, each pulse drawing me deeper. My vision blurred at the edges until all I could see was the curve of her spine, the way her skin glistened in the moonlight. The sound that tore from my throat wasn't human—a primal claiming that echoed through the valley as my release built from the base of my spine. When I finally erupted inside her, my entire body convulsed, every muscle seizing as I flooded her, marked her from within. Annie's body arched beneath me, her inner walls clamping down so tight I saw stars, milking every last drop as she sobbed my name. I bent over her, teeth grazing the nape of her neck, tasting salt and surrender as my seed sealed our bond—the most ancient magic there is.

For a long time, I just stayed there, panting into the back of her neck, my body fused to hers, the world reduced to the taste of her skin and the rough throb of her pulse against my cheek. I didn't want to let go, didn't want to ever risk the chance she'd slip away.

We stayed like that. Naked, filthy, fused together, facing each other in the bruised blue shadow of the creekbed, while the sunset bled out over the rocks and the air cooled. My knot was still locked inside her, and every tiny squeeze or twitch sent a jolt up my spine, so I let myself sag over her body, molding to every sharp angle, every sticky patch of torn flesh and sweat. My wings draped over us like a tent, blocking the wind. Neither of us spoke.

When I finally softened enough for the knot to slip free, she made a noise—somewhere between a whimper and a laugh—and tensed, as if she expected the emptiness to hurt. I eased out as gently as I could, watching her body twitch and clench, then collapse with a wet, exhausted sigh. She rolled to her side, hands tucked between her knees, and looked up at me with a face so ruined it was beautiful. Hair a mess. Dirt in her teeth. Eyes bright and unrepentant.

She laughed, and the sound was perfect—unpretty, but so real it made my chest ache.

"Fuck you," she said, but she let me gather her up in my arms, let me carry her back up the slope like a trophy.

Her legs were covered in scratches, her ass red with claw marks, and her whole body shook with the effort of holding together. But she didn't complain. She curled against my chest, face pressed to my neck, and let me haul her up through the rocks, across the moonlit scrub, all the way back to the deck.

CHAPTER
ELEVEN

Annie

I felt claimed.

My body still throbbed with the memory of his hands pinning me down, his teeth grazing my neck, the delicious stretch of his knot locking us together. Every inch of me felt marked—not like property, but like territory worth fighting for. My skin still burned where he'd touched me, like he'd left invisible fingerprints that only I could feel.

When he looked at me now, I could see the hunger hadn't faded—that same primal need to possess me completely, to make me come apart under him again and again until I couldn't remember my own name. And God help me, I wanted him to. I wanted to be ruined and remade by those hands, that mouth, that perfect, brutal tenderness that saw every desperate, needy part of me and wanted more.

That was the part that made my head go fuzzy as Samiel carried me up the last switchback, my shorts bunched in one hand and the rest of me bundled against his chest like I was something fragile. The air was starless and blue-black, the sky above the valley so endless it felt like I'd slipped out of the world entirely. Sweat dried on my skin, dirt crusted on my knees, but the heat in my chest never cooled. Everything felt too sharp: the scrape of his calluses, the wet pulse between my legs, the sting of rock dust and sage in my lungs. Every step he took, I remembered the way he'd held me down—*pinned* me—I wanted to make it happen again, even if I had to let him win every time.

By the time the lights of the house came back into view, my brain was half shut down from aftershocks. My thighs still shook, and every little jolt set off a secondhand quake in my stomach. I'd never come like that; I didn't think it was possible for a person to lose it so completely, to be so ruined and want more. I was used to sex as performance, as leverage, as a means of getting what I wanted (even if what I wanted was sometimes just to feel wanted). This wasn't that. This was: you lose, and you win anyway.

At the top of the deck, Samiel slowed, then stopped, wings drooped so wide they blotted out the porch lights. He waited, breathing hard, as if he was afraid to set me down and risk the spell breaking. I let my face rest against the curve of his neck, inhaled the furnace of his skin, and made a low, involuntary whine. He tightened his grip, like he was scared I'd be snatched away.

"Do you want to go inside?" he asked, his voice frayed around the edges.

I shook my head. "Not yet."

He sank down to the deck, folding his legs under us, and set me in his lap. It was colder up here, the wind off the lake smelling like wet iron and desert, but I didn't care. I was still slick with sweat and him; my scalp was a mess of snarled hair and dust. I sat there, leaning into his chest, and let the silence fill up with the sound of our synchronized breathing.

His scent was still all over me, marking me as his in a way no human man ever could. I ran my fingertips over the tender bruises forming on my hips, pressing lightly to feel that sweet ache bloom again. My body remembered the weight of him, the way he'd covered me completely. I thought of the run—how my heart had hammered against my ribs on the descent when I realized I wanted him to catch me. My legs had kept pumping anyway, making him work for it, making him prove how badly he wanted me. I imagined us years from now, me darting through these same trails, him always just a few strides behind, both of us knowing exactly how it would end. His. Mine. Ours.

We didn't talk for a while. The wind rattled the porch railing, and the moon came out, a pale coin caught on the edge of the clouds. Eventually, Samiel shifted, tucking the tangle of my hair behind my ear. His hands, so brutal a few minutes ago, stroked the side of my face with a care that made me want to cry.

"Do you want a bath?" he asked, and the question was so out of place, so gentle, it made me snort.

"Are you offering to scrub the dirt off, or just watch?"

He considered. "I could do both. But I'll stay outside the door, if you want. Just in case it's too much." His voice shrank on that last word, his wings drawing in tight against his back. I twisted in his lap until I could see his face—the downturned eyes, the tight line of his mouth.

"I wanted you to claim me, Sam. Every mark, every bruise." I traced my fingers along his jaw where the muscle pulsed beneath my touch. "I ran so you would chase me. I fought so you would pin me. I wanted all of it."

He nodded, but I could tell he didn't believe me. He was holding me so carefully now, like I was some piece of glass he'd just learned was already cracked. "Still. You should have a bath. You need it more than I do."

I pushed up, tested my legs, and nearly laughed when my knees buckled. "You going to help, or just watch me crawl?"

He stood, scooped me up—no warning, no effort, just hands under my thighs and back, wings curled to keep out the cold. He carried me inside, through the kitchen and up the stairs.

He carried me all the way to the upstairs bathroom, the one with the sunken black marble tub and the rack of fancy towels I'd been too chicken to use this morning. He set me down on the counter, careful to keep my knees from banging the edge, and started the water. I watched his face in the mirror as he tested the temperature with the back of his wrist and frowned, like he was worried it wouldn't be perfect.

He filled the tub, then rummaged through the cabinet for bath salts and a tiny bottle of bubble bath, which he uncorked and sniffed before pouring a cautious glug into the running water. The smell was sweet, like gardenias and petrichor, and the first curl of steam made the whole room soften around the corners.

He hesitated, wings tucked tight, hands balled into fists at his sides. "You want me to help you in?" he asked, but there was a wariness in his voice, like he thought I might say no, or worse, that I'd changed my mind about everything that happened outside.

But I wanted him. Here, now, even in this. "Stay," I said, reaching for his hand. "I don't want to be alone."

He blinked, processing, then let his shoulders drop. I saw the relief on his face, but also something softer, almost embarrassed. He helped me peel off what was left of my shirt, the fabric stiff with dust and sweat. He was careful with his claws, always, and when he touched my skin, it was with the gentlest pressure, as if afraid to leave another bruise. He saw the red prints on my hips, the bite marks on my shoulder, the rawness between my thighs. For a second, his jaw clenched like he wanted to apologize, but he didn't—he just met my eyes in the mirror and waited for me to flinch.

I didn't. I wanted every mark, every aching patch of skin. I wanted to know he'd been there.

He helped me into the bath. The water stung at first, in all the places he'd left his mark, but the heat numbed it quickly. I sank down, let the bubbles rise to my chin, and melted. He knelt beside the tub, one big hand braced on the tile, the other hovering just above my knee, as if waiting for permission.

I reached for him, pulled his hand into the water, and settled it just above my shin. "Get in with me," I said, and tugged at his wrist.

He laughed a little and shook his head. "I'll break the tub," he said, but the protest was half-hearted.

"Try," I said.

Samiel gave a little snort, then kicked off his sweatpants and stepped over the side, careful and slow. He was so broad across the chest that for a second I thought he really would shatter the porcelain, but the tub just groaned and settled, the waterline rising to the very lip. He folded himself behind me, wings draping up and over the towel bar like expensive blackout curtains. I leaned back against his chest, and his hands found my shoulders, thumbs making small circles against the knots there. I traced idle patterns on his forearm with my fingertips, following the ridges of muscle and tendon. Neither of us spoke. We just breathed together, his chin resting on the top of my head, my palm sliding lazily up and down his calf.

I leaned back into him, letting my head drop against his chest. The heat pulled the last nerves from my limbs, replaced with a floaty, narcotic softness. I closed my eyes, wanting nothing but the thump of his heart and the wet slip of his skin against mine.

We said nothing for a while. The fizz of the bath salts and the hush of the air vent were the only sounds. I didn't need him to talk, but I wanted to fill the space with something that wasn't just the ghosts of what had happened outside; I wanted to stitch this moment into a different memory, one that could outlast the bruises.

I reached behind me, found his hand, and pulled it to rest over my heart. "You know you didn't hurt me, right?" I said. "I mean, not any way that matters."

He made a noise—half laugh, half broken sigh. "You say that," he said, "but you're shaking."

"I'd shake worse if you left," I said, and realized I meant it. "It's not fear. It's just—the chemicals, I guess. I've never been claimed before—not like that." I swallowed; the words felt weird in my mouth, but not bad. "Not by someone who actually wanted to keep me."

He nuzzled my neck, lips brushing the place behind my ear that was still raw from his bite. "I want to," he said, quiet but steady. "I want to keep you. Every bit. I don't care if it's a day or a lifetime. I want you."

I let that sit for a second. I could feel my own heart drumming under his palm, a wild, unsteady rhythm, but it didn't scare me. It felt right, even if the rest of me was still a mess.

I twisted in the water, just enough to see his eyes, dark now but not empty. "There's something you should know," I said, water lapping at my collarbone. "I've never done this before—not with a demon, but with anyone. I'm usually the one who stays too long, clinging to relationships like life rafts even after they've sprung leaks."

He grinned, the old arrogance back but softer at the edges. "So you're a stubborn one," he said.

That made me laugh, which hurt in my chest and then made everything better. "You like that I don't know when to quit?"

"I love it," he said, honest and quick. "I love that you hold on when others would let go." His finger traced slow circles on my sternum. "That's how I know you're real. That's how I know we won't end before we've even begun."

I let the water work its way between my toes, the heat seeping into joints and muscles I hadn't known I'd used. My eyelids felt heavy, the weight of everything—sex, chase, food, this—piling up on top of the last two days of not knowing how to relax without first being wrecked. I tried to sit up, but Samiel's arms just tightened around me, pinning me with a gentleness I wanted to sob about.

"You think this is going to stay good?" I asked him, not quite a whisper, but softer than anything I'd said before. "You think you won't get bored? Or annoyed by having me around?"

He didn't answer right away. His chin rested on top of my head, his breath slow and steady. "I think there's a version of me," he said, "that could live a million years and never get tired of you. I think there's a version of you that would get tired of yourself before I ever did." He paused, like he was afraid to keep going, but then he did. "I'm not a good liar, Annie." He squeezed me once, just enough to make my ribs creak. "I want you. That's the only real thing I've ever had."

I made a noise. "You'll have me. I'll make sure of it." The

words came out slurred, and I realized with a jolt that my whole body was winding down, a clockwork animal that had finally run out of keys.

I must've drifted a little, because the next thing I knew the water was cooler, my skin puckered and soft, and Samiel was holding me upright, his hands solid and careful under my arms.

"You're falling asleep," he murmured, and there was a smile in his voice, the kind you heard on the last day of summer.

"Wasn't sleeping," I lied, but my neck flopped sideways when I tried to shake it, and a giggle snuck out, lazy and loose.

He stood up, water sluicing off his chest, and scooped me out with zero effort, not even a grunt. He toweled me off, his hands methodical, and I wanted to protest, wanted to be awake for the part where he carried me to bed and tucked me in, but my eyes wouldn't stay open. I remember the brush of his claws on my scalp, the gentle way he plaited my hair so it wouldn't tangle in the night, the way he tucked the sheets in around me like I was precious.

When he climbed in beside me, the heat of him made the whole bed feel like a nest. I rolled toward him, no thought, no plan, just the gravitational certainty that this was where I belonged. He wrapped my whole self into him, arms wrapped around his ribs like a life vest. He kissed my forehead, then my eyelid, and finally the corner of my mouth. The taste of him, clean and metallic, lingered there as I faded hard and fast.

CHAPTER
TWELVE

Samiel

I watched her sleep. The night pressed in at the windows, blue-black and absolute, but the bed was a bubble of heat, Annie's breaths rising and falling in the rhythm of trust. I lay behind her, a hand spread over her ribs, counting the flex and give of her lungs. She'd curled herself backward into me, tangle of hair pillowed on my shoulder, the arch of her ass resting against my lap like she was daring me to wake her with teeth. She didn't know what she was doing to me. Or maybe she did and wanted it anyway.

The marks I'd left on her already darkened: a purple-and-red necklace on her throat, bite impressions on her shoulder, a fan of bruises blossoming across the backs of her thighs. Underneath the covers, I traced them with a claw, not breaking skin this time, just outlining where I'd taken her and where I'd stopped. She flinched in her sleep, a shudder running up her back, and I stilled—not wanting to pull her out of whatever deep, dark place she'd gone. She deserved the rest. She'd earned it.

But if I was honest, I liked seeing my claim on her. I'd never wanted to own anyone, never felt the impulse that turned men into monsters or monsters into gods. But with Annie, the idea of someone else's hands on her, someone else's mouth, was enough to make my pulse spike and my cock stiffen even after hours of wringing her dry. I wanted to keep her. Not just tonight. Not just for the ninety days. I wanted to keep her forever, if she'd let me.

She shifted, rolling onto her back, and the sheet slid down to her hips. Her chest rose, bare and marked, the right nipple swollen and red from where I'd sucked and bitten her until she'd begged for mercy. The skin there was raw, but not broken. I felt a weird, slow pride at the sight. She wasn't fragile. She was fucking indestructible. I wanted to see how far that went, how much more I could give her before either of us broke for good.

I pressed my mouth to her shoulder, careful, and she stirred again—this time drifting toward waking. Her lips parted and a string of low, lazy syllables slid out, half-words and half-moan. She blinked up at me, the whites of her eyes shock-bright in the dark.

"Time is it?" she croaked, voice gone hoarse.

"Just after three," I said. "You can sleep if you want."

She made a face, skeptical, then rolled toward me, nuzzling her cheek to my chest. "Don't wanna miss anything," she mumbled, then slid a hand down to my hip and squeezed, like she was checking if I was still solid. "Can't believe you're real," she added, and I laughed, a low rumble under her ear.

I watched her drift off again, the hand at my waist slackening, her cheek mashed into me. I wanted to ask her if she felt safe. I wanted her to answer, to say it in words. But I realized, as her breathing dropped back into the long, deep troughs of unselfconscious sleep, that she already had—she'd trusted me enough to lose, and then trusted me again to bring her home.

I lay there, not sleeping, feeling the steady burn of her body against mine, and realized—for the first time in decades, maybe ever—that I didn't want anything else. Not power or freedom or even peace, exactly. Just the simple, ancient pleasure of having her here, right now, and the knowledge that I could keep her safe from every other hunger that stalked the world.

This was the part I hadn't planned for, the part no one prepared me for in all the years of reading human manuals or watching sitcoms on late-night cable. The part where wanting became needing, and needing became a quiet, unkillable promise lodged somewhere behind the ribs. I stroked the inside of her arm, letting my claws graze the softest skin, and imagined a thousand different futures with her—most of them messy, all of them better than anything I'd ever managed on my own.

I listened to the way her breathing synchronized with mine, until the rhythm was indistinguishable: two animals, one pulse. I let the thought settle, let it root deep and coil around every other want I'd ever had. If anyone tried to take this from me, I'd burn the world to the ground.

I closed my eyes, finally, and drifted down with her, both of us tangled in the raw, sweet aftermath of the Chase. I would wake before her, I knew, and I'd hold her through the small hours, and when daylight came, I'd start all over again. I wasn't ever letting her go.

∿

Annie woke before I did, or maybe I just let her think she had. I could have listened to her heartbeat for hours, the faint double-hitch as she rolled away from my chest, the way her breath caught when she stretched. I let her go, feigning sleep, until the sound of her feet on the floor—soft, deliberate, like she was sneaking out of a one-night stand—triggered something old and territorial in my chest. I almost reached for her, almost dragged her back into the tangle of sheets, but I stopped myself. I wanted to see what she'd do, how she carried herself now that she'd been claimed and marked and wanted.

She didn't run. I heard the water in the bathroom, the rattle of the faucet, then the hiss of the shower. I imagined her standing there, steam curling around her bruised neck and battered thighs, my print still fresh on her hip. The thought was almost too much. I closed my eyes hard, willed myself to stay put, and listened to the world tick by in the soft, slow increments of morning.

When she came back, hair towel-twisted and skin flushed, she found me standing at the window, in only my boxer briefs. The desert was a furnace outside, heat already crawling up the glass, but Annie's gaze swept past the horizon and fixed on me. She didn't say anything at first— just padded across the carpet and slumped onto the bed beside me, letting her towel slip to her shoulders.

I reached out, traced a finger down the side of her neck. The bruise there was spectacular, a smear of violet and gold. "I like seeing myself on you," I said, voice thick, and she snorted, but didn't pull away.

"Possessive much?" she said, but the smile on her face said she liked it.

I let my hand drift to her jaw, thumb resting on the hinge of bone. "Only with you," I said, and it was the truth.

We sat like that for a minute, the silence companionable, until she broke it:

"Is today the last day of the trial?"

I nodded. "Sunset. Mayor comes by for the final check-in, and we tell him if we're a match or if we want to call it quits."

She pulled her knees up to her chest, wrapped her arms around them. "What happens if we say we're a match?"

I shrugged, trying to hide the way my pulse banged in my neck. She already knew my answer—I'd made it clear. My claws flexed involuntarily against my thigh, leaving tiny half-moon indentations in my skin. "You stay. We do the ninety-day trial." I swallowed, mouth suddenly dry. "We move into my house on the other side of the Valley. See if we still like each other at the end of the next trial."

She mulled that over, turning it around in her head like a coin. "And if I say no?"

I didn't flinch. "You go home. You're free. No strings, no consequences." I tried to sound casual about it, but the words felt brittle in my mouth.

She chewed on that, then looked up at me, her eyes sharp and blue as a Nevada winter. "So we're really doing this? Ninety days?" She flexed her toes against the carpet, making small divots. "Are you sure you're ready for that much of me? Because I get clingy and weird when I'm nervous, and this whole situation is..." She gestured between us, at the marks on her neck.I grinned, slow and deliberate.

"Ninety days of weird sounds perfect," I said, tracing a claw lightly down her arm. "It's the quiet I can't stand."

"You're such a liar," she said, but there was no accusation in it. She lifted her chin, letting the sun hit the side of her neck. "I'm reserving the right to change my mind, but for now, I vote yes. Ninety days."

I felt a weird, electric shudder in my chest. I wanted to grab her, toss her on the bed, and pin her until she screamed again. Instead I only nodded, letting the words hang in the air between us like a rare desert butterfly that might disappear if I moved too quickly or breathed too hard in its direction.

I cleared my throat. "So, want to see where I live?" I said, trying to sound casual. "It's not far. Plus, I have this ridiculous espresso machine I've been dying to show off to someone who might actually appreciate it." I glanced at her, then out the window. "Might give you a better idea of what you're getting into. You know, before you decide." I shrugged, as if it didn't matter much either way, though the tightness in my chest suggested otherwise.

Annie gave me a look, half skeptical and half amused. "You have a house?"

"Of course I have a house," I said, trying to sound offended. "What did you think I did, sleep in a cave?"

She snorted. "Honestly? Maybe." She reached over and laced her fingers with mine, her thumb tracing the strange ridges of my knuckle. "Show me, then. If you want me to say yes, you have to let me see where the demon goes when he's not breaking the headboard."

I grinned, all fangs and delight. "Deal. But we're flying."

Her face lit up. "Are you sure you won't drop me?"

I leaned in, nose brushing her hairline. "Did I last time?"

"Okay, fair." I could hear the grin in her voice.

The sky over the Valley of the Damned was a hard, glassy blue. I lifted Annie in my arms—she scoffed at first but then clung to me with both arms and both legs the second her feet left the ground, which was exactly what I hoped for. I took her straight up, wings beating until the world dropped away beneath us and the lake shrank to a blue coin. She shrieked once, then started laughing, the kind of wild, unstoppable laugh that people sometimes mistake for terror but is closer to prayer.

We cut straight through the heat shimmer, the wind flattening her hair against her skull, but she didn't let go; she didn't even try to pretend she wasn't loving it. I wanted Annie to see every inch of the Valley, to know the rim of it the way I did—the scar of the old mine, the smattering of the human neighborhoods, the way the roads circled the town like a noose. While this town was filled with demons, there were a fair few humans who chose to live in the Valley of the Damned, who liked the quiet, living off the grid without entirely living off the grid.

I banked low over the Devil's Throat, dropping altitude until the wind whistled through my ears. Annie whooped, hair streaming behind her, and when I looked down, she was grinning so hard I worried her face might split open.

"You're a maniac," she screamed, and I tucked my wings and let us fall, just for a second, before catching the air again and skimming along the canyon edge.

I pointed out the landmarks as we went—the abandoned casino, the old stone amphitheater, the solar array that powered the town and also half the demon-run coffee shops. My house waited at the far end of town, past the last run of tract homes and the grid of paved streets that only barely belonged to the desert. The land rose here, sloping up to a bluff where the wind never stopped and the view took in the whole valley—lake, casino, playground, cemetery, all the stuff of both afterlife and real life crammed together. I landed on the flagstone walk, Annie still clamped around my waist, her laughter trailing off as she looked past my shoulder at the house itself.

"This is it?" she said, twisting in my arms to get a better view.

I set her on her feet and let her take it in—two stories, adobe and black timber, long lines of smoked glass windows that reflected the sky so completely that you could never tell if they were looking out or looking in. The front door was dark, thick wood, carved with symbols so old they'd stopped being threatening and started looking like someone's grandma had taken up whittling. The roof was sharp and slanted, with a row of solar panels along the southern edge—enough to power the entire grid, which I did, and billed the HOA for the surplus. I'd had forty years to make the place mine, and every inch of it bore the stamp of someone who'd never really expected to show it to anyone else.

Annie stared for a second, then turned to me, eyebrows jacked up to her hairline. "You built this?"

I shrugged, a little sheepish. "I had help. Demons don't get weekends. But I wanted something that... lasted."

She ran her palm over the doorframe, feeling the relief of the carvings. "You have taste," she said, and there was something in her voice I hadn't heard before—respect, maybe, or the first edge of curiosity that wasn't just about fucking or fighting.

Inside, the house was cool and shadowed, even with the afternoon sun pouring through the windows. The floors were broad, dark planks, worn smooth as river stone. The walls were lined with books—thousands of them, old and new, some imported at criminal expense, half of them annotated and dog-eared and spilling from the shelves like they'd outgrown their bounds. There were couches big enough to sleep on, battered leather armchairs, tables made from slabs of local wood with the bark still attached. The kitchen—my favorite room—took up half the main floor, with black marble counters, an island the size of a pool table, and racks of copper pots that gleamed in the filtered light.

The only real decor was art—dark, brooding oil paintings in heavy frames that somehow made the space feel larger rather than smaller. One wall held a triptych of a storm-churned sea at night, all blacks and indigos with just a hint of phosphorescence where the waves broke. Another featured a charcoal landscape of what might have been Hell's Valley before humans arrived, the canyon rendered in such deep shadows that the eye had to adjust to see the details hidden within. There were no photos, no old trophies, no weird infernal memorabilia. Just the layers of a life lived with the assumption of solitude, now abruptly exposed.

Annie did a slow circuit, trailing her fingers along the spines of books, the backs of chairs, the curl of a lamp cord. She paused at the kitchen island, then turned to face me, arms folded loose over her chest.

"You ever throw a party?" she asked, genuinely. "Or is this just for you?"

"Mostly just me. Most demons are terrible guests—eat all the food, start arguments, never leave before dawn. Humans never make it past the first drink." I watched her scan the room, looking for signs of life, and wondered if she'd ever lived in a house this silent.

She picked up a battered copy of *The House of the Seven Gables*, thumbed the margin notes, then put it down and wandered into the kitchen, where she immediately rifled the fridge.

"You cook in here?" she said, like she'd need proof. "Or is this just for show?"

I grinned. "Open the freezer."

She did, and a cascade of vacuum-packed steaks and tubs of homemade pierogi nearly avalanched onto her toes. "Oh, Jesus. You meal prep."

"Forty years in exile," I said, "you figure out how to feed yourself." I watched her take it in, the scale of my hoarding, the little ways I'd tried to make a space that was mine, and felt strangely proud. Not many people got to see this part of me. Fewer stayed long enough to remember it.

She grabbed a bag of frozen gnocchi and eyed me over the rim. "You ever make these for someone else?"

"Not yet," I admitted. "But I'd try if you asked."

"So this whole place, just for you?" She eyed the giant kitchen.

"Mostly just me. And Fluoxetine."

She cocked her head. "Is that... a human?"

I stooped by the woodstove and scratched at the seam underneath, whistling once, sharp and low. Out from the shadows came a shape—sleek, black, with a tail like a bull-whip and eyes that glowed green in the light from the window. She stalked across the slate in perfect silence, then hopped onto the counter with all the confidence of someone who'd paid the mortgage herself. She eyed Annie, then me, then Annie again, before winding between her ankles and rubbing her skull against Annie's shin.

"That's Fluoxetine," I said. "Stray. Wouldn't leave, so now she's head of the household." I watched Annie try to hide a smile, but the cat had her number. "Mara came by to feed her while we were at the lake. Otherwise, she'd have staged a coup." I reached out, let Fluoxetine butt her head into my palm, then watched as Annie scooped her up with careful hands and forearm support. Fluoxetine melted, a heap of purr and indifference, and Annie's eyes went soft in a way I'd never seen.

"You have a cat," she said, like it was the punchline to a riddle. "A demon with a cat."

I shrugged, feeling silly. "In Hell, the only pets you get are things that can survive you. Here, it's a little easier." I watched the cat settle in Annie's arms, kneading the air and purring loud as a motorcycle. "Honestly, she owns most of the furniture. I just pay the bills."

Annie grinned, all delight and disbelief. "You're full of surprises, Samiel. You live in a fortress and collect stray animals." She scratched Fluoxetine behind the ears, then shot me a look. "Is this your play? Lull me into a false sense of safety with tiny, adorable mammals?"

I leaned against the kitchen island, arms crossed. "Is it working?"

She set the cat down, then prowled over to where I stood, close enough that her knees almost touched mine. "I don't know," she said, voice quiet but not shy. "I think I was already safe."

She tapped the counter, restless energy vibrating from her fingers. "What do we do now? Just… wait for the mayor to show?"

"We could," I said, "but I was hoping you'd pick the next move. I want to show you the town. I want you to know every inch of it. No secrets." I hesitated, afraid of sounding desperate. "Unless you want to just stay in."

She scanned the room, weighing the merits of a day outside versus one last round of just us. I watched her eyes roam over the books, the paintings, the perimeter of the kitchen, and I could almost see the calculus in her head—the odds of encountering something that might break the spell, or worse, expose her in a way she wasn't ready for.

She looked at me, then at the cat, then back at me. She squared her shoulders, like someone about to walk into a final exam, and said, "Is it weird if I want to just... skip to the end? Like, call the mayor now and tell him I'm not going anywhere?" She punctuated it with a little half laugh, but I could see she was dead serious.

I blinked, caught off guard. "You don't want to see the rest of the Valley?"

She traced a fingertip through the condensation on her water glass, drawing little figure-eights as she talked. "I do. I really do, eventually. But right now, it feels like—if I go out there, if I see the bingo parlor or the casino or whatever, it's going to fuck up the perfect run we've had. Like I'll see something I shouldn't, or someone will say something, and it'll just..." She shrugged, unable to finish, but I understood. She wanted this moment sealed, preserved, before anything outside could dilute it.

I felt relief—a big, dumb rush of it—because that was exactly what I wanted too. The kind of permanence that didn't come from a contract or a ritual, but from a shared, secret refusal to let the world fuck things up.

"I can call the mayor," I said, voice careful. "But you sure? Usually people want the full tour. The games, the shopping, the weird tourist traps. Some go to Lake Purgatory twice in a day just to say they did."

She smiled, but it was a private kind of smile, built for one person only. "I just want to stay here. With you. And the cat," she added, as Fluoxetine slithered around her ankles again, insistent as a shadow.

I pulled out my phone, scrolled to Vepar's number, and hit dial. He answered on the first ring, as if he'd been pacing in his office, waiting for the call.

"Samiel," he said, voice flat. "You're early."

"We're ready," I said, unable to keep the grin out of my voice. "Come by whenever you want. She's made her choice."

There was a long pause, then a noise that might have been approval—or just a demon clearing his throat through sinus congestion. "I'll see you in twenty," he said, and hung up without a goodbye.

CHAPTER
THIRTEEN

Annie

I spent the next nineteen and a half minutes in a state of dumbfounded domesticity, feeding the cat, and washing my face in his bathroom. It was black marble, mirrors cut to angles so you could see every possible version of yourself. Samiel, I realized, lived under a barrage of reflection, undistracted by vanity.

Then I just sat on the velvet couch, legs tucked under me, Fluoxetine purring like a little generator against my calf. Samiel disappeared for a few minutes, then returned in a crisp black T-shirt and jeans, looking every bit the suburban demon dad.

He hovered in the kitchen, refilling a glass of water for me and then, in a show of nervous energy, slicing oranges into perfect, identical segments as if expecting a yacht party rather than a government check-in. I watched him, resisting the urge to go full sitcom wife and wrap my arms around his waist, bury my face in his back, and hum nonsense just to break the tension. Instead, I watched Fluoxetine with a hand on her strong, improbable spine, grounding myself in her animal patience.

I was happy. No—*happy* didn't even touch it. I was... okay. Not afraid. Not waiting for the next shoe to drop, or the lights to come up and reveal the joke. I was sitting in the one house in the world where I could actually see myself living, with a man who looked at me like loss was not an option, and a cat who didn't want to kill me in my sleep. It was a feeling so foreign I almost didn't trust it, but there it was—the shape of a future.

The doorbell buzzed at exactly twenty minutes. Samiel tensed, then exhaled, then swept to the door with a certain ceremonial bravado. I padded over behind him, wearing a pair of his socks that went to my mid-thigh, the T-shirt I'd grabbed from his closet, and absolutely nothing else.

Mayor Vepar stood on the stoop, all business and goat hair, his suit immaculate and his clipboard at the ready. The sight of me—bare-legged, braless, a demon cat in my arms—made him pause, a momentary hitch that was more surprise than judgment.

"Ms. Harris," he said, managing a polite nod. "Samiel. May I enter?"

Samiel stepped aside, the picture of demonic hospitality. "You're the first to ever ask," he said. "Respect."

The mayor regarded the interior with a practiced eye, noting the cat, the open books, the oranges, the lived-in feeling that wasn't here yesterday. He set his briefcase on the kitchen island and opened it, revealing an actual stack of legal papers and a single red pen. He made a show of flipping to the top sheet, then leveled his gaze at me.

"This is the finalization of intent," he said. "You sign here. Samiel signs here. There is a ninety-day review at the end, after which either party may opt out with no legal consequences or supernatural retaliation. Please take a moment to confirm your intentions." He flipped the page and handed me the pen. It was heavy and a little warm, the kind of pen that made you want to sign in cursive and never look back.

I didn't ask to read the fine print; I didn't even hesitate. I signed with a flourish, making the A in Annie so large it looped halfway down the page. I handed the pen to Samiel, who looked at me once. He signed right below, his script a surgeon's nightmare, sharp lines and impossible angles. The mayor witnessed both, added a stamp in gold foil, and then closed the folder with the finality of a gavel drop.

"Congratulations," he said. "You are now contractually bound for the next ninety days, subject to mutual review and the usual clauses." He scanned the room, maybe expecting a cake, maybe waiting for us to burst into flames. When nothing happened, he packed his briefcase and made for the door. At the threshold, he turned and fixed us with a look that was almost human.

"Try not to kill each other," he said, half joke, half warning. "It reflects poorly on the community."

The door shut with a hiss of displaced air. Silence pooled in the space he left behind, slow and syrupy. I sat on a kitchen stool, suddenly aware of the way my heart jackhammered against my ribs.

"Well," I said, "that was weirdly anticlimactic."

Samiel's face broke into a smile. "You wanted fireworks?"

"I wanted a little more drama. Maybe a blood oath. At least a handshake that could cause a small earthquake."

He set the pen down, walked over to me, and hooked his claws into the stool's seat so he could drag me closer.

"We can do better than that," he said, voice velvet and smoke. He braced a hand on my thigh, thumb circling just above the hem of the T-shirt, and leaned in so close I could count the flecks of gold in his eyes. "How do you want to celebrate?"

I considered. "We did the food. We did the sex. We did the running and the Netflix binge." I looked down at my lap, then up at him again. "What's left?"

He grinned, slow and sure. "I can think of a few things." His hand slipped to the inside of my knee, drawing lazy, electric lines up the bare skin. "But I want you to pick."

I let the question stretch out, chewing my lip as I tried to land on something that didn't sound corny or like a test. It wasn't that I didn't want to fuck him again, or eat more, or see how fast we could make Fluoxetine run laps around the living room. It was that the part of me that had always felt temporary—provisional, even in my own body—suddenly craved permanence with a hunger that surprised me. I wanted to see if this was real. If I was real to him.

I said, "I want to see if the closet's big enough for both of us."

Samiel's eyes flicked up, a micro-expression so brief I might have missed it if I hadn't been watching for exactly this: hope and terror, in equal measure. Then he nodded and held out a hand. "Come on," he said, and led me down the hall like we were about to go on a tour of a crime scene.

The master bedroom was big, with floor-to-ceiling windows setting the walls on fire with the Nevada sun. The bed was a fortress of sheets and pillows, the kind of place you lost afternoons. The closet was at the far end, behind a sliding door that looked like a repurposed piece of old mining equipment—iron, worn smooth, etched with sigils I didn't recognize but wanted to learn.

He opened the door, and what hit me first was the smell: linen, cedar, the faint echo of smoke and something sweet, like the memory of a dessert. The second thing was the sight: his clothes were ordered by color and function—black, then gray, then rare shocks of blue or wine; crisp shirts, jeans, tailored trousers, all of them hung with a precision that bordered on neurotic. At the end was a stretch of empty rail, six hangers waiting, plus two deep drawers with nothing in them but sachets of cedar and a single, folded white T-shirt.

I put my hand on the hangers, just to feel the cool weight of them. "Did you think you'd jinx it if you put my stuff in here?"

He looked away. "Demons are superstitious," he said, so quietly I almost missed it. "And I didn't want to make it seem like I was expecting you to stay. In case you… didn't want to."

I turned, meaning to tease, but his face was still a little too raw. So I just stepped in, wrapped my arms around his ribs, and pressed my cheek to his chest. "You want me to move in?"

He didn't hesitate. "I want you to move in so much it's embarrassing."

I laughed, and the sound vibrated between us. "Give me a suitcase and I'll make it official."

He pulled me tighter, then let go and ducked out, returning thirty seconds later with my duffel from the first place. He set it on the bed as an offering, then stepped back, giving me the floor. I unzipped it, started hanging my clothes—the only clothes I had packed. It took all of three minutes and then there, in the closet, was actual evidence I was going to be part of this place.

Samiel hovered in the doorway, watching me like I might bolt. He didn't say anything until I paused to finger the last hanger, which was made of polished black wood and heavier than the rest. "That one's for if you ever get something fancy," he said, and it was both a joke and not. I could imagine it now: me in some blood-red dress, him in one of those crisp shirts, both of us trying to survive the world outside the glass.

I hung the hanger back on the rail, stepped out of the closet, and squared off with him. "What's next? You going to show me the bathroom or just wait until I start snooping?"

He rolled his eyes and led me down the hall, swinging open the door to a bathroom that was not just a bathroom, but a cathedral to water. Black tile, glassed-in shower big enough for a rugby team, and a steel soaking tub that looked like it had been rescued from a mad scientist's lab.

The counter was black stone, the sink a basin deep enough to drown a toddler. There was a little lacquered tray, already lined with my sunscreen and eyeliner and the ancient bottle of toner I never remembered to use. Next to it was a box of cotton swabs, and what I recognized as my peppermint toothpaste. My toothbrush rested in a new holder, still in its shrink-wrap. I touched the tray, smoothing the bottles like they might vanish if I looked away.

Behind me, Samiel hovered, then ducked his head, that strange rush of embarrassment again. "I asked the mayor if it was okay to get your mail forwarded. He said it was fine."

I stared at him. "You're better at domesticity than any man I've ever met."

He looked at me sidelong. "I read a lot of women's magazines during the lockdown," he said. "They said the key to a happy home was mutual respect and clear boundaries. I figured—if you were going to stay, you should have a place for your stuff."

I spun to face him, half wanting to punch him in the chest, half wanting to… something else. "What would you have done if I said no?"

He shrugged. "Kept the drawer empty. Or filled it with more pasta." He smiled, a real one this time, not baring his teeth but letting the edges crinkle, soft as a human. "I'm adaptable."

I was stunned, almost embarrassed at the gut-punch sweetness of it. I dropped my bag on the counter, hopped up to sit next to it, and just looked at him. "You're ridiculous," I said, but what I meant was: *You're perfect. You're dangerous.*

"Do you want to see your office?"

I blinked. "My what?"

He grinned and gestured for me to follow. Down the hall, past the kitchen, past the living room full of sunlight and the cat sprawled on her back like a dead possum, he opened a door I hadn't noticed before. The hinges didn't even squeak. Inside was a room with two enormous windows, both overlooking the rim of the valley and the lake, the light so bright it was like stepping into another state. There was a desk— black steel, glass top, wide enough for two people to work shoulder to shoulder without ever touching. Two monitors, one a massive, curved gaming beast, the other a vertical number I recognized from every productivity blog I'd ever hate-read. To the side was a rolling rack of office supplies and, next to that, a single, battered Aeron chair that looked like it had survived a decade of boardroom battles.

On the desk was a set of new notebooks, still shrink-wrapped, my laptop, already plugged in, and a jar of pens, half of them the expensive kind that bled like a paper cut.

I walked to the window and stared out at the impossible blue of the lake, then back at him. "How did you get this?" I asked. I remembered telling him about my job, but not that I would need two monitors—or a chair that wouldn't make my spine give up before lunch.

He shrugged, almost embarrassed. "You said you worked

from home. I thought you'd want a space that felt like yours." His eyes slid away; I could see the nerves behind the bravado.

I ran my hand over the glass. "Did you... build this?"

He shook his head, but the pride was there anyway. "I had Mara find you something when you mentioned working from home. I am pretty sure this is from an abandoned casino." He grinned, sheepish. "Demons are resourceful. And I wanted you to have everything you need."

The silence stretched out. I could see myself tomorrow, sitting here with coffee and the cat, the sun burning in through the glass, a version of myself I didn't quite recognize but desperately wanted to meet.

I turned, hugged myself, then blurted, "You don't have a job, do you?"

Samiel cocked his head, as if considering. "Not... like this," he said, gesturing to the monitors. "I don't need one. But if it makes you happy, I could get one. I could bartend, or work at the lake. I could sell timeshares to the other side."

The image of Samiel in a cheap suit, hawking desert condos to infernal retirees, made me snort so hard I almost lost my balance. "You'd be terrifying at sales," I said. "Nobody would dare call customer service if you messed up their contract."

He leaned in the doorway, wings loose, gaze fixed on me with an intensity that should've felt claustrophobic, but didn't. "If you want me to work, I'll work," he said, honest-to-god earnest. "But you don't have to, either." I didn't realize I was smiling until he smiled back, slow and tentative. "I'm serious," he said, and he was. "The money just... happens. I've been here a long time. Investments are easier for us." He said it with offhand confidence. "You could write a book. Or raise a goat. Or just make art. You never have to work again if you don't want to."

It was so blunt, so honest in its disregard for the whole human nightmare of hustle-and-grind, that it stunned me. No performance. No apology. Just the quiet, terrifying certainty.

I sat in the desk chair, spinning it once, twice, then fixing him with a look. "So I could quit my job right now and you'd just… let me be a kept woman?"

He tilted his head. "If you wanted. Or you could run the town, or open a bakery, or start fires for fun." He grinned wolfishly. "Whatever you want, Annie. I don't care. You're not here to pay my bills."

For a second, I forgot how to breathe. I thought about every boyfriend who'd ever made me feel like I had to justify my existence—what I brought to the table, how pretty or useful or resourceful I was, always competing for a seat at the smallest table in the world. And now here was this monster, this literal hellbeast, offering me the one thing I'd never even thought to ask for: unconditional permission to just be.

I spun again, head swimming with the possibilities. "I might actually quit," I said, half-joking, but the words felt so good I almost moaned. "I could spend my days baking, or reading, or I don't know, terrorizing the HOA board for all eternity."

He looked at me like I'd just solved an equation he'd been working on for decades. "If you want that, I'll make it happen," he said. "But if you want to keep working, I'll build you a better office. I'll wire the whole canyon for internet, if you want. I'll—"

I cut him off with a laugh, losing my grip on the chair and nearly launching myself into the bookshelf. "You're out of your mind," I said, but it was the best thing I'd ever heard.

He crossed the room, caught me before I could tip over, and set me back on my feet. His hands were gentle, steadying me with no more effort than it would take to hold a feather. "I'm just trying to prove you made the right choice," he said.

I reached for him, hooked two fingers in his back belt loop, and gave a tug. "If you really want to prove it, you could take me upstairs and fuck me in our bed."

CHAPTER
FOURTEEN

Samiel

My body tensed at her suggestion, heat coiling low in my stomach. But I had one more surprise I needed her to see first—something that would make what came after even better. I took her hand, my thumb brushing over her pulse point, and led her through the kitchen. The cat slipped between her bare legs as we stepped onto the sun-warmed patio stones. Annie's hair caught the light, and I fought the urge to bury my face in the curve of her neck.

"You want to fuck in the yard?" she asked, voice husky and teasing. Her eyes flicked to the expanse of privacy beyond the patio, teeth catching her bottom lip in a way that made my wings twitch.

I took her hand, my thumb brushing over her pulse. "I want to show you something." The yard unfolded before us, black rock and crushed granite sloping away in terraces that caught the light like obsidian. No tidy lawn or fragile flowers—just wild sage and wiry grass that bent and straightened in the wind, resilient as desire.

At the far edge, black pines stood sentinel, beyond them nothing but the lake's silver shimmer. But here, I'd carved something else. Her eyes traced the perimeter, lingering on the half-hidden alcoves I'd built—private nooks nestled between boulders, soft depressions lined with blankets, a hammock strung low between two ancient timbers. A path wound through it all, connecting each secret space.

"Is this for...?" She didn't finish, her fingers tightening around mine as understanding bloomed across her face.

"Hunting," I said, and let the word hang between us like smoke. Annie's hand tightened in mine, her pulse quickening against my thumb. I watched her pupils dilate as her gaze traced the uneven track, lingered on the cover points, the places where someone my size could drop from nowhere and pin her to the earth.

"You made a fucking obstacle course for hunting people?" Her voice caught, breathy and low, as she pressed her thighs together.

"Only if they want to be caught." I pulled her against me, one hand sliding to the small of her back. Annie's heat radiated through her thin clothes. "For when you want me to chase you again. For when you want to feel what happens after I catch you."

She stared at the track, teeth dragging across her bottom lip. A flush crept up her neck as she trembled against me, her body remembering. "And when you catch me?"

"When I catch you," I murmured against her ear, "I take what's mine." My fingers splayed possessively across her hip, and I felt her breath hitch. "Not every day. But some-times—" I inhaled against her hair, helpless against the primal hunger that surged through me at her scent, at the memory of her surrender.

She looked at me, her pupils dilating as her gaze traveled down my body and back up again. Her teeth caught her bottom lip, releasing it slowly as she considered the hunting ground I'd built for her.

"I might let you chase me," she said, voice dropping to a husky whisper that made my wings twitch beneath my skin. "But only if I get a head start. And only if you promise not to tear my clothes... every time."

I leaned closer, close enough to feel the heat radiating from her skin, but not touching. "That's a promise I'll try very hard to keep." The lie tasted sweet between us.

She stepped off the patio, bare feet crunching on the rock. The curve of her calf flexed as she turned a slow circle, arms spread wide.

"The house, the cat, the monster who built me a play-ground." When she faced me again, the wind plastered her hair across her flushed cheek. "I never thought I'd crave staying somewhere this badly."

I followed her down the slope, hands in my pockets, letting her set the pace. Fluoxetine bolted ahead, tail high, prowling the path like it was her own personal speedway. We walked in companionable silence. At the far end, Annie stopped and looked back at the house—a black raft at the edge of the world, every window now reflecting not just the sky, but the two of us, small and improbable, on the wrong side of forever.

I trailed Annie back up the yard, watching the way her hair snagged in the sudden gust, the curve of her bare legs dusted with fine black gravel. My hands twitched at the sight of her, a primitive urge to pick her up and drag her back into the house, where she'd be shielded from every single thing that might want even a taste. I wanted to keep her, to lock her down inside my domain, but I also wanted to show her off—maybe even more. The monster in me wanted both—for her to be seen, and for everyone who saw her to know she was already taken.

She was halfway to the porch when I coughed, awkward, and said, "I should probably take you out on a real date. If only to prove I'm not just here to keep you locked in the closet."

She stopped, turned, and eyed me up and down. "A real date? With dinner and drinks and small talk about the weather?"

I shrugged. "If that's what you want. I can do dinner, drinks, and also provide a running commentary about the weather." I caught up to her, the cat winding between our ankles, and added, "There's a place in the old town, just past the amphitheater. They serve actual food. You'd be the best thing in the room, but that's not new."

She considered, then, "You know I'll have to wear something that doesn't immediately say 'I spent the afternoon getting railed in the dirt,' right?"

I grinned at her. "Not for my sake."

"Not for the mayor's, either," she said, arching a brow. "Who's the audience, Samiel?"

I wanted to tell her the truth: the audience was anyone who might dare look at her twice, anyone who'd think she was up for grabs, who didn't know she was already hooked deep and permanent. I wanted her to know how good she looked with my marks, but also how much I wanted her to walk into the bar and have every eye—demon and human—turn and smolder, only to have her come home with me.

She must have read the thought on my face, because she

laughed and said, "God, you're going to snap if someone puts a hand on me, aren't you?"

"No," I said, a lie so thin it barely held. "Unless you want me to."

She smirked, then nudged my hip with hers. "What if they just look? Are you going to kill a guy for looking?"

I considered, then: "They shouldn't, not after this morning." I looked down at her collar, tracing the edge of the bruise, then leaned in, voice low in her ear: "But yes. I might."

"Are you going to get in trouble for that?" she said, looking at me sideways. Her tone was almost casual, but I could see the tension in her jaw. "Choking out another demon on your porch. What's the demon equivalent of excommunicated?"

I laughed, then shrugged. "Not unless I kill him. Then it's paperwork." I wanted to laugh again, but she didn't, so I reached for her hand to anchor the conversation in something solid. "It's different here than where you grew up. Clem knows the rules. He crossed a line."

She made a little sound, not quite agreement. "The rules," she echoed, and I could hear the skepticism. "So you can just grab people by the throat if you feel like it?"

"If they touch what's mine," I said, and the words came out more jagged than I meant them. I saw her eyes narrow, searching my face for what kind of claim that really was.

She didn't let it slide. "I'm not your property, Samiel. I'm not a car or a cat." She glanced down at Fluoxetine, who was busy licking the empty bowl of cream I'd set down. "Well, actually, you treat your cat with more respect, so let's start there."

I took the hit, my jaw tightening as I swallowed back the growl rising in my throat. "I know," I said, voice dropping to that register that always made her pupils dilate. "But it's not the same as when I was on my own." I stepped closer, close enough to feel the heat radiating from her skin. "I don't want to own you. I want to... keep you." My fingers brushed her wrist, tracing the delicate blue veins there. "Safe. Close." The word in demon tongue burned on my tongue, unspoken—a sound like thunder breaking over mountains.

Annie's breath caught. She pressed the heel of her palm to her forehead, then looked at me, her lips parted.

"It's not your job to keep me safe from everyone," she reminded me, her voice husky as she leaned in until our chests nearly touched. "I don't want to be something you have to guard." Her fingers found the edge of my shirt, playing with the hem. "I want to be your equal. Not your favorite thing." She tilted her face up, eyes dark with challenge. "Your favorite person."

I felt the old, burning urge to argue, but I sat back and let her words dig in. I tried to picture a world where she was just a person, not a miracle, not something I'd been waiting half a century for. It scared the shit out of me, but I wanted her to trust me with more than just her body, more than just the soft, defenseless part she gave me at night.

"Okay," I said, and meant it. "You're not a thing. You're not mine. But you're still the only one I want."

She rolled her eyes—hard—but I saw her mouth twitch, the faintest smile at the corners. "You're such a disaster," she said. "But you're my disaster now, so you better not fuck it up."

"Wouldn't dream of it," I said, and leaned over to kiss the top of her head.

We fooled around for a bit on the deck—Annie, barefoot and backlit by sunset, daring me to chase her through the kitchen while the cat attacked her ankles in solidarity. I let her tackle me onto the velvet couch, let her smother my face with kisses, let her grind against my thigh until both of us were a little lightheaded from laughing. It wasn't sex, not really, but it was something I'd never had: the play-fighting, the soft wrestling, the kind of intimacy that didn't require fangs or claws or any sort of violence. I didn't know how much I wanted it until I had it.

But I'd promised her a real date, and the thought of it—Annie, out in the world, on my arm, the whole Valley watching—lit up every stupid, competitive, territorial circuit in my brain. I told her to get ready, that I'd take care of everything, and she wandered off to shower again, humming some pop song I'd never heard but would now remember forever.

I called in another favor with Mara, who was not just in charge of the actual Bingo games, but the whole program. Annie would need a dress she could stun in, and I was going to have to rely on Mara to get it for me. There were more than a few shops in town that carried Annie's aesthetic. I shot off another text to Mara, then went to figure out what I was wearing while Annie showered.

I went to the wardrobe, digging out the clothes I hadn't worn in years. The shirt was black, collared, tailored but not tight, and I left the top buttons open because she liked my chest, and I wanted her to have easy access. The pants were black too, pressed, nice enough for a funeral or a wedding or the kind of night that could turn into either. I pulled them on, checked myself in the mirror, and realized—surprise—there were nerves. Not hunger, not bloodlust, just the taut, hopeful anxiety that I might fuck this up by caring too much. And beneath that, something territorial and raw—the thought of every demon in the Valley seeing her, wanting her, knowing she'd chosen me.

Mara's knock came just after five—three sharp raps that somehow managed to sound both impatient and smug. When I opened the door, she stood there with a garment bag draped over one arm, her silver-tipped nails tapping against the plastic.

"You're welcome," she said, thrusting it at me before I could speak. "She'll look devastating in this. The color will make her skin glow like she's lit from within." She leaned closer, lowering her voice. "And it'll show off those lovely marks Veeps told me you left on her neck."

I rolled my eyes. Of course there was already gossip about me and Annie. Not a lot happened in the Valley of the Damned, and a new match was always the talk of the town.

I waved Mara off with my thanks, then took the garment bag to the bedroom and opened it. Inside was burgundy crushed velvet, soft and dark as old blood, with a plunging neckline that would frame her collarbones perfectly. The dress had a slit that would ride dangerously high on her thigh and tiny straps that would showcase the marks I'd left on her shoulders. A note from the shop in town read simply, "Wear with attitude." I carried it upstairs, the weight of the fabric absurdly satisfying in my hand, already imagining how it would cling to her curves.

Annie was in the bathroom, steam curling out from under the door. I waited, pacing the hall, until she emerged in a towel and caught me staring. She wrinkled her nose. "Is it time already?"

I held out the box. "Put this on."

She eyed it, suspicious, then lifted the lid. The dress slithered out, pooling in her hands like liquid sin. Her eyes widened, but not with shock—with something hungrier.

"Jesus Christ, Samiel," she breathed, running her fingers along the fabric. "You trying to get me arrested or laid?"

I grinned, slow and deliberate. "Hotel on the lake. Dress code is 'look like a sin or don't bother coming.'"

She bit her lower lip, already holding the dress against her body. "Give me ten minutes."

I waited in the living room, feeding the cat and pretending not to listen for sounds from upstairs. The slide of fabric against skin. A low, appreciative "damn" that wasn't meant for my ears. Then heels on hardwood, deliberate and confident. She appeared at the top of the stairs, one hand on her hip, the other trailing down the banister. The way she moved in that dress—like she owned the air around her—made my mouth go dry.

The dress clung to her like a second skin, the velvet catching the light as she moved, revealing the curves of her hips, the swell of her breasts, the dip of her waist. The color deepened when she breathed—more red than purple, more sin than wine. Her hair was still damp, slicked back to expose the elegant column of her throat where my teeth had been. Her eyes, dark and hungry, met mine through lashes thick with mascara.

"Do I look ridiculous?" she asked, but her voice had dropped to that register that made my skin tighten.

I shook my head, heat crawling up my spine. "You look like everything I've ever wanted to taste," I said, voice rough. "And everything that's going to get me in trouble tonight."

She smirked. "That's the plan, isn't it?"

I offered my arm, she took it, and together we stepped into the dusk, the wind off the lake already brushing goosebumps up her arms. I wanted to wrap her in my jacket, but I liked the way the cold made her press in closer.

We walked the path to my car—the real one, not the loaner from the mayor's pool. It was a vintage GTO, electric yellow and rebuilt with more than a little help from the other side. Annie slid into the passenger seat, the dress riding up her thighs, and ran her finger along the dash as if reading Braille.

"You love this thing more than most people, don't you?" she said, but her voice was warm. "I'll try not to spill on the seats."

I started the engine and let it rumble, then peeled out onto the crushed gravel, the headlights cutting a pale V through the deepening dusk. Neither of us spoke on the way to the hotel, but the silence wasn't hollow—it was electric, a fuse burning down to something neither of us wanted to name. I kept a hand on the shifter, but every other muscle in my body was tuned to her, to the shape of her mouth in the window reflection, to the way her bare shoulder pressed against the seatbelt.

The hotel on the lake was a piece of old Las Vegas exiled to the desert. Neon script spelled out "The Infernal," and the sign was a three-story demoness in a sequined dress, one leg cocked, tail wrapped around a martini glass. Inside, it was all red velvet and gold leaf, mirrors that made you look twice, and carpets so plush you could lose a shoe if you weren't careful. The lighting was dim but intimate, designed to make everyone look just a little more expensive.

I held the door for Annie, then draped my arm over her shoulder, letting the world see us together. Every demon in the lobby turned to look—and not just the demons, but a handful of humans who'd come for the spectacle of it, the thrill of spending a weekend somewhere that still felt lawless. I watched them take her in, the way their eyes slid over her body, the dress, the marks I'd left. I felt a flicker of violence; I met every stare until it turned away, and Annie caught the edge of my smile.

"You don't have to glower at everyone in the zip code," she whispered, but she sounded pleased.

"I want them to know you're with me," I said, voice low enough for only her.

She rolled her eyes, but she laced her fingers through mine and led me to the bar. The place was packed, a spill of bodies in every color and configuration: lesser demons, humans in everything from business casual to leather harnesses, a pair of succubi in matching couture. The bartender was a demon I knew—Neph, tall and marble-skinned, with hair the color of copper wire and a knack for making a martini that actually burned on the way down. He clocked me from across the bottles, then Annie, and his mouth curled into a grin.

"Samiel," he called, voice big enough to rattle the glassware. "And this must be the prize."

Annie raised her brows, smirking. "I'm afraid he's oversold me," she said, but Neph's grin only grew.

"Not possible." He wiped his hands on a towel, shook our hands, and poured two drinks without asking. "On the house. This one's for the archives." I watched Neph size up Annie, not with the predatory edge I expected, but with a kind of respectful curiosity. Like he was trying to figure out why a human would ever put up with someone like me.

We took our drinks to a table by the window overlooking the lake. The water was glass-dark, reflecting the neon and the fat, lazy moon. Annie slipped into the booth, sliding right up against me even though there was plenty of room. I liked it. I wanted her next to me, always.

We ordered food—a charcuterie board with so much raw meat I thought it might try to bite back, plus fries, plus a dessert that was just called "Crème Infernal." The menus were printed on black leather, the font so Gothic it was barely legible. Annie squinted and pursed her lips trying to make out each word, which made me want to drag her under the table and fuck her until she screamed.

But I wanted to do this right. A real date. A normal night, if either of us knew what normal meant.

She sipped her drink and made a face. "You know, in the world I come from, this is the part where we talk about our exes—and probably our families."

I choked on my whiskey, the burn of it almost as sharp as the twist in my stomach. "Is that a requirement?"

She shrugged, eyes bright. "It's tradition. You tell me about yours, I tell you about mine, and then we either get jealous or decide everyone in our past is trash."

I tried to think of a single demon I'd ever fucked who qualified as an "ex." I tried to picture Annie, sitting across from some other man, laughing at his jokes while acting like her smile wasn't the best thing in the room.

"You first," I said, and braced myself.

CHAPTER
FIFTEEN

Annie

I went for maximum flippancy, because that was how these games went. "My last boyfriend was a barista with a demon complex. He had a Satan tattoo on his thigh and kept a bootleg bottle of absinthe under my bathroom sink." I propped my chin on my fist, giving him the look that said, *Go ahead, judge me, I dare you.* "He moved into my place after, like, a month. We played house for almost a year before I realized he actually thought I would do his laundry forever. Seth would leave his dirty socks on my coffee table and then text me from work asking what was for dinner." I paused, not sure how much I wanted to say. "When we broke it off, I expected to be broken-hearted, but I think I felt relief more than anything. The joy of finally giving up on something that had been long dead."

Samiel listened, eyes on my mouth, not my eyes. For a solid beat, he didn't react—like he was buffering, trying to make sense of a story that probably sounded as alien to him as "I once fucked a centaur" would to a regular guy.

"What was his name, again?" he said, not moving.

I almost lied. The urge was there, sudden and ancient and leftover from every time I'd watched a new boyfriend's face try on the shape of the last boyfriend's name. But I didn't want to start this thing with a lie, not even a dumb one. "Seth," I said. "He was... present. I wouldn't call him an ex so much as a roommate with benefits and boundary issues."

Samiel nodded, but his jaw flexed, like he was chewing over the name and not finding it to his taste. "He wasn't good to you."

It wasn't a question, but I answered anyway. "He was fine. Just small. Like, his world was a studio apartment and a coffee shop and three friends who all hated each other. I wanted more." I looked out at the lake, at the black mirror of water and the way our reflections flickered in the glass. "I always want more, I guess."

He was quiet for a second. Then: "Did you love him?"

I shrugged, but the answer surprised even me. "No. I don't think I've ever been in love, exactly. Not the way people sing about it." I rolled my glass between my palms, letting the cold bite my skin. "I wanted to be seen. I think that's all. He saw what he wanted, not what I was."

Another silence, this time with teeth. I risked a glance at Samiel, and the look on his face was rawer than I'd expected. Not just jealousy—though there was a jagged edge of that— but something like confusion, or maybe even grief. "Have you ever been in love?" I asked, and it came out sharper than I meant.

He stilled, the kind of stillness that meant a hundred gears were grinding in secret. "Not really," he said. "Demons don't do love. Not... the way you think. Sex, yes. Loyalty, sometimes. But the closest thing I've felt to it is right now." He looked up, square in my face, and there was no joke. "I've never done this before. Not the food, not the house, not the…" His hand, big and inked with veins, hovered over mine but didn't touch. "I've never had a relationship that wasn't a game, or a fight. Or a contract with a time limit."

I stared, waiting for the punchline, some hint that he was exaggerating. But he wasn't. I realized with a jolt that I might be his first—his actual first shot at more than just sex, or violence, or whatever demons counted as a social life. He'd been with other people, sure, but the way he said it, the way he looked at me, made it clear. Nobody had ever let him try, or wanted him to try. Nobody had ever made him want to.

I reached out, slow, and set my hand on top of his. It felt like petting a sleeping tiger—risk and reward, both in the same breath. "You're doing okay so far," I said, and the joke landed, because his lips twitched in relief.

He squeezed my hand, careful not to leave marks. "Who else?" he said, and I realized he wanted the rest of the list— not out of jealousy, but because he genuinely believed that love was a numbers game, and that each ex was a rung on a ladder he didn't know how to climb.

I thought of the guy before Seth, a grad student in Tampa who'd once proposed to me after a music festival, too high to remember it the next day. I thought of my first girlfriend, a girl named Sammi who had dyed both our hair with box bleach in eighth grade and then kissed me behind the choir room. I thought of the bartender who'd let me drink for free and called me his "dark muse," which sounded romantic until I realized he was dating three other muses at the same time.

I gave him the highlights reel. "A music nerd. A girl with good hands, a bartender who couldn't keep a secret." Then, because it felt wrong not to say it, "None of them ever lasted. I was always too much." I looked down at our hands, my chipped black polish against his red skin. "Or maybe they were just not enough."

He nodded, looking thoughtful. "I like that you're too much," he said at last. "I like that I can't predict you. If I could, I'd be bored already."

"Does it bother you?" I asked, and my voice came out lower than intended. "That I've fucked other people. That there have been... well, not a ton, but enough to make a dent."

It was the kind of question I'd flung at men before—usually at the bitter end, a lit match in a room I was already planning to torch. But with Samiel, I wanted the answer. I needed it from him, unfiltered, because I didn't want to wake up a week from now and find out my past had started to rot the foundation.

He didn't answer right away. His hand stayed on mine, palm warm, thumb moving in slow arcs over my knuckles. When he finally spoke, it was quiet but brutal as always. "I hate it." He didn't look away from me, not even to blink. "I hate that anyone else has ever touched you. I hate that they got pieces of you and didn't even know what they had." He flexed his fingers, and I realized he was fighting the urge to squeeze, to leave a mark on me that would outlast every other handprint. "But it's only fair," he added, softer now. "You had a life before this. So did I."

"Did you?" I said, and realized I genuinely wanted to know. "You ever have anyone... serious? Before now?"

He shook his head, smiling with just the right amount of self-loathing. "No. I told you—demons don't really do love.

Not unless we're starving for something. And I didn't even know I was hungry." He paused, then: "You're my first real thing. The first one that matters."

I should've found that terrifying. Instead, I felt it settle in me like a shot of whiskey—a little burn, then a clarity that cut through every other noise. "I don't care if you get jealous," I told him. "But you can't do the thing where you treat me like an object. If I'm your first, I still have to be a person."

He grinned, but there was no menace in it. "I'm learning," he said. "But you have to be patient. Sometimes the urge to break things is all I have." He let go of my hand, just enough to cup my face, thumb tracing the line from cheekbone to jaw. "If I get too much, you have to tell me. Or punch me. I can take it."

"That a challenge?" I said, letting him see the spark of mischief that always made men underestimate me.

"It's a promise," he said. "And I hope you hold me to it."

I let the moment hang, let the weight of his confession fill the space between us. Then I leaned in, resting my forehead against his. "Next time you get the urge to break something," I said, "try me first. I might like it better."

He laughed, and it was a real laugh. Under the table, he squeezed my thigh once, then let go.

Wanting to shift topics, I asked, "Can I ask you something weird?" I stared out at the traffic of demons and humans moving through the bar, all pretending not to obsess over each other. "Where's your family in all this? I mean, do you have parents? Siblings? I've never met a demon who wasn't just, like, born fully formed out of a volcano or something."

Samiel nearly choked on his whiskey. "You want to meet my family? Annie, that is a threat, not a privilege."

"I'm not saying I want to meet them," I clarified, grinning. "I just want to know if you have a mom out there who's gonna show up and judge me for coming to dinner with chipped nail polish and a healthy fear of organized religion."

He made a show of rolling his eyes. "My mother's barely on this plane. She comes around once a year for the HOA meeting and then bitches for six months about the paint on my house." He tilted his head like he was rifling through a mental Rolodex. "There's my dad, but he's mostly retired. Spends his days building model trains and arguing online about politics. The only thing that sets him off is when people disrespect railroad infrastructure."

I burst out laughing. "Your dad is a train guy?"

"Oh, absolutely. He's got a whole basement layout." Samiel's face twisted with mock horror. "Once he cornered the mayor for a solid hour about switching the town's public transit to light rail. The mayor nearly exorcized him out of boredom."

I grinned so hard my jaw hurt. "Tell me there's a picture," I said. "If there's not a photo of your dad in a conductor hat, I'll be crushed."

"You'll get your photo," Samiel said, "but prepare yourself. If you meet him, there is a ninety percent chance he'll try to induct you into the 'Friends of Railroads' club, which is not a euphemism. It's just a bunch of retired demons and a handful of confused humans who genuinely love trains more than oxygen." He sipped his drink, then gave me a look: "If you want to really play with fire, ask about my brother."

"Oh, god. There's a brother?" I leaned in, hand on his thigh. "How have you never mentioned this?"

He shrugged, but it was the kind of loose-tendoned motion that said this was a topic he'd spent years defusing.

"Azazel doesn't come around much. Technically he's older, technically he's the better son, but honestly? He spends most of his time in Hell because he thinks Earth is 'too loud' and the coffee is shit. When he does show up, it's only because the old man guilt-tripped him into it, or because he's bored and wants to prove he still knows how to ruin a party."

I tried to picture it: an even more demonic version of Samiel, somehow less interested in humans, maybe even allergic to small talk. "He sounds like fun," I said.

"He's miserable," Samiel agreed, but there wasn't heat in it. "He's also the one person on the planet I count on if something bad happens. Not even Vepar. If ever there was a demon who'd help you hide a body, it's Azazel. But you'd better believe he'll judge your shoveling technique."

"Oh my god," I wheezed, clutching the edge of the table. "Samiel, you're telling me you're the normal brother?"

He bared his teeth in a guilty, delighted grin, then reached for my hand, folding his claws around my knuckles. "Not normal. Just... adaptable." His thumb swept back and forth, slow and thoughtful. I could see the shape of his family in this—the contradictions, the stubbornness, the way he clung to me like I was an answer to a problem he hadn't known he was solving.

Samiel turned it around on me. "So, I've told you about mine. What about yours?"

I took a second to answer because I wasn't used to this kind of interrogation. Boys wanted to know what you'd done, not what had made you. Samiel watched me with that never-blinking stare, and I felt the urge to perform, to cut my family down to bite-size sitcom anecdotes, but for some reason I wanted to give him the whole thing.

"My family's boring," I started, but he made a face and I

had to recalibrate. "Okay, not boring. Normal. But, like, Florida normal, which is not actually normal."

"Three of us kids. I'm the youngest, so my personality is half attention-seeker, half diplomat. My oldest brother, Tyler, does HVAC; he's built like a walk-in freezer and has the emotional range of a Roomba. My sister, Keri, lives in Orlando and has three kids. If the world ended, she'd still find a way to get to soccer practice. Our parents are still together, and still living in the same double-wide in Tampa where the air is permanently blue with cigarette smoke, no matter how many pamphlets on lung cancer I've left on their coffee table. Dad's always got a Marlboro dangling from his lip while he tinkers with his conspiracy boards, and Mom's Virginia Slims leave lipstick rings on everything she touches."

Samiel's face contorted in delight. "So you're saying a demon would fit right in?"

I laughed because honestly, yes. "My dad's the kind of guy who cornered Jehovah's Witnesses on the porch and tried to teach them about cryptids. There's a solid chance he'd see you, horns and all, and just want to know if he could smoke in your kitchen. Mom would try to feed you the minute you walked in—"

"Perfect," Samiel said with a wicked grin. "I love food, and people who feed me. You ever bring a demon home for Thanksgiving?"

I tried to picture it: Samiel ducking under the fake cobwebs strung across the porch light, Fluoxetine inevitably smuggled in under my arm, my mom squinting at him across a folding card table crowded with Pillsbury biscuits and three kinds of Jell-O salad. The visual was almost too much. I laughed so hard I snorted my drink.

"I'd pay good money to see you try to smoke out back

with my dad," I said. "He'd ask if your horns got TV reception."

Samiel looked so genuinely delighted I wanted to drag him home right then, just to watch my parents' heads explode. The strange part was how little I felt I had to hide. Some gnarled shame-knot down in my spine started to loosen; the idea that he'd fit, or at least want to fit, into my version of "home" was so outrageously comforting that I had to take a second to let it register.

We let the silence settle as we both recalibrated, now knowing where each of us came from. Samiel's hand stayed warm on my thigh.

Finally, he reached for the check and paid in cash, not even glancing at the total, then slid out of the booth and offered me his hand. The gesture was old-fashioned, but I liked the way his palm fit around mine, careful but inexorable. We walked out through the lobby, past the mirrors and the sequined demoness, and into the sharp chill of the desert night.

In the parking lot, he pinned me against the hood of the GTO, wings spread to block the wind, and kissed me hard enough to leave me gasping. I bit his lip, because I could, and he smiled into the kiss, fangs sharp and perfect on my tongue. When my hands tangled in his hair, he groaned—an actual, honest-to-god groan—pressing his hardened cock into my stomach, and I wondered if he would tear my dress off then and there.

"Get in the car," he said, voice shredded, and I did, legs shaking. We drove home in a silence that wasn't really silence at all—just the sound of want, burning so loud it filled the whole car. His hand never left my thigh, thumb tracing circles until I thought I might combust.When we finally pulled into the driveway, he killed the engine but didn't move, just sat there with his forehead pressed to the steering wheel.

"I've wanted to do this since the second I saw you," he said, and the words were stripped of every flirtation or pretense. "Not the Chase. This. Bringing you home."

We stumbled through the front door, and I didn't wait. The moment the lock clicked, I twisted in his arms—sudden, hard, a pivot that shoved him against the wall and put my face less than an inch from his. He blinked, surprised, and I felt the dark, deep satisfaction of catching him off guard for once.

"You're not the only one with claws, Sam," I said, and hooked both hands in the collar of his shirt, dragging him down so I could bite his jaw. Not a nibble, not a tease—a real, hard bite that left a line of teeth in the skin just under his ear. He shivered, a full-body tremor, and I knew I had him.

I pressed him deeper into the wall, a hand splayed flat on his chest, pinning him. My heart was hammering, blood so hot it felt like I could have burned him from the inside out. "You said I'm yours," I said, kissing a line down to his throat, "but you're mine, too. You get that, right? I want all of you."

He nodded, but it wasn't enough. I scraped my teeth along the tendon of his neck, trailing down to the rip of his shirt where his skin burned under my nails.

"I want to ruin you the way you ruin me," I whispered, hungry for the moment he finally shattered.

I sank to my knees in the narrow foyer, my velvet dress pooling around my thighs. With the precision of a bomb squad technician, I undid his belt. He tried to speak—probably my name—but I pressed a hand hard into his stomach and the sound died.

His cock sprang free, flushed and slick. Heat blazed through my palm. I licked from root to crown, tasting salt and the echo of our earlier want, then took him as deep as I could on the first try.

A broken moan ripped from him, and I felt triumphant. I started slow, then turned deliberately mean, letting my teeth graze that sensitive ridge. His hand tangled in my hair, holding tight, every muscle in his body coiled like piano wire.

I met his gaze when he teetered on the edge. "Do you want to cum in my mouth?" I asked, humming his name around the thick of him so he felt every vibration.

My knees went numb on the tile, but I didn't care. Palm and tongue worked together to pull him apart—pulsing knot swelling at the base. I paused to spit once—just to be filthy—then sank lower, fighting my own gag reflex as his length filled my throat. His claws bit into the drywall, paint splintering, but he stayed perfectly still beneath me.

"Annie—" he warned, breathless.

I popped off, lips slick, jaw throbbing. "Don't hold back," I challenged, wrapping one hand around his shaft, the other cupping his balls. My grip tightened, twisting just enough. He bucked, the shaft flaring with that dark knot.

He grabbed my hair and pushed me down, not cruel but demanding. I opened for him, spit pooling at my chin, as he stretched me wide. His cock thickened further; I welcomed the burn. Tears slipped down my cheeks when he drove deeper, the tip battering my palate until I couldn't even breathe. I choked on purpose, then pulled off, coughing, mascara running, grinning through the mess.

"You like ruining me, don't you?" I rasped.

He leaned over, wings unfurling, dragging his thumb across my lips. "I want you ruined for everyone but me," he murmured, then claimed me again—steady, forceful. I squeezed his balls, tugged the knot until he yelped, and sucked him into my mouth as he burst.

His flood filled me, warm and unstoppable. I swallowed it all greedily until the last pulse faded. When he finally stilled, I lingered—lips ghosting over him—then wiped my mouth on the back of my hand, spent and utterly his.

CHAPTER
SIXTEEN

Samiel

I hauled her upright by the elbow, and in one easy motion, threw her over my shoulder. She kicked once, a reflex, but then laughed—a bright, filthy sound that went straight to the back of my skull. She clawed down my spine, not hard enough to break skin, but enough to make my cock twitch back to life.

The stairs were a blur. I took them two at a time, Annie's ass leveled at my mouth, the velvet of her dress bunched high. I bit her through the fabric, just to hear her yelp.

"Where are you taking me?" she demanded, voice muffled by my back.

I carried her where she belonged, to my—our—bed. I wanted her sprawled across those sheets, gripping that headboard, my hands and mouth claiming every inch until the memory of any other touch was erased from her skin. I kicked the door open, tossed her onto the mattress, and dragged her dress up those thighs that had been tormenting me all night.

She rolled over, hair a wild tangle across my pillow, lips swollen from my kisses. "You planning to fuck me through the box spring?"

My wings unfurled as I crawled over her, casting us both in shadow as I caged her between my arms. "You're not getting my cock until you come twice on my tongue." I let my fangs show when I said it. "I want to taste how wet you get for me. That's my price."

Her breath caught, pupils blown wide. "You're serious?"

I lowered myself until my lips brushed her ear, letting her feel the hard length of me pressed against her thigh. "You want it, you earn it. And when you finally get this cock, I'll ruin you so thoroughly you'll still feel me inside you next week."

A visible shiver ran through her body before she twisted her fingers in my hair and yanked me down with surprising strength. "Then stop talking," she whispered against my mouth, "and get to work."

I shoved her knees apart, palms biting into the soft flesh of her thighs. When I dragged her ass to the edge of the mattress, her heat was already radiating against my face. The velvet bunched at her waist, revealing black panties soaked through, the fabric clinging to every curve and fold of her cunt. I inhaled deeply before pressing my mouth against her, tasting her arousal through the thin barrier.

Her body went taut as a bowstring, one hand flying to the headboard, the other twisting in the sheets as if anchoring herself against the storm. I growled against her center, letting her feel the vibration travel through her core. My tongue traced the outline of her lips through the fabric, deliberately slow, savoring how her wetness seeped through with each stroke. When I finally slipped a finger beneath the edge, she was so slick I nearly lost control. Her clit swelled against my tongue, begging for attention as I teased around it, never quite giving her what she needed. She tried to grind against my mouth, desperate for more pressure, but I pinned her hips down with one arm across her stomach.

"Mine," I whispered against her flesh, my breath hot against her most sensitive spot. "My pace." Her thighs began to quiver uncontrollably as I sealed my lips around her clit and sucked, feeling her pulse against my tongue until she cried out, then caught herself—shocked at how quickly I could make her unravel.

"You're delicious," I said, tongue flicking over the cloth, letting the words vibrate right against her cunt. "You get this wet just sucking my cock?"

She nodded, then shook her head, then nodded harder, like she couldn't decide which answer would get her what she wanted. I slid one claw up the line of her panties, cutting them in half so the fabric snapped back and left nothing but the bare, swollen lips underneath. I sucked her clit, slow and deliberate, while I worked two fingers into her, knuckles grinding the roof of her cunt until she started to lose the thread of language.

"God, fuck, don't stop," she said, but her voice was gone, shredded and hoarse.

I didn't. I wanted to break her open, to pull every last ounce of want out of her until she couldn't stand the thought of anyone else ever between her legs. I curled my fingers, tongue never leaving her, watching the way she twisted on the bed, how her face went slack with every pulse of my hand. I bit her inner thigh, just enough to leave a mark, then covered the spot with my mouth and sucked hard, so she'd feel it every time she sat down for the next week.

She came hard the first time, nails raking my scalp, dragging me deeper, grinding her cunt into my mouth until she drowned the sheets in slick. I lapped it up, pulling her through every aftershock, not letting up until the tremors faded and she collapsed back, boneless and shaking. I sat up, chin slick with her, and let her see the mess she'd made out of me.

"One," I said, and the look in her eyes—hazed, ruined, hungry—almost undid me.

She tried to catch her breath, but I didn't let her. I pulled her forward, yanked the dress over her head, and laid her flat on the mattress. She was trembling when I slid back down, mouth open and ready, but this time I didn't tease. I ate her like I was starved, every lick harder, deeper, letting the pressure of my mouth draw a new, desperate sound from her every time I sucked her clit between my lips. She tried to twist away, but I grabbed her by the thighs and held her to my face, tongue fucking her until she sobbed my name and begged me to stop. I didn't. Not until I had her shaking against my tongue, cunt spasming in a rhythm that felt like it might never end.

"Fuck, Sam, I can't—" she gasped, but it was a lie. She rocked her hips to match me, greedy, hips fighting mine for control. I hooked her thighs over my shoulders and drove my tongue deeper, fingers curled inside her, and every time I pressed the flat of my tongue to her clit, she jerked like I was shocking her with a live wire.

She came again—this time louder, shameless, a sound so raw it made the fine hairs on my arms stand up. She convulsed, thighs locked around my head, and I let her ride it out, licking slower now, gentler, until the quake rolled down to aftershocks and sweat puddled in the small of her back.

When I pulled away, she was limp, eyes glassy, mouth half-open. Her hair stuck to her cheeks in wild black-and-blonde ropes, and her chest sawed air in and out like she'd just finished a marathon. I crawled up the bed, braced myself over her body, and let her feel the weight of everything I wanted to say.

"Two," I said, voice gone to gravel. "You're perfect. You know that?"

She managed a laugh, weak and incredulous, but she didn't look away. "You're going to kill me," she said, and her voice was full of awe and delight and something that felt almost like fear, but better.

"No," I said, "I'm going to keep you alive forever. That's what you do with something you can't stop wanting." I meant it, every word. I let my mouth drift down to her throat, kissed the bruise blooming there, then tasted the sweat on her jaw and the salt at the corner of her eye.

She cupped my face, fingers shaking, and pulled me down for a kiss. The taste of her on my tongue made her moan, and she bit my lower lip, a little payback for every mark I'd left on her. I kissed her back, slow and deep, until I felt her body start to wake up again, her hips shifting under mine with that helpless, greedy want.

"Do you still want it?" I asked, not sure who I was teasing more.

I lined my cock up with her slick entrance and pressed in, watching her body yield to me—her flesh parting, stretching, swallowing me inch by inch. Her walls gripped me, molten silk contracting around every vein and ridge. When the thick knot at my base nudged against her, I held there, letting her feel how it pulsed with need, how it would lock us together when I finally gave it to her. Her eyes, wild blue rings around black pools, locked onto mine as her breath caught.

I withdrew almost completely before sinking back in, savoring the wet sound of her taking me. My hand found her throat—not squeezing, just feeling her pulse hammer against my palm while my other hand lifted her ass, tilting her so I could drive deeper. When I bottomed out again, she raked her nails down my back hard enough to draw blood, her cunt clenching around me in perfect rhythm.

"The way you take me," I growled against her ear, teeth grazing the shell. "Like your body was carved out just for this cock." I rolled my hips in a slow figure eight that made her gasp and arch. Her wetness coated us both, the scent of her arousal making my head swim. "Every inch of you dripping for me."

"Please," she whimpered, her thighs trembling against my sides. "I need—I need—"

I stared at her, memorizing every line, every freckle and bruise and bead of sweat. "You're going to have it," I said. "It's yours. I'm yours." I kissed her, slow and deep, letting her taste herself on my tongue.Thrusting into her mouth languidly, in a way that mimicked my cock.

I kept at her, letting the friction build, the heat rising between us in a steady, perfect spiral. Every time I thought she was spent, she fired again—hips rolling up, hands yanking at my hair, teeth on my shoulder, the kind of want that never died even after the body begged for mercy. I loved it. I wanted to live in the space between her gasps and curses, the way she shuddered every time my knot pressed against the entrance and then slid just inside.

She was slick everywhere—skin to skin, sweat matting her hair to her face, a wet sheen on her chest that made her freckles pop. I wanted to cover her in it, to mark her in every way a body could be marked. So I did. I fucked her through the mattress, slow and ruthless, until she was clawing for air and the headboard rattled against the wall. When I felt her start to come again, I pressed all the way in, letting her feel the full, brutal stretch of the knot, and just held her there, deep as I could go.

She broke. She fucking shattered—arched up off the bed, back bowed, mouth open in a scream that probably woke every demon in a mile radius. Her cunt clenched so hard I saw stars, and in that moment, I let the last bit of control go and came inside her, every pulse of it a promise, a seal, a surrender. We stayed locked together, shaking and gasping, until the aftershocks faded and the sweat cooled on our skin.

I almost couldn't move, but I wanted to see her face, so I rolled us to the side, keeping us tied together. She gave a low, exhausted moan, then started laughing, a wild, delirious sound that made my chest ache.

"That was…" she started, but the words fell apart. "You're going to actually kill me one of these days, Samiel."

I kissed her forehead, careful, then her eyelids, then the tip of her nose. "No," I said, "I'll just fuck you back to life if I do."

She giggled, then winced, legs trembling as she tried to shift. "I think I'm stuck," she said, which was technically true—my knot still anchored us, and every little twitch sent a new spark up my spine. I tried to shift and failed, so I just let myself collapse on her, the full weight of my body draped over hers, sweat making us both slick as raw steak. I could still feel the knot, the way it pulsed inside her, a living fist clamped tight to her want, keeping us fused together even though every muscle in my body was screaming for sleep. Annie's breath came shallow, a laugh and a gasp tangled up, and she reached behind to slap my ass, weak but proud.

"I'm going to need so many electrolytes," she muttered. "And an ice pack. Possibly a wheelchair."

I laughed, but my voice was ruined—just a scrape of

sound. "I'll carry you anywhere you want to go. But you're not moving until I say you can."

She wiggled her hips, which sent a shockwave up my spine and nearly made me see double. "Don't think I can't get up by myself, demon. I'll drag you through the house like a dead dog."

I bit her shoulder, lazy and lingering, then nuzzled the mark I'd made. "Try it."

The knot loosened with a soft, viscous pop, and I slid out of her, rolling to the side and pulling her with me in the same motion so she landed on my chest, skin to skin. She laughed again, this time breathless but content, and rested her cheek right over my heart, her hair a wild halo between us.

We lay there, a tangle of legs, sweat, and sheets, for a long time. I stroked her spine, letting my claws trace the heat map of every bruise and scratch, while she idly played with the veins on my forearm, tapping out a rhythm I didn't know.

When the last of the aftershocks faded, she rolled off, stretched like a cat, and stared up at the ceiling with the dazed pride of a marathoner who'd just set a personal record and wasn't sure if she'd ever walk again.

"If you ever wanted to murder me," she said, "that would have been the time. I wouldn't have even noticed."

I dragged a hand across my face, trying to catch up with her. "I'm not done with you yet."

She snorted. "You say that, but I think your cock's going to need CPR."

I propped myself up on one elbow, damp hair sticking to my face, and looked at her—really looked at her. The marks on her chest, the bite prints on her neck, the line of my claws down her side, raw and red and healing already. She met my gaze, blue eyes rimmed black with mascara and want.

"What?" she said, voice soft.

"I just—" I stopped. The words didn't come easy. "I like seeing you like this."

She raised an eyebrow, waiting for more.

I tried again. "I've never seen anyone who looked better when they were ruined. You make destruction look like art."

She smiled, slow and bright, and for a second I thought she might laugh it off, but she didn't. She sat up, pulled her knees to her chest, then slid off the bed and padded to the bathroom, not bothering with anything like a robe or towel.

She left the door open. I watched her in the mirror, the way her body caught the light and refracted it in a hundred shades of bruised and perfect. She didn't look at herself—she looked at me, every time, like she wanted me to see her as she was, not as what she thought she should be. I followed, unable to stay away, and stepped into the shower with her, the spray hot and stinging against my skin. The water hit her marks, and she hissed, but didn't flinch, just braced her hands against my chest and let me wash her. I used my claws like a loofah, scrubbing her scalp, her back, the insides of her thighs, everywhere I'd left a mark. She let me do it, never looking away.

When we were clean, she wrapped a towel around her hair and shook herself off like a dog, then raided my closet for something to wear. She picked a T-shirt first—a black one, vintage and thinned with age, the words "HELL'S KITCHEN" across the chest in cracked red type. But then she found the pajama set I'd ordered, hoping she'd stay—black, soft as sin, trimmed with lace at the hem and sleeves.

She held it up, eyebrows raised, and I shrugged. "I told Mara comfortable but sexy," I said, suddenly unsure.

She pulled off my HELL'S KITCHEN shirt and put on the set, top and bottom. She looked down at herself and gave a little, satisfied hum. "They're perfect," she said, and the way she said it made my chest hurt. She curled up on the bed, knees to her chest, towel turban slowly sliding off her head, and patted the space beside her.

I got in, still naked, and let her tuck herself into the crook of my arm. The sheets were cool, the air outside the window sharp enough to bite, but under the blankets it was pure body heat. She traced lines on my chest with her fingers, lazy and aimless, and for a while, neither of us said anything.

"Are you happy?" she asked, finally, voice so small I almost didn't hear it.

The question shocked me because it had never occurred to me to check. I'd spent so many years hungry, so many more years angry, that the idea of contentment was foreign, like waking up in someone else's skin. But lying there, with her pressed to me and the echo of her laugh still in my bones, I realized I was. I was fucking ecstatic. I was terrified.

I turned and kissed the top of her head, breathing in the smell of her hair, the clean edge of it. "I'm not just happy," I said. "I'm ruined for anything else."

She laughed, but it was a soft sound, and I felt her relax all at once, every muscle going liquid in my arms.

We slept that way—her heartbeat in my ribs, my wings folded in around us, the cat a warm weight at our feet.

CHAPTER
SEVENTEEN

Annie

The next few weeks spilled out in ways I never could have predicted: a collage of sun-drenched mornings, midnight snacks, and sex that got so good it was almost boring how often we ended up on the floor, the countertop, or the front seat of the GTO.

The days stopped keeping themselves separate. I learned the sound of Samiel's walk, the way the floorboards groaned under his clawed feet when he was being deliberate, even, in his attempt to sound less like a beast and more like a boyfriend.

Was that what he was? My boyfriend? My fiancé? My... lover?

I learned the cat's routines, which were as precise and occult as any demon: Fluoxetine liked a spoon of cream at dawn, and exactly two cubes of ice in her water dish or else she'd drag the dish to the bedroom and dump it on my socks, a warning shot across the bow. I learned I loved waking up before sunrise, loved it so much it made my chest ache, because there was a blinding, still blue to the world at that hour. And every time I rolled over, there was Samiel, looking like he'd been waiting for me to acknowledge his existence since time began.

It was domestic, but not boring. Samiel alternated between treating every day like a honeymoon and every night like a wrestling match. We cooked together in the kitchen. Sometimes I'd find a recipe on my phone and he'd scowl at it, then make it from memory, better than the photo in the app. He had a truly perverse love of breakfast casseroles—like, Midwestern church potluck level—and an actual knack for sourdough that I found almost offensive. His hands were big enough to knead three loaves at once. The first time I saw him braid a challah, I wanted to fuck him on the kitchen counter, and then I did, and then the only real problem was picking the dough out of our hair and from under my nails before the bread went in the oven.

We went to town sometimes, but never for long. The world outside felt less real, less concrete, than the one we'd made for ourselves. The first time we went to the grocery store together, he spent the entire trip glowering at the other customers, like he was daring the senior citizens in the produce aisle to challenge his right to buy spinach. I made a game of it, seeing how many times I could get him to laugh in public before someone called the manager. By the time we got to the checkout line, he was red-faced from trying to stifle his laughter, and I was heated with the rush of being able to undo him so completely, so easily.

One Saturday morning about four weeks in, Samiel drove into town. He'd gotten weirdly obsessed with the farmer's market—maybe it was the way the produce stands looked like offerings to a minor god, or the fact that every time he went, he picked up gossip about the demon and human sides of town and came back smugger than a cat in sunshine. I watched him load up the GTO with empty baskets and every reusable bag we owned, then kissed him goodbye, tasting the anticipation on his skin.

"Don't start any fights with the vendors," I warned, and he just grinned, promising nothing.

He was barely gone ten minutes before the doorbell rang.

I froze. There was no reason for anyone to show up—no deliveries scheduled, no neighbors who'd ever come closer than the property line, not even an HOA dweeb with a bad attitude and a fresh stack of warnings. I padded barefoot to the window, peeking through the slit in the blinds.

It was Seth.

I recognized him instantly, even with the new mustache and the dumb black tie. I'd blocked his number, never once replied to the DMs or the "hey you up?" emails, but somehow he'd found me out here on the absolute edge of the void, where even the cell reception had to be paid for in blood. I watched him shuffle his feet on the front step, then check his phone, then look up at the house like he half-expected it to bite him. He was carrying—no, this was unreal —a fucking bouquet of gas station sunflowers, already starting to wilt at the tips.

I thought about hiding. I could have bolted for the mudroom, texted Samiel to come home, or even just waited for Seth to leave, like a raccoon playing dead on the kitchen floor. But the old me—every version of Annie that had ever existed—hated being cornered more than anything. I put on the Hell's Kitchen T-shirt, jammed my feet into Samiel's slippers, and opened the door.

He almost dropped the flowers. "Annie?" He blinked, jaw agape. "You look... You look amazing."

I ignored that. "How did you find me?"

He shuffled, looking past my shoulder for a glimpse of something I couldn't imagine. "You never answered my texts," he said, "so I called your mom. She said you'd joined a witness protection program or something. I thought she was joking."

She was, but that didn't matter. I'd have to thank her later. I leveled a glare at him, arms crossed. "You drove all the way here?"

"It's not that far," Seth said, and I could feel the lie in his voice. "I just had to see you. I made a mistake, Annie. I want to fix things. I'm better now. I'm in therapy. I got a raise at work. I—"

His voice trailed off as he stared at my neck, at the constellation of hickeys Samiel had left there like some kind of demonic Rorschach test. I resisted the urge to cover them or explain that last night had involved a very athletic session with the headboard. Seth's eyes went so wide I half-expected them to fall out and roll across the welcome mat like cartoon marbles. God, I hoped he wouldn't faint. I wasn't about to perform CPR on my ex while wearing my boyfriend's demon-sized slippers.

I didn't move. "You need to leave, Seth."

He tried to push past me, a hand on the frame, already invading. "Who did this to you?" It came out too loud, like he was auditioning for a role he didn't understand. "Did he hurt you? Is someone here?"

I wanted to laugh, but it curdled in my throat. "No one hurt me," I said, clear and cold. "I'm happy, Seth. You need to go."

He shook his head. "You're not safe here. This place is dangerous, Annie. There are, like, actual demons in this town—"

I smiled. "Yeah. And I'm fucking one of them."

He shut up, mouth working soundlessly. The color drained from his face.

"That's not funny," he said, finally.

I stepped closer, tilting my neck like I was an actress in a vampire B movie. "It's not a joke. Samiel has matching bruises, plus a bite mark that looks like Nebraska. Turns out I'm into guys who can bench-press a Buick and don't need WebMD to find a clitoris. Geography lesson's over, Seth—get in your sad little rental car and MapQuest your way back to Tampa."

His eyes snapped up—stunned, almost comically, like it had never occurred to him I might be serious. For a second, I could see all the old gears working, trying to fit what I'd just said into the shape of the Annie he remembered. The one who rescued him from his own messes, who wouldn't so much as jaywalk if it meant hurting someone else's feelings. He didn't get it. Maybe he never would.

"You're… you're not joking." His voice was so small it almost made me feel bad. Almost.

I kept my arms crossed. "No, Seth, I'm not. And it's none of your business."

He took a step back, nose wrinkling like he smelled something bad. "Jesus, Annie. You're in some kind of— what, a cult? Is that what this is?" He held up the flowers as if they could shield him from reality. "This isn't you. You're not this person. You hated the desert, you hated weird shit, you—"

I cut him off. "Don't tell me who I am." I was shaking a little, and it pissed me off that I still cared enough to be angry. "I get it, okay? You showed up because your life is a mess and you can't imagine a world where I don't drop everything to fix it. But that's over." I leaned forward, voice low. "If you cared about me at all, you'd leave."

He looked at me, then at the bruises, then back up at the house, half-expecting some demon to pop out and drag him to hell. It would've been funny if I hadn't wanted to do it myself.

"This guy," he said, almost a whine, "he's clearly not safe."

I laughed. "Not safe for you, for sure. Which is why you should leave. He'd love to watch you run. But he'd love it even more if you stayed, because then he'd have an excuse to break every bone in your body." I felt a little dizzy, like I was watching someone else's hands punch out the words. "I'm in love with him, Seth. And if you stay here, he'll tear you apart."

The second I said it, I felt it land—*in love*. I didn't need to look for the recognition in his face. It was in mine. I held the stare for a long time. Maybe a minute. The silence got so thick you could frost a cake with it. Seth looked like someone had smacked him. Then, in the saddest little motion I'd ever seen, he tucked the sunflowers under his arm, nodded, and just... left.

I watched him get into a rental car that probably cost more than his month's rent and pull a three-point turn so wide he nearly mowed down the mailbox. The whole drive down the gravel, he didn't look back. I waited until the car was out of sight, then shut the door—hard—and leaned against it, breathing like I'd just run the obstacle course in the backyard. My knees gave out and I slid to the floor, back pressed to the wood, head in my hands.

I knew I should tell Samiel. I knew if I did, he'd take it as a threat. A challenge. Something to fix by force, or by fear. The idea of that—of Seth mangled on the side of some county road, or Samiel pacing the living room like a caged animal—made something heavy thud in my chest. I sat there for a long time, thinking about it, about all the ways this could go wrong, about what happened to people who carried secrets in towns like this.

I didn't move until I heard Samiel's car in the drive.

By then, the kettle had boiled itself dry, and the cat had meowed herself hoarse at the pantry door. I got up, wiped my face, and tried to look like I hadn't just had a near-miss with my own bad patterns. When Samiel walked in, arms full of produce, overheated and sweating, I met him with a smile and a kiss and a joke about how he'd forgotten the avocados, everything was just as it should be.

Except it wasn't. Not quite. Not for the rest of the day, or that night, or the next week. I kept waiting for the other shoe to drop, for Seth to show up again, for a police cruiser or a neighbor or a demon in a cheap suit to knock on the door and say, "Hey, there's a problem. A human one." I kept waiting to feel like myself again, but what I mostly felt was a kind of sick, sweet relief.

I didn't tell Samiel.

CHAPTER
EIGHTEEN

Samiel

Annie and I were brushing our teeth side by side, staring at each other in the mirror when something shifted in my chest. Annie caught my eye, foam at the corner of her mouth, and winked.

My toothbrush froze mid-stroke. I was totally and completely in love with her. The realization hit with such force, I nearly choked on mint. I'd never been in love, not even close. And now I was standing in my house—our house if she decided to stay—plotting ways to move mountains for her until the heat death of the universe.

I hadn't gotten up the courage to ask if she'd decided to stay at the end of ninety days. I didn't want to pressure her. And though I was almost certain the answer would be yes, she'd been... distracted for the last few days. I'd catch her looking out the window, lost in thought or petting Fluoxetine while gnawing on her lip aggressively. She'd started leaving half-drunk cups of coffee around the house, something she never did before. Twice I'd found her phone face-down on the porch, like she'd set it there deliberately to avoid checking it. Yesterday, she'd jumped when the mailman came, then laughed it off too loudly. Was something bothering her? Was she trying to decide if she was ready to say yes to forever?

In what I thought was an excellent display of personal growth, I finally decided to ask her if something was bothering her, rather than ruminate on worst case scenarios.

I rinsed, spat, then met Annie's eyes in the mirror. "Breakfast?" I said, aiming for casual, but I could see she already knew something was coming.

She grinned, but it went weird at the edges. "You're not making me eat another breakfast casserole, are you? Because I still haven't recovered from the last one. My pancreas is staging a protest."

I grinned back, forcing a brightness I didn't feel. "We'll go to the place in town. The one with the blueberry donuts you said were better than sex." I said this with a straight face, which made her snort toothpaste foam out her nose and half the tension in my chest evaporated.

We dressed—she in a faded band shirt and my softest flannel, me in jeans and a T-shirt that somehow still smelled like her after the wash—and walked out to the car. The GTO roared to life, satisfying as ever, and she did the thing she always did, cranking the radio to something loud and forgettable and rolling the window all the way down. The wind blew her hair straight back, and she turned to me with cheeks pink from the cold, looking so alive it almost hurt.

I parked us in front of the bakery and walked Annie up the ramp so she wouldn't slip on the dust-slick tile steps. The place was full of morning—sugar and yeast and strong coffee in the air, and a clatter of voices from the counter and patio. Annie headed for an outside table, dragging me by the hand like a kid desperate to stake out the playground. Her hair whipped around her face, wild and perfect, and I wanted to eat her more than anything on the menu.

We sat, and the server—human girl, barely of age, eyes rimmed with glitter liner—brought menus and stared at me like I was the first demon she'd ever seen up close. Annie ordered for both of us, two blueberry donuts, an iced coffee for her, an Americano for me. She didn't let go of my hand the whole time.

I waited until the plates were down, the server gone. "You're acting weird," I said, going for gentle but missing the mark and landing more on the side of interrogation.

Annie blinked, then snorted, "Wow, thanks, Sam. Most guys just tell me I look tired."

"You don't look tired," I said. "You look like you're waiting for the ground to open up and eat you."

She smiled, but it was all teeth, no warmth. "That's because it's Valley of the Damned. The ground does that sometimes." But she was winding herself up for something, I could tell. She was spinning the spoon in her coffee so hard the handle vibrated, which wasn't her usual nervous tic. She was about to say something, maybe confess the thing that had been ghosting between us for days, when a shadow slanted across the table and a voice cut in—thin, nasal, and absolutely unwelcome—cut in.

A guy, human, wearing a rental car windbreaker and a haunted, sunburnt face. As soon as I saw Annie's body language—stiff, then a snap to angry—I knew who it must be. I didn't recognize him, but he looked like the kind of guy who'd collect Funko Pops and wear ironic socks to funerals. He was carrying himself like the idea of confidence, without any of the substance.

"Annie." He stopped right in front of the table.

Annie's whole body jerked, like she'd been zapped. Then she went steel-cold, the way I'd seen her in the split second before she decided to run or punch. She set her coffee down, slow and deliberate, and folded her hands on the tabletop.

"What are you doing here, Seth? I told you we are through," she said, voice so flat it could have been a warning label.

He looked like he'd practiced a speech but lost the script. "I couldn't leave," he said, then darted his gaze to me, lingering on my veins, arms, face, then back to Annie. "Not after seeing you in his house. This isn't what you want."

Now I was doubly shocked. Not only was Seth here—but he had been to my house. And Annie had kept it from me. I could see Annie's jaw flex, a twitch at her temple like she wanted to take a swing at him. But I didn't care about that— not right now. What I cared about was the fact that this loser had been in my house. Our house.

I wanted to believe he was lying, that this was just human drama, not what it sounded like. But Annie's face did a thing—a tiny, almost nothing spasm at the corner of her mouth—that told me he wasn't.

"When were you at our house?" I said, as calmly as I could manage. My voice came out low and cold, nothing of the human-friendly rumble I practiced for customer service or the driveway block parties.

"Last week," Seth said. "She didn't tell you?"

My hands curled under the table, claws pressing into my palms. The world shrank to the space between Annie's silence and my rage. The bakery noise went thin and tinny, voices fading until all I could hear was the echo of my own pulse, and the scratch of Annie's thumbnail against her coffee cup.

"Annie?" I said, not trusting myself to make it a question.

She looked at me, and I saw her make a choice—fight or flight—but this time, she didn't run.

"He showed up," she said, not looking away. "He brought flowers and a speech. I didn't let him in. He left." She swallowed, and her voice dropped. "I didn't tell you because I knew you would hunt him down and kill him."

I watched Seth take me in. I wanted to rip his head off. I breathed through my nose, trying to rein myself in. I waited —long enough for the silence to go from tense, to brittle, to a vacuum that hurt your ears if you moved.

Seth broke first. I watched him really look at me for the first time, the way my shirt barely contained the mass of my shoulders, the black veins crawling up my forearms, the claws that could slice through skin. I could see the moment he clocked the horns under my hair, the color of my skin, the eyes that didn't quite work like a human's. He looked at me, then at Annie, then back at me. I could see the math in his eyes—height, reach, bite force. He blinked hard, then tried to compose himself, the way men do when they know the brawl is lost but want to salvage their pride.

"You don't have to do this," Seth said, voice low, as if he wanted to block me from hearing. "You don't have to stay with... with him." Not even the nerve to look at me when he said it. "I know you. This isn't you. You're afraid—"

Annie's eyes went cold as she cut him off. "You have no idea what I want, Seth, and you never did." Her voice was a deadly whisper. I'd never seen Annie so angry.

"I'm not afraid," she said. "Not of him. I'm staying, Seth. I'm in love with him. And before you ask? He doesn't need me to fix him, or pretend to be less, or apologize for breathing. He actually likes it when I talk back. He treats the cat better than you treated me on your best day." She took a breath. "You can go."

My mind was whirling chaos. Annie loved me. She loved me. We'd yet to say those words to each other. But now was hardly the time to tell her the feeling was mutual. Not with her ex-boyfriend standing there.

He stood there stunned, like he was waiting for a punchline. Then his jaw set. He looked at me, and for a second, I thought he might do the thing men do—try to assert dominance, square off, make a scene. But he did something perhaps even more foolish and grabbed Annie by the wrist.

He did it without thinking, or maybe without thinking enough. He reached for Annie in a way that was both desperate and familiar, a move you make when you think the person is still yours. His hand closed around her wrist, not hard, but insistent. I saw red.

The world contracted. I was out of my chair before the screech of wood on tile finished echoing. My hand wrapped Seth's throat, not gently, not with any attempt at subtlety. I felt the pulse against my palm, the dance of fear beneath the skin, every muscle in his body going slack as the oxygen started to drain. I lifted him off the ground like he weighed nothing—because he did, to me.

The entire patio went silent. All the humans, the demons, the staff—everyone watched me, watched Annie, watched stupid Seth dangle like a sideshow prop in my grip. I could have crushed his trachea in a blink. I wanted to. I started to squeeze.

Not hard, not at first. Just enough for Seth to realize who held him, to let the certainty travel up his spine and register in the pupils blown wide with panic. He scrabbled at my wrist, nails biting skin, but I barely felt it—my hand was three times his, and it was built to break, not to be broken. I squeezed harder, the way you test a piece of fruit for ripeness, until his face went blotchy and the veins at his temples bulged and fluttered. His feet left the ground. The sound he made was small and ugly, a child's whimper squeezed through a grown man's larynx.

"Samiel!" Annie's voice split the air, sharp and unafraid. "Let him go."

I didn't. I watched Seth's eyes roll, watched his hands flail for purchase, watched the way the bakery staff dialed 911 but didn't dare come any closer than the window. The world had gone silent; even the cars on the street slowed to see who would win.

This was what I was built for. Not the house, or the sourdough, or the novelty of a girlfriend who made me laugh and fucked me raw and wore my shirts with nothing underneath. This was the real me, the one made for violence, the one who'd spent eternity learning that the only way to be heard was to leave a mark that never faded.

"Sam." Annie's voice again, closer, and this time there was no fear, just a low, steady current of command. "Put him down. He's not worth it."

I looked at her. Really looked. She stood there, hair snapping in the wind, hands curled into fists, but she wasn't afraid. Not of me, not of the scene I was making. She was angry, yes, but she was also pleading—for me, not for the sack of shit dangling in my hand.

"If you kill him," she said, "he wins. Is that what you want?"

I hesitated just long enough for Seth to make a desperate, wet gasp. His lips were blue now, the whites of his eyes a bloodshot maze. I wanted to keep squeezing. I wanted to snap the little column of bones and watch the life drain out of the first and last man who ever made Annie feel small.

But I wanted her more. I wanted what we'd built, the house, the running track in the yard, the stupid cat and the even stupider hope that I could be something other than what the world had always told me.

So I loosened my grip. Just barely. Seth collapsed to his knees, coughing and retching, spittle running down his chin. I watched him crawl, watched him clutch at his throat like he thought the damage wasn't permanent. He looked up at Annie, not at me, and I could see the fresh terror there, the knowledge of how close he'd come. I wanted him to remember it every time he swallowed, every time he tried to speak in a room that wasn't his.

CHAPTER
NINETEEN

Annie

I didn't see Samiel's face at first—all I saw was the human shape of Seth, retching on the bakery tiles, and the impact that my boyfriend's handprint had left on his neck, already staining purple. For one cold second, everything in my body collapsed inward. I'd always known what Samiel was, but some desperate, soft part of me had needed to believe in the boundary between monsters and men, and now I wasn't sure there was one.

The rest of the world came back in pieces. The clatter of an overturned coffee cup. The echo chamber of silence as everyone on the patio stared, waiting for the post-mortem. Seth staggered upright, clutching his ruined voice box, and spit something at my feet that might have been blood or just humiliation. He didn't look at me as he turned, lurching out of the bakery straight-legged and angry, disappearing around the corner in a daze.

I rounded on Samiel as soon as he let go, voice barely above a whisper but shaking with everything I was suddenly, violently aware of. "What the fuck was that, Sam?"

He looked at me, eyes two open wounds. "He touched you." Like it was a full explanation, as necessary and obvious as breathing.

I felt my hands shake, but not from adrenaline—terror, maybe, or just the understanding that this was the real him, the one who'd warned me from the beginning. "You could have fucking killed him. In front of all these people."

"Only if you'd asked," he said quietly, and I saw the ugly truth—he meant it.

For a second I wanted to run, wanted to get in the car and keep driving until the world fell away on both sides. Even now, even with everything I'd already seen, it stunned me how thin the line was between love and annihilation.

But this was what I'd chosen. This was what I wanted, wasn't it? The honesty, even when it sliced.

"He's not worth it," I said, the words tasting like blood. "I told you. I don't want you to protect me from myself. Or from him. I want you to trust me."

His jaw worked, the muscles rippling under his skin, and I saw he didn't know how. He didn't know how to let go, any more than I did.

We left the donuts half-eaten, the coffee still hot in the cups. The car ride home was a mutiny of silence—Samiel gripping the wheel so hard I thought it might snap, me staring out the window, counting the seconds until the ache under my ribs became something I could name.

When we got home, he killed the engine and just sat in the driveway, head bowed, hands locked at ten and two on the wheel. I didn't wait for him to speak.

"I said it at the coffee shop and I'll say it here," I said. "I didn't tell you Seth came by because I knew you'd do exactly this. I knew you'd hurt him or scare him or worse. And I didn't want to see that. I meant what I said. I love you. I don't want this… possessive whatever it is you have going on to ruin it."

He turned, slowly, the veins under his skin black and rising like he was about to break the glass just by looking at it.

"You're right," he said, each word landing like a metal object on tile. "You're right, Annie. But you don't get it. I can't stand knowing anyone else even looked at you, much less touched you. I can't let someone walk into our house like it's nothing—like you're an option, like he could just… take you back. Because I love you too. I love you more than I thought it was possible to love."

I didn't know what to do with that. The intensity was a compliment, a curse, and a confession in equal measure. Part of me wanted to rage back, to say I wasn't a trophy, not a prize to be won or lost. Another part—the secret, greedy part —loved it. I wanted to hate that part of myself, but I didn't.

I settled on, "It's not your decision who gets to find me. It's not up to you to get rid of the things that scare you. That's not love, Sam. That's just control."

He let out a breath and the windows fogged up, both of us slick with sweat and leftover adrenaline. "I don't want to own you," he said. "I just can't stand the thought that someone would come after you and not understand that you're… that you're—"

"Not property," I finished for him.

He flinched a little but nodded. "Not property," he repeated, voice softer. "But not… at risk, either. You're all I have worth a shit in this world. I don't know how to do it any other way." He flexed his hands, watched the black veins fade back under his skin. "I'm sorry. I am. I just—if anyone ever hurt you, Annie, I'd tear down the fucking sky to make it right."

I stared at him, at the big stupid architecture of his body, the bruised lips from where I'd bitten him last night, the faint mark of blue from my nail against his jaw. An entire arsenal designed for violence, and all of it pointed at me like a shield. It didn't excuse what he'd done, but it made sense of it.

I wanted to stay angry, but my voice came out tired, flat. "I need some air." I opened the car door and just walked, heat punching through my sneakers as I crossed the crushed granite. The sky was cautious blue, the light too bright and unforgiving. I didn't know where I was going, just that I needed to move, to let the edges of myself stop buzzing with adrenaline and settle into a shape again.

Samiel didn't follow. When I looped back to the porch, he was sitting on the steps, elbows on knees, chin in his hands. He looked up only when I made it to the top step, concern mapped in the set of his jaw.

"Don't say you're sorry again," I said, before he could start.

He didn't. Just looked past me, at the wild yard, the splintered rocks, the horizon shimmer beyond.

"I could give you space," he said, with the practiced neutrality of someone who'd read it in a book about People with Feelings.

"You wouldn't like it," I said, sitting down beside him.

"Doesn't mean you don't need it," he answered, and that almost undid me.

I picked at a scab on my elbow. "Remember the isolation house? The one up near the ridge? The mayor said any time a match needed a reset, they sent them there for a couple days. No contact, no drama. Just enough time to hear your-self think."

He blinked, frowning. "You want to go there?" The ques-tion was gentle, almost fragile.

I could have lied. I could have said no. But the truth was, it felt like I was living in a slow-motion landslide. I didn't want to leave him, but I also didn't want to keep breaking myself apart every time I flinched at his temper or the thought of his hands on someone else's throat.

"Yeah," I said. "I think I need to."

He was quiet for so long I thought he might just get up and drive away, which would have been its own kind of mercy. But then he said, "You can take the car. I'll walk you up there."

I half-laughed, half-choked. "You're not going to lock me in the trunk and drag me back, are you?"

He shook his head, and I saw a flicker of a smile at the corner of his mouth. "You're the only thing I've ever wanted to keep safe. That's the whole problem."

We drove in silence. The isolation house was farther than I remembered, perched above the main drag of the Valley like an outpost in some cold war. There was no road, just a winding dirt path and the crunch of tires over dust and bone. When we arrived, he killed the engine and sat for a minute, then turned to me.

"I want you back," he said, eyes sharp and unblinking. "But not if coming home means you have to pretend every time I lose control." He put a hand on my knee. Not posses-sive—just contact, trying to say goodbye without making it hurt more. "But if you decide to stay up here a while... I'll check in from a distance. I'll send the cat."

I wanted to argue, to say it was a terrible idea, but I could see the way he was shouldering his own want, trying not to pressure me even with his presence. It was such a Samiel thing—brutal devotion, and the willingness to let me break his heart if it meant I'd come back stronger. I had to look away so I wouldn't crack.

We went inside together, me trailing his shadow, and found the place exactly as advertised: a single room, a bed with clean sheets, a desk, a mini fridge stocked with every imaginable flavor of seltzer. The windows looked out over the whole Valley so that if I wanted, I could watch the world end and begin again a hundred times before lunch. I paced, not sure what to do with my hands.

He set my bag on the end of the bed, then hovered in the doorway like he didn't trust himself not to follow. "I'm leaving the car," he said. "And the keys. I'm leaving your phone and your charger. You want to ghost me, you can." His jaw flexed. "But if you want to come home, you come home."

I nodded, so sharp I felt it in my teeth.

He turned to go, then stopped, staring at the floor like he was conjuring the words from somewhere deep and volcanic. "You know," he said, "I'm technically supposed to be the one in isolation. The record was, this was always for demons, not—" He looked up, shrugged. "Not like it matters. If you want the house, stay in the house. I'll stay here. I'll check in with the cat."

He was giving me the out, handing me the keys to our whole fragile kingdom and saying, it's yours, *even if you don't want me in it*. I wanted to break his nose for it, but more than that, I wanted to wrap my arms around him and not let go. Instead, I watched him stand by the door, every muscle at war with every other muscle.

He said, "There's food, and blankets, and I'll bring up

more if you want. You don't have to text if you don't want to. I just—I need you to know you're not trapped."

The way he said it, I knew he understood the difference between being kept and being wanted. Between possession and care.

I stood at the window until Samiel's shape blurred to nothing on the dust road, just a dark thread unraveling over sun and distance. I waited for myself to feel relief—some click of "finally, he's gone"—but the second the door shut, the silence struck so hard I actually whimpered, a noise I hadn't heard from myself since childhood.

I tried to fill the space the way I always did: rearranged the mini fridge a full three times (alphabetized by seltzer flavor, then by color, then back to flavor), put my books on the desk and stacked them and restacked them in order of least to most embarrassing. I sat on the bed and scrolled my phone, but there was nothing to scroll. My friends wouldn't understand, my family was on another planet, and the only person whose notifications mattered had made it explicit I could ghost him at will.

I wandered the little house, which smelled like bleach and empty, and tried to remember the last time I'd really, truly been alone. Not the kind of alone where someone was a text or a shout down the hall away, but isolation, pure and perfect, where the only echo was your own heart and fear. I let myself have the panic attack, right there on the floor. My brain spun every worst-case scenario: Samiel furious, Samiel gone, Samiel snapped and turned into the kind of monster people braced for when they heard a demon moved in next door. But the real horror was that I couldn't stop picturing him—not as the brute with his hand around a throat, but as the man who'd left me in this house with every comfort and none of his own, just to prove he could try to give me what I needed.

I didn't sleep much that first night. Maybe an hour. I walked the perimeter four times, made up three different elaborate cereal recipes, read the entirety of a romance novel I found in the closet (*Bride of the Blood Moon*—so, so bad), and then watched the lake go from onyx to the same red-gold as Samiel's eyes when he let his defenses down and just looked at me. I spent the first day furious. The second day, I cried so hard I thought I'd give myself sinus damage.

On the third morning, the cat arrived. Fluoxetine, tail up and confidence high, stalked up the path and headbutted the door until I let her in. She sniffed the walls, pawed at the blanket, then flopped on the end of the bed and glared at me like, *Get a grip*. I tried to make her leave, but she just bit my ankle, so I gave up and let her have half the cereal. She was better company than most people I'd known.

I spent that day really thinking—about Samiel, about me, about the way I kept running from one version of love to another. What scared me most wasn't the violence—it was the way that, with Samiel, the violence wasn't the point. I knew what it felt like to be the target of a man's anger, and this wasn't it. What he'd done to Clem, to Seth—yeah, it was pure animal, but if I was honest, what I'd felt from Samiel was something closer to instinct too, the wild protective urge that made you want to take a bullet for a friend or throw yourself between a kid and a moving car.

But that was the problem, wasn't it? That I kind of craved being wanted in a way that bordered on dangerous. The idea twisted in me like a knife: I didn't just want to be chosen, I wanted to be kept.

I hated myself for it. I hated that deep down, I wanted to run right back home and crawl onto his lap and let him cage me in with his arms and his body and the shadow of his wings. I wanted the impossible—to be free, and to be claimed. I wanted to have it both ways, and I knew the world did not actually work like that for girls like me.

The cat glared up at me as if to say, *get over yourself.*

So I did what I always did when my emotions threatened to swamp me—I went looking for the edge, the line I could walk until I either fell off or learned to balance. I put on my shoes and just started running, tracing the cliffside above the lake, until the air in my lungs was sharp and every muscle in my legs howled for mercy. It wasn't about exercise, not really. It was about beating the storm in my head into something quieter, smaller, a set of problems I might eventually be able to solve.

I ran until the sun was high and the sweat had dried salt in my eyebrows. When I finally slowed to a walk, the world felt different. I'd outpaced the worst of the anxiety, leaving a more manageable, solid core beneath. I stood at the brim of Hell's Valley and looked back at the sprawl of human houses, the faint glint of glass where the demon enclave started, the GTO still parked crooked in the drive, a mile and a half below. I stood there for a long time, arms wrapped across my belly, and wondered what it would take to hold both parts of myself at once.

When I finally went back inside, I crashed face-first onto the bed and slept for six hours straight. I dreamed of nothing, which felt like a gift.

Day four, I called my mom. I hadn't expected to, but I found myself dialing her without thinking, as if some vestigial survival instinct needed reminding that the past I'd run from wasn't all bad, or at least that it existed out there, waiting for me. She picked up on the first ring.

"Are you alive?" she said, skipping hello.

"Definitely alive. Just… decompressing," I said, and realized my voice sounded normal. Like me, not like someone drowning.

"Well, that's something. Is it the demon? I'm not against alternative lifestyles, sweetheart, but if you're being held against your will, cough twice."

I laughed, hard, and felt the last of the tension melt out of me. "He's not holding me hostage, Mom. He's actually giving me space. Which is more than can be said for certain ex-boyfriends."

She went quiet for a beat. "Is that what this is about? The pest ex?" She meant Seth, but she never said his name if she could help it.

"Kind of." I sat on the bed, pulled the blanket over my knees, and looked out at the stitched-together patchwork of lake and sand and demon-warded suburbia. "He showed up. I told him to get bent, but it… complicated things." I hesitated, then decided to just say it. "Samiel almost killed him. I mean, he didn't, but he wanted to. And I thought I could handle it, but—I don't know."

My mom inhaled, a sound like the start of a verdict. "So you left."

"Not exactly. I'm just… in a timeout," I said. "I needed to figure out if I was actually safe, or just addicted to the drama."

She laughed. "Oh, honey. Those are the same thing."

There was a pause while she no doubt lit a cigarette and exhaled a perfect ring. When she spoke, her voice was wickedly clear. "Let me give you some motherly advice," she said, and I braced myself for either the worst or best speech of my adult life. "If he ever puts a hand on you that you didn't ask for, you call, and I will drive straight to Nevada and blow his head off. No questions asked."

"Jesus, Mom—"

"But if he never does, and you love him, who cares if the rest is a mess? You do not have to fix his wiring. You just have to decide if the risk is worth the heat. Men like that, they're all or nothing. They don't do safe." She paused as if she might sob, but of course she didn't. "You're my daughter, Annie. You were never going to be happy with a guy who just listened and made you chamomile tea and sent you Valentine's jokes on Instagram. You need a man who can take it and give it right back."

I lay back on the bed, phone clamped to my ear, and pictured Samiel in the kitchen, pummeling bread dough or dropping oranges for the cat to play with. "He scares the shit out of me sometimes," I said. It was a confession and a prayer.

She snorted, delighted. "Good. Keeps you sharp."

We were quiet awhile, both of us chewing on it. Finally, she said, "I know you, Annie. You don't want normal. You want someone who will burn a city down for you and expect you to rebuild it with him. If Samiel's that guy, stop trying to be someone else's version of safe."

I breathed in, out, and realized I was crying—not the ugly kind, but relief, given permission to exist exactly as I was. "Thanks, Mom."

"If you run, you'll just find another man who's worse at hiding it," she said. "At least this one's honest." She coughed once, then said, "You got your pepper spray?"

I grinned, wiping my cheeks. "Always."

"Then go back to him," she said. "You've made him wait long enough."

CHAPTER
TWENTY

Annie

I thought about her words long time after I hung up with my mom. I watched the sparkle of the lake and the shimmer of heat off the demon sands, and I tried to picture what my life would look like if I went back right now, right this second. I didn't feel fixed, or braver, or even especially together. I felt the same as always—too much and not enough, too loud, too hungry, too ready to throw myself into the fire even if I knew it would burn.

But the thought of seeing Samiel again made my entire body buzz, a frequency so high I could barely sit still. The cat, sensing my mood, pawed at the front door until I got up and opened it, then promptly planted herself on the door-mat, as if to say *It's about damn time.*

I threw my stuff in the GTO, scooped Fluoxetine into the passenger seat, and cranked the ignition. She yowled the entire way down the mountain, a banshee howl of complaint that made me feel less alone. The wind through the open window tangled my hair and dried the sweat on my upper lip, and all I could think of was how, in less than fifteen minutes, I'd be home.

Our home. I wanted it to be that, and I wasn't going to pretend otherwise, not anymore.

I barely parked the car before I was out of it. The cat launched herself from the window, claws out, and immediately began patrolling the perimeter with the focus of a military scout. I stood in the driveway, heart raw and wide open, waiting for the first flicker of movement from inside.

He was at the door before I even knocked, like he'd been standing there the whole day, like he'd known I would come back as soon as the sun hit high noon. I braced myself for some speech, but he just reached for my face and held it like I was the last piece of glass left in a shattered cathedral.

"I missed you," he said.

I tried to say something cool, or make a joke, or even just speak, but instead I started ugly-crying on his shirt. He smelled like oranges and dust and the salt I'd left behind on his skin, and I felt his arms go gentle-wild around me, holding me up, holding me tight, holding me like he'd already decided we were forever and was just waiting for me to catch up.

"Don't ever do that again," he said, but there was no threat in it. Just a splintery relief, sharp and honest.

"You are a fucking disaster," I said, which made him snort laugh against my hair.

"Your disaster," he said. "If you want."

I wanted. More than anything.

We stood on the porch for a long time, neither of us moving, like the moment might disappear if we stepped away. The cat wound around our ankles, tail high, and I thought: *This is it. This is what I came here for.*

He pulled away just enough to look at me, wiping with a

careful thumb the mascara tracks from my cheeks. His hands were trembling.

"I love you," he said, and I felt it crack through me like a bullet. "I love you, Annie."

The words landed so hard I nearly laughed, but it came out as a kind of hiccup, a mess of relief and terror and joy. "I love you too, you absolute monster," I said, hands fisted in his shirt, and I could feel him exhale, every muscle in his stupid, dangerous body finally letting go.

We didn't say anything else for a while. I pressed my forehead to his jaw, breathing him in. He kissed the top of my head, then my eyelids, then the place just under my earlobe where he said my skin tasted like cold stars. I wanted to say a hundred things, all at once—that I was sorry for running, that I'd always come back, that I wanted to spend the rest of my life arguing with him over nothing and fucking him against every surface we owned.

We didn't even make it to the bedroom. The front door slammed against the wall, and Samiel lifted me with hands that burned against my thighs, his claws pricking through the denim. My back hit the kitchen counter hard enough to rattle dishes, my legs instinctively wrapping around his waist, feeling the rigid heat of him press against my center. His mouth crashed into mine, all hunger and possession, fangs grazing my bottom lip as I arched into him. The low growl vibrating from his chest sent electricity straight between my legs. He tasted like every dark fantasy I'd ever had, his tongue sliding against mine as his hands gripped my ass, pulling me harder against him.

He broke the kiss, pupils blown wide in those red-gold eyes, a thin trail of saliva connecting our lips.

"Say it again," he demanded, voice rough as gravel. His hips ground against me in a slow, deliberate circle that made my eyelids flutter. The hard ridge of him pressed exactly where I needed it, and I couldn't stop the desperate sound that escaped my throat as his fangs extended fully, gleaming and deadly against his flushed lips.

"I love you. I love you more than anything." It came out cracked and needy, and the second I said it, the mask slipped. He made this noise, half-groan, half something wild and wordless, and hitched my thighs up until my ass was right at the edge, body spread open for him, trusting he wouldn't let me fall.

He tore my jeans off—not just a figure of speech, literally shredded them on the diagonal with his claws, the fabric unraveling in a spiral of blue and white over my skin. I shrieked, then started laughing, then shrieked again with the shock of bare air on skin, and he just pressed his face straight between my legs, shoulders pinning me to the countertop, tongue hot and alive.

He ate me out like he'd spent four days thinking about it, like every second apart had been rehearsed with his mouth on air, waiting for the taste of me. His forked tongue flickered against me—two precise points of pleasure that somehow reached everywhere at once. I clung to him, knuckles white, as he worked me slow at first, then with inhuman speed and dexterity, each split tip finding separate nerves to torment simultaneously. The more I bucked against his mouth, the deeper he moaned, the hungrier he got. When both tips of his tongue circled my clit in opposite directions before he sealed his lips around it and sucked, I thought I'd bite through my own tongue. The pressure was unreal, and I could feel the edges of his fangs graze, careful but there, reminding me what I was giving myself to.

I lost the thread of language. I was just sound and heat and shaking, every nerve in my body ratcheted up to the point of pain. Then he slid two fingers inside me, then three, working me with a precision that was obscene in every sense. He curled them just right, and when he dragged his tongue up the seam of me with his other hand pinning my hips, I saw stars—not metaphorical, actual bursts of white behind my eyelids. Then something happened I'd never experienced before—a sudden, intense release that shocked me as much as it soaked him. I gasped, mortified and exhilarated all at once, certain this wasn't supposed to happen outside of porn. But his tongue never stopped, not even to catch a breath. He just buried his face deeper and groaned like he'd discovered something precious that had been hidden from him until now.

I twitched so hard I nearly rolled off the counter, but he caught me with one massive hand, holding me in place while he licked me slowly, up and down, savoring every aftershock. When I finally went limp, every muscle in my body spent, he nuzzled his face against my thigh and breathed out, "I love you." It was muffled and wet and so vulnerable that I almost cried.

For half a second, all I wanted was to let him keep going until I disappeared. But the greedy, competitive part of my brain fired back to life. I remembered the way he'd looked at me the night we met, starving and certain at the same time, and I realized I wanted to wreck him again, to see if his hands would shake the way mine had.

"Incredible," I gasped, hair damp and clinging to my cheeks, legs trembling like jelly. "But if you think I'm letting this be all about me, you're delirious."

He lifted his head, the tip of his tongue gliding over his lower lip, eyes dark with challenge. I cut him off, pressing my palms to his broad shoulders and shoving until he stumbled back. Sliding off the counter, I landed soft on the cool tile. My knees nearly buckled, so I braced myself on the sink's porcelain edge, laughing in ragged breaths. Then I let myself drop, kneeling on the kitchen floor.

He hadn't seen it coming. He was still undoing his jeans when my hand found him—rock-hard, pulsing. I spat in my palm—raw, impulsive—and wrapped my fingers around the length of his shaft, reveling in the taut swirl of veins beneath. I wanted him undone, to dissolve four lonely days with the warmth of my mouth alone.

I took him in slowly at first, then relaxed my throat and welcomed him deeper, letting him glide past that tight ring of resistance until my nose brushed against the coarse curls at his base. My eyes stung with tears as I fought the instinct to pull back, drawing him down into my throat, feeling his pulse throb against me. He emitted a low, savage groan—part growl, part plea—one hand gripping the countertop, the other tangling in my hair, pulling me closer until every nerve ignited.

He set the pace now. His grip tightened, and he thrust forward, driving me down his shaft with wanton desperation. The knot at the base of his length bounced against my lips, growing thicker with each powerful push. I surrendered completely—my mouth, my throat, my will. Spit glossed my chin like molten silk as he hammered a punishing rhythm. Through tear-blurred eyes I met his gaze, felt the raw possessiveness there, the unspoken agreement that this was our reckoning. I moaned around him, urging him deeper, faster.

With each flick of my tongue and twist of my wrist, he grew louder, more ragged.

"Annie," he rasped, voice thick with need. "Annie, I'm—"

His plea cut off as he drove home in one final, shuddering thrust. My vision blurred, my body quivering around him as he emptied himself in fiery pulses—some swallowed, some dribbling down my chin.

My legs gave way, and he scooped me up, carrying me toward the bedroom. My head lolled against his chest, every nerve humming in a delicious afterglow.

CHAPTER
TWENTY-ONE

Samiel

I dumped her, not gently, onto the bed, and every cell in my body burned for more. Annie sprawled on the sheets, eyes wild and blue as lightning, hair a tangle of platinum and black against my dark sheets. Her lips parted, swollen from our kisses, as she smirked at me like she hadn't just come undone on my tongue minutes ago.

"Get on your hands and knees," I growled, voice thick with need. She moved instantly, the curve of her ass rising in the air, back dipping into a perfect arch that made my cock throb painfully. A thin sheen of sweat made her skin glisten in the half-light, every muscle quivering with anticipation.

I tore off my remaining clothes, the fabric a forgotten whisper on the floor. Gripping her hips hard enough to bruise, I lifted her until only her fingertips touched the mattress and dragged my length against her slick heat— teasing her entrance but not pushing in, savoring how wet she was for me. She tried to press back, to take me inside, but I held her firmly in place.

"Stop fucking around and put it in," she demanded, voice breaking with desperation. I laughed darkly against her ear and brought my palm down on the curve of her ass, watching the flesh redden instantly beneath my hand.

The sound she made—half pain, half pleasure—sent electricity straight to my groin. I grabbed her chin, turning her face so I could see her eyes, pupils blown wide with desire.

"Say please," I commanded, brushing my thumb across her lower lip.

She bit the pad of my thumb, then whispered, "Please." The word dripped like honey.

I positioned myself and thrust forward in one brutal stroke, burying myself to the hilt. Her body seized around me, so tight I nearly lost control. She collapsed forward with a strangled cry, face pressed into the sheets as I established a merciless rhythm. Each time I drove into her, she clenched around me, her body greedily pulling me deeper.

When I slowed to prolong the torture, she looked back over her shoulder, hair clinging to her flushed cheeks, eyes glazed with pleasure. "More," she begged, voice raw. "Harder."

My body screamed for more. I flipped Annie so she sprawled on the sheets, eyes wild and blue as lightning, and she had the nerve to smirk at me like she hadn't just begged for mercy five minutes ago.

"You want to be used?" I gritted. "You want to be ruined?"

She nodded so fast her hair stuck to her lips. "Fucking ruin me, Sam."

I wanted all of her. All of it. So I hauled her up to her knees and reached around, pulling her hair back so her throat arched. Then I let the tip of my tail flick up between her legs, teasing her clit while I still pounded into her from

231

behind. The moment she felt it, her whole body tensed, and the whimper that escaped her lips was pure need.

"You like that?" I taunted, and ran the pointed tip around her entrance, circling, then snapping it against her with a pop. She jerked and tried to twist away, but I pinned her, cock never leaving her cunt as I toyed with her with my tail. I trailed it higher, flicking, dragging it up and then down, until it pressed hard against her ass.

Annie froze, then relaxed so I let the tail press in, just a little, just enough that the thick tip breached her rim and she hissed through her teeth.

"You want that?" I said, and her moan answered for her. I worked it deeper, inch by inch, and the noises she made— wet, frantic, almost embarrassed—drove me wild. I let her feel the full girth of my cock as I twisted the tail, slow and patient, working it in and out until she started to shake, thighs clamped taut, hands fisting in the sheets like she was hanging on for dear life. I'd always wanted to try this but seeing her take it—seeing her whole body shudder and collapse under the dual stretch—sent a shiver up my own spine. I wanted it for her, but I also wanted it for me. The obscene, greedy part of me wanted to leave her so fucked out she'd never look at another man, human or demon, and even thinking about it made the base of my cock throb in anticipation.

She moaned, desperate now, voice hoarse, "Holy fuck, Samiel, don't stop." Her words were mush, little more than gasps, and every time I pumped my hips, burying myself deeper, her cunt spasmed around me like it had learned my rhythm by heart.

I licked down her spine, left a hot trail over the dip of her back, and bit her shoulder—enough to leave impressions, not enough to break skin. With one arm, I pulled her upright, chest mashed to my own as I impaled her on both cock and tail. The motion sent a fresh wash of wetness over my thighs, and I realized she was close, closer than ever before. I fucked her harder, bracing my hand across her shoulder blades, teasing her with the tail and using the last shreds of my control to not come first.

"Good girl," I said, a pulse of pride in my voice, and she writhed in my arms, every muscle working to meet me. "You're taking it so well. Look at you—made to be fucked like this."

She tried to talk but all that came out was a series of sobs and a whimpering, "I can't—" and then she broke.

She shattered. The orgasm hit her so hard I felt it in my own bones, a clamping, rippling vise that milked my cock and squeezed the tail so tight the plates of my spine almost spasmed. Her whole body seized, then went limp, a dead-weight collapse that would have dropped her to the mattress if I wasn't holding her up. I let her fall this time, watched her shake and claw into the sheets as I kept up the rhythm, not letting her come down, not even for a second.

She screamed. Not a word, not a plea, just a raw animal sound, and the pulse of her cunt around me was enough to bring me over the edge. I felt the knot at the base flare, let it lock into her, and came so hard I thought I was going to black out. The world narrowed to the point of our bodies joined, the feverish grip of her around me, the evidence of my own need dripping out as I filled her past the point of leaking. She was still shaking, sweat and tears streaking her face, but she arched her back and took every last thrust and twitch of my cock.

CHAPTER
TWENTY-TWO

Samiel

I collapsed on my back, pulse hammering in my skull, and stared up at the ceiling while Annie melted across the sheets. I couldn't remember a time when my body had felt so empty and so full at the same time, every nerve fried to glass, every bone melting under her weight. For a long stretch of minutes, neither of us spoke. The only sounds were her breath, the gentle snort of the cat nestling onto the pillow by my feet, and the blood still roaring in my ears.

Annie rolled onto me, a slick, beautiful mess, and flopped her face into my chest. "If anyone else can make me black out from sex, I don't wanna meet them," she mumbled, voice muffled in my skin. "I'll die happy never knowing."

"Good," I said, still panting, "because you're not allowed to meet anyone else. Ever again."

She snorted, which vibrated across my ribcage like a threat.

"Possessive much?"

"Only always," I said, and I meant it with every ruined, grateful cell in my body.

She raked her fingers through my hair, tugging at the roots, and let them drift down to my chest, where her nails traced the upraised marks from the last few hours.

"You know," she said, "when I left, I half-thought you'd turn into a werewolf and come after me. Or eat the cat and leave her paw on my pillow as some sort of fucked-up apology."

"I missed you more than I missed air," I confessed, before I could think of something clever. "It was Hell on earth."

She made a noise, half a purr, and curled up tighter. "Guess you're stuck with me then."

"Would you trust me enough to say I will be right back?" I asked, expecting her to laugh or call me a cocky bastard. Instead, she released me, and I sauntered casually out of the room, still completely naked.

The return to the bedroom was almost ceremonial: ice cream, crackers, two spoons, and maybe two ounces of pride left. Annie sat cross-legged in the center of the bed, one hand pressing a towel to her inner thigh where I'd left an impression that looked like a bite mark and a meteor strike at the same time.

I crawled on the mattress and dumped the food between us. "Your electrolyte solution, madam." I popped the lid off her ice cream and jammed the spoon into the carton at an obscene angle. She grinned, digging in, still flushed from sweat and laughter. The first bite made her eyes flip up, and she made a sound so pornographic I nearly pounced on her again on the spot.

"I can't believe you," she said, around a mouthful of melting ice cream. "You're a monster."

"That has literally never been in dispute," I replied, and

tore open the Cheez-Its. I shoved a handful in my mouth, crumbs dusting my chest, and watched her eat.

It was impossible not to think about how she'd looked twenty minutes ago, body pinned and trembling, then about how it'd felt to nearly lose her. I was desperate, not just for her body, but for every weird piece of her—every compulsion, every sharp angle, even the human drama she'd dragged in with her.

~

Annie

Samiel knew exactly how I craved junk food after sex. Showing up like some demonic Adonis with ice cream and Cheez-Its was practically foreplay for another round. I shoveled chocolate fudge brownie into my mouth like I was being timed, letting it drip shamelessly down my thighs.

"Mind-blowing orgasms followed by processed cheese products?" I said, licking my spoon clean with religious devotion. "This is how cults get started. If you proposed right now, I'd not only say yes—I'd let you pick the wedding colors."

He put the ice cream down, and for a second it looked like was going to say something. Then he reached over to the nightstand, rummaged with those ridiculous hands, and pulled out a box so tiny that I didn't even clock what it was until he held it, black velvet and trembling, between us.

My mouth froze open around the spoon. "No," I wheezed, a sudden, real panic blooming in my chest.

He grinned, almost apologetic. "I told myself I wouldn't do this like a cliché," he said, popping the lid. Inside, crimson silk cradled a ring like nothing I'd ever seen: a blood-red ruby, roughly the size of my thumbnail, caged in wrought gold and flanked on either side by three tiny black diamonds. The kind of ring that said "I want to own you, but only if you eat me alive first."

He looked at me, then at the ring, then back to me. "I never wanted to do the thing people do. The wedding, the contract, the forever promise." He exhaled, the sound almost a laugh, but not. "But then I met you, and I realized I was already ruined for anything else. I don't know how to be good, Annie. I don't know how to be normal. But I know I want you, and I know I want to keep you, and—" He looked away, down at his hands. "If you want it, I want forever. With you. And the cat, and the stupid car, and all the junk food we can eat before we both die of cholesterol poisoning."

I stared at it. Then at him. Then back at it, because the alternative was looking him in the eye and having my brain splinter.

Then I lunged, nearly toppling the entire bed, and slammed into him, bare thighs straddling his hips. I buried my face in his neck, soaked through with all the things I could never say. I must have made some kind of strangled seal-bark of a noise, because Samiel started to panic.

"You don't have to—if you're not sure, or if this is too much, just—"

"Shut up," I said, tears streaking down my cheeks, "and give me the goddamn ring."

He laughed and jammed it on my finger. It was cold, then molten, then part of my entire hand—giant, ostentatious, dramatic. Absolutely perfect.

"You know," I said, blinking at it, "most guys would hide this thing in a donut or something. Not just, like, haul it out after a marathon hatefuck with Cheez-Its."

He grinned. "I don't own a donut big enough for you. Or

a box." Then he watched my face—waiting, with a terror that made him so much less monster and so much more boy.

"Yes," I said, and the word ricocheted around the room, louder than my own orgasm before. "Yes, you idiot. Yes, yes, yes." I couldn't stop repeating it. I didn't want to.

He let me tackle him. He tucked me under his chin, arm heavy and possessive across my waist, and for a long time neither of us said a thing.

When I finally caught my breath, I twisted the ring so it caught the light. "We're really doing this," I said. "I'm going to have to introduce you to my parents, aren't I?" The thought was so outrageous, I started laughing again.

He did not laugh. "I'll meet them. Whenever you want." Then, softer, "Who do you want to tell first?"

I thought about it. My mom was the obvious answer, but weirdly I also wanted to show Mayor Vepar, to include the cat somehow, to maybe send a mass email to every ex I'd ever had, subject line: SORRY, YOU LOSE.

But mostly I wanted to stay there, in that room, with the man who brought me ice cream and ruined my body and put an actual demon's engagement ring on my finger, and never, ever leave.

"I don't care who knows," I said, stroking his cheek. "It's my favorite secret. Let's keep it for just a little while."

He nodded. "Our secret," he said, and I realized it was the first time he'd ever said *ours* without sounding like he meant mine alone.

We lay there in silence, sticky and exhausted, and I thought, *This is what it means to be claimed, not caged.* I'd found the line. And I'd decided, for once in my life, to stay.

The cat, sensing the shift in power, jumped up on the bed and immediately began licking the ice cream off my leg. I let her. I let the world be as strange and perfect as it wanted.

And for the first time in forever, I felt safe enough to want more.

EPILOGUE

Six Months Later

Annie

Though Samiel and I signed the paperwork the day our ninety days were up, we didn't have a wedding. We wanted to wait. After our legal ceremony, we were given a binder labeled "Unholy Matrimony" with a sticky note from Mayor Vepar reading, "Congratulations! Our wedding planners can accommodate any request, from blood fountains to human sacrifice (decorative only)." I flipped through glossy photos of couples—some with horns, some without—exchanging rings under moonlit gazebos and dancing in ballrooms with chandeliers made of what looked suspiciously like bones.

"I want the lake," I said, pointing to a sunset ceremony where lanterns floated on dark water. "Just us, the dock, and maybe twenty people who won't ask if your tail is real."

Samiel agreed with me easily, and we planned a wedding for our families and only a handful of friends.

The night before, we hosted a dinner for our families to meet. Samiel insisted on catering. Your only job tomorrow is to show up and make me the happiest demon in existence."

My parents arrived first, Dad's pickup crunching on the gravel. Mom burst out with her arms already open, enveloping me in a hug that smelled like cinnamon, Virginia Slims, and home.

"My baby girl," she whispered, voice catching. My brother arrived with a homemade cake wobbling precariously in his hands. My sister followed minutes later, having driven six hours straight from Orlando, leaving behind what she affectionately called her "mini-monsters" with the in-laws just to be here for me.

Next, Samiel's parents arrived. His mom was tall with angular features that she accentuated with a cat eye to die for. His dad was a carbon copy of Samiel—just with salt and pepper hair. The last to arrive was Azazel, Samiel's older brother. Though he had the same coloring as Samiel, he was bulkier with short-cropped hair, much smaller horns, and a full black beard. He seemed gruff, but hugged me all the same. Samiel had dinner set up on his deck so everyone could sit together.

I was shocked at how normal it felt. It wasn't a rehearsal dinner—just the weirdest blend of humans and demons you could find in North America, passing paper plates and laughing at "in-law" jokes like the fate of two worlds didn't rest on a seating chart. If you squinted, you could pretend it was just a big family barbecue, not a peace summit for the descendants of Hell and Tampa's most tenacious smokers.

My mom took one look at Samiel's mother and latched on like a remora, dragging her away from the grill to compare hand creams and eye shadow tips. They were the same kind of alpha, just with different evolutionary pressures—Mom wielded guilt as a weapon, and Samiel's mother used withering sarcasm and a stare that could turn coal into diamonds.

Dad and Samiel's dad, on the other hand, found a common language in trains, and both of model-train dads yammered together until Samiel's dad went inside for a moment and came back with what looked like an HO scale freight set, and the two of them vanished to the garage, only to emerge twenty minutes later with a completed figure-eight and a blood orange IPA in each hand.

My sister and Azazel disappeared too, winding up on the roof, tipsy and howling at the moon like a pair of teenagers. Even the cat went feral, darting between bare ankles and occasionally dropping at Samiel's feet to yowl for another piece of salmon.

It was surreal how quickly these families—mine loud and unfiltered, his dark and barely restrained—found a common, weird groove. And it was a relief. For the first time maybe ever, I felt like a grown woman with a future I had actually chosen, surrounded by people who might not understand it, but wouldn't leave. I spent the whole night cycling from the kitchen to the deck to the living room, chasing the laughter, never once feeling out of place. Samiel, meanwhile, alternated between talking to my parents and his, and fending off every attempt by my sister to get him to take a Jell-O shot. By the end of the night, he looked weirdly relaxed—a big soft slab of demon in a linen button-down, all sharp angles sanded down by the sound of my people, our people, making themselves loud and at home.

As the sunset sunk into twilight our families headed for their hotels, leaving Samiel and me alone together.

"For the record," he whispered, "your sister is terrifying."

I laughed and almost snorted wine out my nose. "She could take you, easy," I said. "If you underestimate Florida girls, you do so at your peril."

He kissed the top of my head, then reached down to the cat, who rolled onto her back and presented her belly.

"I'll never underestimate any of you again," he said softly, and I got the sense this was the kind of vow he meant to keep.

When the last of the goodbyes had been said and the night was finally ours, he took my hand and tugged me upstairs—we'd both agreed we weren't spending the night before our wedding apart just because of "tradition." We brushed our teeth together and climbed into bed, arranging me as the little spoon and him as the big spoon. Sleep arrived quickly and my last thought before I lost consciousness was, *How did I get this lucky?*

Samiel

The morning of the wedding, I was a bundle of nerves. I shouldn't have been—Annie and I had already signed the legal paperwork the minute our ninety days were up, so we'd been legally married for more than a few months. I tried to pin down the anxiety, and it was really just my hope that Annie got everything she wanted out of the day.

I was easy. I wanted to see her in her the dress she'd insisted on keeping hidden, celebrate with our family and friends without anyone getting into a fistfight, and then spend time with her. Since we kept it small, she also said more casual. I was in a black suit, open at the neck, no tie.

I wondered what she would show up in. I doubted

sincerely that she'd show up in a traditional all-white wedding dress—that just didn't seem like Annie.

Before I knew it, I was standing at the end of the dock, with Mayor Vepar, who was presiding, waiting for Annie to walk down the aisle.

When Annie approached the dock, the chatter died away. Everything in me stilled. She walked toward me in a sheer, deep purple, off-the-shoulder lace dress, with a cream underlayer that made my heart nearly stop. Her eyes never left mine as she approached, that familiar, determined stride carrying her down the aisle alone. The sight of her fierce smile—the one I'd fallen for months ago—made my throat tight. This wasn't just the woman I loved; this was Annie choosing to be mine forever.

I forgot how to breathe. She seemed to float down the aisle, eyes locked on mine as if no one else existed. Walking herself down the aisle—answering to no one—in a move so unmistakably Annie. My Annie: strong, independent, and now coming straight to me with absolute certainty. This strange and perfect mix of elegance and shadow was exactly how forever should look.

Our vows were simple promises to cherish and protect each other—equals in all things. When the mayor pronounced us married, I took Annie's hands in mine, careful not to catch her lace sleeves with my claws. I kissed her with all the tenderness I'd been saving since the moment I first saw her walking down that aisle. Her lips tasted like cherry lip balm and promises. When we finally parted, Annie's eyes were shining with tears that matched my own, her fingers reaching up to brush one from my cheek as our guests erupted in joyful applause.

The rest of the night was a blur of champagne, food, and dancing. My mother insisted we perform the traditional

Flame Blessing, where Annie and I held hands over a small blue fire that burned without consuming our joined fingers. When Annie's laugh bubbled up as the flames tickled her palm, I felt my heart swell impossibly larger.

It was well after midnight by the time everyone left, the moon hanging like a silver pendant above our new home. Azazel gave me one last pat on the back, his eyes softening as he watched Annie kick off her shoes by the door.

"You found a good one," he whispered, something wistful in his voice I'd never heard before.

When I closed the door behind our last guest, Annie padded across the floor in her bare feet and purple dress. "Hey, husband," she said softly, reaching up to straighten my collar with gentle fingers. "You know, you clean up real nice." Her smile was so tender, it made my chest ache.

My voice came out rougher than intended. "You're breathtaking," I growled, though I'd told her repeatedly all night. The purple lace clung to curves that made my claws itch to tear fabric. Heat pooled low in my body as the demon part of me stirred—the urge to claim, to possess, to devour. I traced one talon down her bare arm, watching goosebumps rise in its wake.

"Tell me something," I murmured against her ear, letting my fangs graze the sensitive skin beneath it. "How much would you miss this dress if it didn't survive the night?"

She grinned and bit her lip, leaning close enough that her breath was wine-sweet and reckless. "Rip it," she said, voice low and dangerous. "See if I can outrun you before you do."

Holy shit. I felt my heart, real and metaphorical, seize up with want.

She was already halfway across the living room by the time I registered her dare. The purple lace flared out, alive with motion. I followed, not running at first, just prowling, watching her dart barefoot onto the deck, laughter trailing behind like spilled glitter. She vaulted the steps into the backyard darkness striped silver by the moon. There was nothing more beautiful on this earth or any other than the woman I loved, arms out, head back, dress floating, daring me to catch her.

I stretched my wings wide, letting the wind fill them, and leapt from the deck in a single beat, boots skidding in dirt. She shrieked, real joy and terror mashed together. She barely cleared the iron gate before I closed the gap, the thump of my feet shaking the whole world.

Our backyard maze waited for us, the one I'd built just for these moments—a series of towering cacti and desert succulents arranged in winding paths across the sand. Annie disappeared inside, purple lace flashing between spiny sentinels, and I heard her laugh echo across the open night before she dropped into a crouch behind the stone lion with the missing jaw—her favorite hiding spot. Her pulse called to me—loud, frantic, deliciously close.

I circled the perimeter, moving slow, claws leaving trails in the sand. I let the anticipation build, let her think she had a chance in this playground we'd created together. The night air let the scent of her fear and excitement mix, let it curl up my spine until every muscle in my legs begged to give chase. I moved slow at first, dragging each step through the sand so she'd hear how close I was. The wind shifted, and I caught the sharp, electric tang of her sweat, her feral want, her laughter trembling just out of reach.

As I carefully approached her, the sand crunching beneath my feet gave away my proximity. The wind shifted, allowing me to catch the scent of her sweat, tension, and laughter just beyond my reach. She was luring me in, and I was more than happy to follow.

Annie thought she could easily maneuver through the dense cluster of barrel cacti due to her size, but I had other plans. With a grin and a mighty display of my wings, I stepped off the path and charged through the cacti as if they were made of tissue paper. Pain seared through my thigh as spines dug deep, but it hardly mattered as the mix of blood and pheromones heightened my senses, driving me forward.

Hearing me closing in, Annie shrieked and tried to outrun me by darting towards the opposite side of the clearing. Despite trying her best to escape, she glanced over her shoulder to gauge my distance. In that split second, I took advantage, jumping forward with arms outstretched. Grabbing her waist in a full tackle, I lifted her off the ground as she let out an exhilarated scream.

I carried her a few more feet before pinning her down onto the sand, my claws encircling both wrists above her head. She arched against me, her body a perfect curve beneath mine as I straddled her hips. When she bucked upward, I growled low in my throat and tore the skirt from her dress with one fluid motion, the sound of ripping lace like thunder in my ears. The scent of her arousal hit me instantly—she'd worn nothing underneath, the minx. Moonlight caught the slick evidence of her desire as she writhed beneath me, her eyes challenging even as her body betrayed how desperately she wanted this. Wanted me. But my Annie would never surrender too easily.

With my free hand, I traced a single claw down the center of her bodice, the sharp tip catching on purple lace.

"Last chance to save this dress," I growled. She arched her back in response, pressing herself against the point of my claw. I sliced downward in one fluid motion, the fabric parting like water, exposing her completely to the night air. Her sharp intake of breath was all challenge, no surrender.

I released her wrists but fixed her with a look that burned. "Keep them there," I commanded, voice rough with desire. "Don't move them."

Only when she nodded, eyes half-lidded and defiant, did I begin my descent. I traced the curve of her throat with my mouth, lingering at her collarbone, then lower still. I circled one pebbled nipple with my forked tongue before drawing it between my teeth, applying just enough pressure to make her gasp. The second nipple received the same attention, my fangs grazing the sensitive peak until her back bowed off the sand. Her body arched beneath me as my tongue finally found the heat between her legs. Each time her hands twitched, instinctively wanting to reach for me, I paused—a sweet punishment that made her curse and writhe against the sand.

I growled against her inner thigh. "Tell me what you want."

She gasped as my tongue traced dangerously close to her center. "Please," she whimpered, hips rising desperately. "Use your words," I demanded, breath hot against her slick folds.

"Make me come with your mouth," she finally commanded.

I devoured her then, my forked tongue working its dual magic—one side circling her clit while the other plunged inside her, creating a rhythm that had her thighs trembling against my horns. "Don't stop, don't—" she cried out, her words dissolving into incoherent pleasure as the twin sensations overwhelmed her. She shattered completely, back arching off the sand, her body convulsing around my tongue as I continued my relentless attention to both spots at once.

Without warning, I slid up her body, my claws digging

into her hips as I flipped us over. I positioned her above me, her slick heat hovering just inches from my mouth.

"I need to taste more of you," I growled, pulling her down. She gasped as my tongue found her again.

"My turn," she purred, and before I could react, she'd pivoted above me, her hair cascading down as she bent forward. "I want all of you," she whispered, her breath hot against my throbbing cock. When her fingers wrapped around me, I bucked involuntarily. "So responsive," she teased, her tongue flicking out to taste the tip.

I was slick with sweat , breath heaving in the hot night as Annie slid her mouth down my cock in one smooth motion, so deep the tip hit the soft back of her throat. I clutched at her thighs, greedy for her taste, locked on the pulse fluttering under the skin just above her knee. She braced herself on my hips, the heat between her legs smashing onto my face with a confidence that made me want to destroy and worship her in equal measure.

"Fuck," I groaned, as she tightened her grip at the base, twisting her wrist while she sucked me down to the hilt. I let my tongue find the slick seam of her cunt and split it open, tracing lightning patterns over her clit. My tail wrapped her calf, pinning her there as I focused all the chaos of a week's wanting into the flick and curl of my tongue.

She moaned around me, the vibration shuddering up my cock so hard it nearly ended me then and there. I dug my claws into her ass, pulling her down as if I could swallow the whole of her into me. I didn't let her up for air, not for a second. Each time she paused to gasp, I buried my face deeper in her, fucking her with my mouth until she was shaking so hard she had to prop her knees against my ribs and hold tight or else risk melting straight into the sand.

I liked her like this: feral and unguarded, her want running wild over the neat borders of her self-control.

But I also liked the way she took me in her mouth: greedy, unashamed, like she'd been designed in a lab for the express purpose of blowing my mind and every other thought out of my skull. For every inch I gave her, she pushed me further, humming my name between soft, wet slurps, her tongue sliding the ridge, the sensitive veins, the thick base of my cock as if memorizing topography.

I flicked her clit hard enough to make her yelp my name.

"You're close," I said. "Close enough I can taste it."

I took her back into my mouth and redoubled the effort, twin tips of my tongue working in tandem: one circling her clit, the other sliding inside to curl up and beckon, right at the spongy spot that made her entire body tense. She sucked air through her teeth, then retaliated, bobbing her head and swirling her tongue under the head, her hands working the knot with a tight, perfect grip.

Her arms started to shake. She balanced on her elbows, jaw working, brain barely tethered to her body. "Samiel— fuck—" she said as she tried to hold back, but her hips betrayed her, grinding against my mouth with uncoordinated, desperate rhythm.

The edges of my vision blurred. Everything narrowed down to the pulse of Annie's body on my tongue, the hot, salt-slick taste of her, the tremors starting in her thighs and rolling up her spine. I locked my hands around her hips and pulled her all the way down until her cunt sealed over my mouth, and I flattened my tongue, working back and forth with a pressure I knew would finish her. The wind whistled over the yard, but I could still hear the wet, obscene sounds of her getting closer, her breath chopping up into animal whimpers.

"Sam, I—fuck—" Her voice split, breaking on the edge of a scream.

She came hard, harder than I'd ever seen her—her whole body a live wire, knees buckling as she arched backward and let loose a sound torn straight from the bottom of her lungs. My name echoing off every wall of the goddamned night. Her body went soft. For a second Annie just sprawled over me, panting and blinking at the sky, pupils so blown that her eyes looked like abyssal pits ringed in blue. Sweat dripped down her back, sawed the rip in her dress into dark rivers. I licked her clean, slowly, and nipped her inner thigh, feeling the tremor that shot straight to her toes.

I could have let her float there. I could have spent the rest of the night under her, letting her cum in my mouth until the sand turned to glass. But I was past the edge. All patience was gone. I needed to be inside her—needed to claim her, brand her, ruin her with every part of me she'd ever touched.

Before she could recover, I flipped her, planting her knees and elbows in the sand and caging her in with my body. The shredded fabric of her dress littered the ground beneath her, framing the pale skin of her back like a torn flag. I pressed my cock to her entrance, dragging the head through the slick mess I'd made of her cunt, and watched her shudder with anticipation.

"Ready?" I growled, voice hollowed out by want.

She nodded, but that wasn't enough. "Say it," I demanded.

"Please, Samiel," she whispered. "I want you to—"

I didn't let her finish. I slammed into her in one deliberate, brutal thrust, burying myself to the hilt. She broke open around me, every muscle clenching to welcome me deeper. I held her hips and pulled her against my groin, the impact reverberating up our spines. She let out a guttural moan, and I grinned into the sweat-wet skin of her shoulder.

"You were made to be fucked like this," I rasped, and started to move.

She met every thrust, refusing to let me dominate the rhythm. Each time I pulled back, she chased me; every time I tried to draw it out, she rammed herself backward so hard her ass slapped against my hips, loud enough to echo. The sound pulsed in my skull, as obscene and beautiful as the night itself.

"Is that all you got, demon?" she taunted, voice ragged with need. "I thought you were supposed to be strong—"

I bent her lower, hands traveling up her arms until I could pin both wrists behind her back with one hand. The move flattened her to the earth, made her arch deeper, sent her tits dragging through the cool sand. With my free hand, I laced her hair into a fist and used it to guide her head back, exposing the vulnerable line of her neck.

"Still think you can handle me?" I thrust harder, letting her feel the full force of me, the knot at my base swelling with every ragged stroke.

She gasped, panting into the ground. "Want to find out?"

I leaned forward, mouth at her ear. "You're going to come again, and when you do, I'm not stopping until you black out."

She gritted her teeth and braced herself, but already her walls were fluttering around me—already she was losing ground, her screams muffled by the sand as her body tried and failed to contain everything I poured into her.

I gripped her hips so tight I thought I might snap bone, the pulse in my cock matching the clench of her cunt in dangerous, perfect tandem. My tail found her clit, circling in frantic counter-motion to the pounding of my hips. I wanted every cell in her body to remember this forever. Every vein, every nerve, every trembling muscle owed itself to me, and she fucking loved it—she was sobbing my name into the dirt, uncaring if neighbors or wildlife or the local sheriff heard the racket. Right at the end, her hands broke free and reached behind her, grabbing at my thighs and digging in so hard her nails left trails of conviction in my flesh.

"Samiel, holy fuck—" Annie's words crumbled as she came again, and this time it was an earthquake, her whole body locked up, skin humming with the rawness only the two of us knew how to conjure. I bent over her, letting my chest crush her back, my cock twitching wildly in the iron furnace of her grip. The knot at the base finally gave, swelling and locking us together in the oldest way known to my kind. I hilted one last time, hips pressed flush to her body, and came so hard I saw flashes behind my eyelids— red, gold, the colors of hell, but here on earth where I belonged.

I didn't stop moving, not even through the aftershocks. I rocked into her, the tide refusing to recede, fucking every last drop of sweat and desperation out of both of us. My mouth found her shoulder, biting down barely enough to break the skin, marking her one final time, a circle closed and sealed for good. Her hands clutched my forearms, and when she went limp, neither of us said a word for a long time.

I held her like that until my own bones softened, her body sunk into mine, two shapes fused by friction and animal want. The sand burned my knees and back, and the sky above wheeled in slow, indifferent arcs, but I didn't give it up, not even when my lungs started to riot for air. I wanted her there, held and spent and certain. I wanted her to know, even at her most broken open, she was the strongest fucking thing in my universe.

When my senses returned, I loosened my grip, careful not to crush her. The aftermath was glorious—her hair wild, skin peppered with bruises, every inch of her branded with marks that meant Annie, mine, always. I bent over her, kissing the sweat at the nape of her neck, then traced my tongue down the curve of her spine, licking the salt from her skin. She shuddered, but this time it was pure relief.

I waited until the knot softened, then eased myself out, catching her before she collapsed. I rolled her over and kissed her, gentle now, letting her taste the heat and hunger that had consumed me. She caught my face in her hands, nails raking my scalp, and pulled me down until our foreheads touched.

She lay there, breathing hard, eyes wild and shining in the dark. "I love you," she said, voice hoarse but clear as anything I'd ever heard. "I fucking love you, Sam."

"I love you too." I kissed her again and again, not stopping even when the cat howled in protest from the porch, or when the moon set and the night went thick with cold. We stayed there, wrapped in ruined lace and sand and sweat, until I couldn't tell where her body ended and mine began.

Eventually, I scooped her up, bridal style, and carried her toward the house. She protested, halfhearted, but curled into my chest as I hiked the whole way. I set her down in the bathroom, filled the tub with scalding water, and slid in behind her. She sat between my thighs, hair floating, the rest of her sinking into me like she'd always belonged there.

We soaked in that bath for an hour, maybe more. She fell asleep with her cheek resting on my arm, lips curled in a smile. I held her until the water went cold, until the sunrise started to color the lake with blood and gold, until I felt a peace I had never known before.

THANKS FOR READING!

Creating the world for *Saving Samiel* was a blast. I fell in love with Annie and Samiel and The Valley of the Damned and I am so glad I don't plan on leaving it anytime soon.

As always, I have to thank my patient husband. He puts up with ridiculous deadlines (that I set myself) and having multiple characters based on him. Maybe one day I'll write our story.

Huge thank you to my editors Ana and Emily, you make me so much more confident in putting out books. It is a pleasure to work with both of you.

Thank you you to my PA Kaitlyn, who tells me I am a *real author* more often than she should have to and saves me from my own dumb decisions on a regular basis.

Finally, to my group of author friends who hold my hand whenever I have to do something big and scary, thank you for pushing me to try something outside my comfort zone. I wouldn't be where I am without you. Lyonne, you are my safe space. I don't know what I would do without you.

ALSO BY JENIFER WOOD

~

Abandoned on Niflheim

Agnarr's Teacher

Agnarr's Jarlin

Steve's Barmaid

Fenrik's Fate

Standalones

Screwed by the Minotaur

ABOUT THE AUTHOR

~

Jen has been reading for as long as she can remember. She used to get in trouble for reading Little House on the Prairie under her desk in elementary school. Jen's day job is advocating for adolescent mental health, something she doesn't see giving up any time soon.

Jen is married to a very polite Englishman she brought back as a souvenir from her college study abroad trip. She has identical twin mutants who make her question her sanity daily. She enjoys reading about alien peens, napping, and watching soothing cooking shows.

She is a goth kid at heart and truly wishes she could wear platform combat boots and black nail polish on all occasions.

~

www.authorjeniferwood.com